Hal Brogn_____ _____ _____ n, well-chewe_ _____ _____ _____ _en locked teeth as he surveyed the Farm's operations center. Against the wall at the front of the room television screens flickered with images. One screen offered an overview of the island from the Farm's dedicated Keyhole satellite. On another screen was the feed from the nose camera mounted in Jack Grimaldi's Comanche attack helicopter. Two additional screens were linked to similar camera systems in the Predator drones controlled by Carmen Delahunt and Akira Tokaido at their respective workstations. The UAVs were outfitted with Hellfire missiles for the engagement.

The screen featuring a topographical map of the island was controlled by Hunt Wethers and showed the individual operators of both Phoenix Force and Able Team in icon form, allowing the Farm to visually follow their progress as the assault unfolded.

Barbara Price stalked back and forth in front of the screens, working her sat-com headset to coordinate last-minute logistical needs. Above her head a digital clock counted down to H-hour.

DON PENDLETON'S

STONY

AMERICA'S ULTRA-COVERT INTELLIGENCE AGENCY

MAN®

TARGET
ACQUISITION

A GOLD EAGLE BOOK FROM

WORLDWIDE®

TORONTO • NEW YORK • LONDON
AMSTERDAM • PARIS • SYDNEY • HAMBURG
STOCKHOLM • ATHENS • TOKYO • MILAN
MADRID • WARSAW • BUDAPEST • AUCKLAND

Recycling programs
for this product may
not exist in your area.

First edition October 2010

ISBN-13: 978-0-373-61993-1

TARGET ACQUISITION

Special thanks and acknowledgment to
Nathan Meyer for his contribution to this work.

Printed in U.S.A.

TARGET ACQUISITION

CHAPTER ONE

Washington, D.C.

Hal Brognola strode down the east hall of the senate. He'd just been called before another pointless meeting with the Senate Subcommittee on Covert Action Oversight. He kept bringing them actionable intelligence and debriefs of successful operations, but they kept questioning the constitutionality of his original Sensitive Operations Group charter. The experience left him feeling like the cardboard silhouette at a shooting range.

He sighed heavily, picked up his pace and for the hundredth time that day wished he'd never quit smoking.

"Hal," a gravelly voice barked. "Can I have a word?"

The highly polished linoleum floor squeaked under the big Fed's feet as he slowed his pace and turned to address the man who had spoken to him.

"Brigadier," Brognola said.

Brigadier General Brooks Kubrick, Joint Special Operations Command, walked up and put his hands on his hips. "We have a problem," he announced.

"Don't we always," Brognola countered.

Kubrick looked up and down the hallway and, satisfied, pulled Brognola over to a quiet corner underneath an oil painting of Andrew Jackson. Kubrick was a big man, ex-Ranger and former Tenth Group Special Forces who'd been with Detachment Delta in El Salvador. His reputation as a no-nonsense operator and premier unconventional strategist preceded him, and Brognola was more than willing to listen to what he had to say.

"I got guys," Kubrick began, "rolling out of four or five tours in the Sandbox or the Rockpile then disappearing into a sensitive security operation for Homeland for months on end."

"Okay." Brognola didn't offer the man any help.

"Something I have on good authority my boys are calling Operation Blacksuit."

"Really?"

"Really my ass, Hal. I got hard-core recon boys and SEALs coming back talking about a gang of cold-eye killers, some of them foreign nationals, doing very wild shit. I got Special Forces sergeants with twenty years in, talking about specialists with crazy mad skills. I got twenty-year-old Airborne Rangers telling me about men twice their age kicking their asses in training runs or during hand-to-hand drills."

Brognola drew his mouth into a flat, sharp line. In the ranking of security clearances the operations the general described were deemed above top secret and were given something called code-name clearances. Admitting that you had knowledge of a code name you were not specifically assigned to was a criminal offense significant enough to have your general security clearance revoked and an internal security investigation launched.

Hal Brognola's connection to the Justice Department was well established in the Capitol, even if the rest of his purview was decidedly murky. Brigadier General Brooks Kubrick had just taken a very big risk by admitting his knowledge of the assignment of special operations personnel to the security of Stony Man Farm.

Brognola knew such a savvy individual would not commit such a faux pas lightly.

"Sounds impressive," he said, voice even.

"Impressive? You're right, what I'm hearing is impressive. I'm stretched to the breaking point for operators, I got more missions than operators, I got casualty rates rivaling my train-up rates, I'm short guys, guns and goods but long on tangos and I discover the Justice Department is sitting on a crew of shooters that make the FBI's hostage-rescue team look like beat cops."

"You're starting to make me feel like a cheerleader who's just wandered into the locker room, Kubrick. Is there a point to this?"

The general turned away and released a pent-up breath. "I got a problem, Hal. I need help. The Agency has dumped a real dog of an operation in my lap. In Pakistan."

"What are we talking about specifically?" Brognola asked.

"You know the KLPD?"

"Khadi Lun Pe Dhoka," Brognola answered automatically. "A sort of 'boys in the basement' bureau in their intelligence agency."

"Exactly, bad mojo boys. Thick with the Taliban back in the day. The only Pakistani intelligence group to have any worthwhile presence in the lawless tribal regions to the northwest. For all the wrong reasons."

"That jives with what I know," Brognola conceded.

"The Agency put a task force into Islamabad. Paramilitary operators, almost exclusively made up by ex-Special Forces communication sergeants. Their job is to do electronic countersurveillance on the Pakistani security apparatus."

"Help us find out who are the bad guys pretending to be good guys."

"Exactly." Brooks nodded. "I've got a list of KLPD agents directing enemy combatant operations. They're working with al Qaeda cells, Taliban splinter groups, Lashkar-e-Taiba. But everyone has a political patron in the government. They have juice or cover or plausible deniability. They're operating with immunity. Every time we turn around they're screwing us. We can't put our boys up into Waziristan without these snakes fucking us."

"What precisely are you asking me for, Brigadier?"

"I got a honey pot operation. I got time, place, an A-list of partygoers. I got a pipeline in and out under everyone's noses. I got a money shot of a direct-action takedown."

"What's the problem?"

"Prince Ziad Jarrah bin Sultan al-Thani."

"He is…what, a Saudi?"

"A crown prince, or the son of a crown prince. His father was very high up in the defense ministry. *Very* high up. So high up I can't get a green light on this op because his highness the son of his highness Hadji son of a bitch is playing sleepover at my hit site. He's dirty as hell, spending his allowance money funding suicide bombers and sport torturers."

Brognola nodded. "You wearing a wire, Brigadier?"

"What?" Kubrick seemed genuinely bewildered, but Brognola wasn't at his first rodeo.

"A wire. You working with a special investigator?"

Brognola slapped him in the chest, feeling for a hidden microphone.

"Jesus, Hal, no! I swear on my kids," Kubrick protested.

In a second Brognola relied on decades of street experience and made his decision. He reached into his suit jacket and pulled out a business card. He reached out and carefully placed it into the JSOC officer's hand.

"That e-address is tight as a nun's habit, Brigadier. You send me what you have and I'll see what we can do."

Stony Man Farm, Virginia

BROGNOLA LOOKED UP at Barbara Price.

"What do you think?"

The honey-blonde Stony Man mission controller sat on the edge of the War Room's massive conference table, a cup of coffee in her hand. She cut her eyes away from Brognola toward Aaron "the Bear" Kurtzman, the head of her cyberteam. From his wheelchair Kurtzman deftly worked at the keyboard built into the unit.

"I think, Hal, that you handed me a complete operation tied up with a pretty pink bow." The former NSA manager began ticking points off on her slender fingers. "Initial intelligence. Field reconnaissance. Logistical support to include transportation. Safehouse with arms, explosives, equipment and fresh changes of underwear."

Brognola, seeing her starting to really warm up, gently interrupted. "Your point, Barb?"

"My point is that it's one thing working with Agency, or Homeland or even Pentagon through SOG's executive charter. It's what, in part, we were designed to do from the beginning."

"But?"

"But." Kurtzman spoke up, "that's not exactly what's happening here."

Price nodded. "This is a JSOC gig from scratch to burn. You're just plugging the boys in as interchangeable with DEVGRU or CAG." She paused and shrugged. "Or the Rangers, for all that goes."

Barbara Price was listing off the premier units of the Joint Special Operations Command. The Combat Application Group, or CAG, was the elite Army counterterrorism and hostage rescue unit usually referred to as Delta Force, while DEVGRU, or the United States Naval Special Warfare DEVelopment GRoUp, was the successor to the more common reference of SEAL Team 6.

"You start doing this in this fashion," Kurtzman added, "then where does it end? Remember Force Recon? The Marines tried for decades to keep that asset to themselves but now it's out of Corps control and in JSOC's."

"The Marines got tired of seeing Green Berets and SEALs getting all the covert action and agreed to the move," Brognola pointed out. "Look, this isn't an attempt to poach our crews. It's our specialty—last-minute, high degree of difficulty, direct action. This isn't an attempt by the Pentagon to piss on our turf—it's a professional favor. We've used and abused their personnel and equipment before, though they didn't necessarily know it was us. What's the problem?"

"I guess *that* is," Kurtzman said. "JSOC initiated this…directly. It wasn't a request or system of briefings channeled through Homeland or the Executive Office.

They've thrown an end run, broken the cone of silence and come to us face-to-face. Something's changed."

"How do we know he's not working with a Senate or Congressional special prosecutor? Times have changed, Hal. They're trying to put covert-ops guys in prison these days."

"Look, I ran Kubrick's name past my Justice contacts. The FBI had nothing on him. Barb's own check with NSA says Kubrick did some questionable things in El Salvador back in the day. He's not a good candidate for setting us up. He checks out, guys. This is about killing bad guys with mass political protection. We're all on the same side. The brigadier's not working with the *New York Times,* people."

Price pursed her lips then folded her arms. "I'll alert the boys."

THE WAR ROOM was crowded.

The five members of Phoenix Force and three of Able Team were arrayed around the conference table. The mood was upbeat and a current of emotional energy hummed in the room, just below everyone's awareness. Clearly a mission was imminent, and the men of Stony Man were ready to take up the challenge.

"The KLPD is running a safehouse on the outskirts of Islamabad. It consists of six rooms, the entire seventh floor of a residential building, about half a block away from one of the largest mosques in the city and a local police precinct," Barbara Price began.

From his wheelchair Kurtzman worked his keyboard. On the large screen recessed into the wall a digitized satellite map of the world appeared. Latitude and longitude readings scrolled down as the head of the cyberteam dialed up first Southwest Asia, then Pakistan, then Islamabad. On the screen, high-definition optics revealed buildings and streets.

Gary Manning, shoulders wide as barn doors, leaned over to Hermann Schwarz. "The resolution on that screen kicks ass."

"That building is your target," Price said.

On the screen the image split to accommodate a text scroll listing building materials, windowpane thickness, door construction, plumbing and electrical diagrams and a schematic drawing of the industrial blueprint.

Manning and Schwarz, the explosives specialist on each of their respective teams, began taking notes. Manning used a yellow legal pad while Schwarz employed a heavily modified CPDA, or Combat Personal Data Assistant.

Rosario Blancanales, a member of Able Team along with Schwarz, turned toward their unit commander, Carl Lyons, a blond and burly ex-LAPD detective. "We can put a sniper position on that building at the intersection across from the target. We'd have exposure on two sides to the building plus elevation on its roof. Also we can cover the major avenues of approach."

"Not perfect," Lyons agreed. "But just about all we can do."

"We are going to ensure police response is down during the time frame," Kurtzman said. "I have my team working on it now. We'll simply crunch through their phone lines and shut everything down. We aren't going there to leave Islamabad cops dead in the street."

"What about any response from ISI assets?" Calvin James asked. The ex-SEAL reached up and stroked his close-cropped mustache with a hand the color of burnished onyx.

"The genesis of this operation is our problems with

ISI boys getting U.S. boys dead. Most especially the KLPD branch," Price said. "I've seen the information the ISA gave JSOC and it's smoking-gun, slam-dunk stuff. The jackasses holed up in that apartment building are jihadists. They're either just coming from some terror mission or they're going to some terror mission. If KLPD wants to protect them, then they're exactly the kind of targets within Pakistani intelligence we want to cull."

"Bang bang," T. J. Hawkins said.

"Numbers?" David McCarter asked. The ex-SAS commando was the leader of Phoenix Force.

"Anywhere from a squad to a platoon," Price answered. "Armed with light weapons, grenades, standard stuff."

"That's a little ambiguous," McCarter pointed out.

"As far as it goes all you're really, really concerned with is *this* man," Kurtzman said.

He tapped a key and a picture of a young Middle Eastern man filled the screen. He was handsome and well groomed in traditional dress. Each member of the Stony Man teams scrutinized the picture closely, committing each detail to memory as closely as they had the target building's industrial specifications.

"Who's this bastard?" Hawkins asked.

"Prince Ziad Jarrah bin Sultan al-Thani," Price replied. "And for the next twelve hours he is your raison d'être."

Lyons leaned over toward Schwarz. "What did she say? The guy is our what?"

"Raisin entrée," Schwarz replied.

Hawkins snorted out loud. "You guys are like Abbot and Costello." The ex-Ranger trooper shifted his gaze over to Rosario Blancanales. "Sorry—Three Stooges."

The Puerto Rican ex-Green Beret gave the Texan a wan smile. "Fuck you very much, T.J."

"Did you say 'Prince'?" Rafael Encizo interrupted.

"Yes," Price answered. "Saudi oil actually—if there's any other kind. His father is very high up in the defense ministry. He is, in fact, Osama bin Laden's second cousin. He is a crown prince."

Encizo leaned his stocky build back into his chair and whistled. He eyed the picture of the Saudi prince up on the screen the way an alcoholic eyed an unopened bottle of liquor.

"Meaning?" Schwarz asked.

"Meaning there are somewhere in the neighborhood of eight hundred princes in the Kingdom Saud, currently," Price explained. "Of those only a very tight handful are even remotely likely to succeed to the throne. Bin Sultan al-Thani is one of them."

Silence greeted her proclamation. Price smirked; she loved it when she was able to shut them up.

David McCarter let out a long, slow whistle as James shook his head in disbelief.

"This explains why the Agency punted to JSOC and JSOC handed off to us," Manning muttered.

Brognola spoke up. "Technically only the paramilitary operations officers of the CIA's Special Activities Division can legally do this. By handing off to JSOC, the Agency hoped to quash the deal. My contact hoped to pull a bureaucratic riposte by coming to us."

"Who cares what's holding up the pinheads. I've always wanted to kill royalty," Lyons said.

"Then I suggest we get cracking," Price replied. "We only have a narrow window to make this work."

CHAPTER TWO

Islamabad, Pakistan

Carl Lyons regarded the target building through his night-vision scope.

He ran the Starlite model attached to his baffled SVD sniper rifle along the exposed windows, putting each dark square in his crosshairs before smoothly scanning onward. He looked for fixed points to use as quick landmarks once the shooting started as he played the optic across the building's roof.

"Able Actual in position. All clear on roof," he murmured into his throat mike.

Across the street on the second leg of their L-shaped overwatch positions Rosario Blancanales nestled in closer to the Pachmayr recoil pad on the buttstock of his own silenced SVD. "Able Beta in position. All clear on primary and secondary approach routes," he replied.

Lyons shifted his scope, running it along the length of a fire escape leading down to the dark alley that would serve as Phoenix Force's primary insertion point. "Able Epsilon, status please?"

"We barely ever get out of the Western Hemisphere," Schwarz answered into the com link, "and you take me to a shithole like this? What? Was Paris blacked out on your frequent-flyer miles?"

"Are we clear on the ground floor, Able Epsilon?" Lyons repeated.

In the back of the blacked-out 1970s model delivery van Hermann Schwarz eased back the charging handle on his RPK machine gun. The muzzle of the weapon was set just back from the access panel covertly placed in the rear door of the vehicle.

"Six o'clock clear," Schwarz conceded.

From his rooftop position Lyons touched a finger to his earbud. "You copy that, Stony?"

"Copy, Stony here," Barbara Price's cool voice responded on the other end of the satellite bounce. "Phoenix Actual, you are clear on approach."

"Phoenix Actual copy," David McCarter responded. "En route."

Carl Lyons pulled his face away from his scope and quickly did a security check of his area. It was very early in the morning and the residential block was like a ghost town. Despite this, the leader of Able Team felt naked and exposed.

Unable to field adequate overwatch because of insufficient personnel assets, the Farm's JSOC liaison had requested additional manpower. Price had no choice but to deploy Able Team as security element for Phoenix Force's raid.

Because the Farm's teams were operating black inside Pakistan, local coordination and cover had been impossible. Able Team had taken their positions only minutes prior to the strike. Dressed as Islamabad riot police to disguise their Western features and delay any alert to the authorities, they would be exposed to a confused, frightened and potentially hostile indigenous population should their positions be discovered.

Speed and decisive of action on the part of Phoenix Force was their best hope at this point.

Across the street from Carl Lyons, Rosario Blancanales shifted his scope and took in the alley running next to the target building. A blacked-out delivery van with a sliding side door identical to the one occupied by Schwarz suddenly swerved into the alley.

Instantly, Blancanales shifted his aim and began scanning his overwatch sectors to provide Phoenix Force with security.

In the alley Phoenix exited the vehicle, leaving the engine running. The dome and cargo lights had been disabled so that the five-man team looked like black shadows leaking from a dark box as they approached the building's side entrance.

T. J. Hawkins produced a claw-toothed crowbar and the countdown began.

ON THE SIXTH FLOOR of the target building Ziad Jarrah bin Sultan al-Thani put his cup of strong coffee down and drew heavily on his cigarette. His eyes squinted against the harsh smoke as he surveyed the room.

Three hollow-eyed men in Western business suits with Skorpion machine pistols were spread across the room while a fourth man, their boss, spoke with quiet tones into a satellite phone. A Wahhabite cleric had a Koran open in his lap and was reading a passage to a sweating teenage boy sitting in a straight-backed kitchen chair.

Two men, explosives experts from the Pakistani terror group Lashkar-e-Taiba, carefully rigged the boy with a suicide bomber vest packed with powerful Semtex plastic explosive.

It was a warm night in Islamabad but all the doors

and windows to the apartment were tightly closed for security reasons. Ziad Jarrah had stripped off his expensive robes and was wearing only a ribbed cotton white muscle shirt, his olive skin damp with sweat.

The Saudi carefully lined up packets of *riyals* on the table. The currency totaled the equivalent of five thousand U.S. dollars. The sum would be paid to the suicide bomber's family upon his detonation. The bomber's rewards would come later, in heaven.

Ziad Jarrah thought how nice and cool the vice dens of Dubai would be, or his palace in Riyadh. But he grew so bored there. He loved being out on the edge of the jihad—not too close, but close enough to feel the vicarious thrill of murder plotted and murder committed.

He placed the last stack of money on the table, made eye contact with the bomber, nodded, then began putting the money into a manila envelope. Once he was done he stubbed out his cigarette and immediately lit another. He smoothed down each side of his thin mustache where it ran into the sparse hair of his goatee.

He drew in deeply, filling his lungs with smoke. Across the room the leader of the KLPD unit abruptly clicked off his phone. He turned toward the kitchen table and his suit coat swung open, revealing his own machine pistol in a shoulder holster.

"Abdul." The security service officer smiled. "My brother, we are ready. You go to glory!"

The bomber looked down as one of the terrorist explosives engineers placed the detonator in his hand. Another Lashkar-e-Taiba operative stepped forward and began to use black electrician's tape to secure the ignition device to the bomber's hand. Neither Ziad Jarrah nor the KLPD officer bothered to tell the martyr in the chair that there was a ignition failsafe built around a Nokia cell phone constructed directly into the bomb.

One push of the Pakistani intelligence agent's speed dial and any hesitation the teenager might feel would disappear instantly.

Ziad Jarrah could feel a sense of euphoria, a giddiness at what was about to happen, surge through him. The illicit thrills of Dubai paled in comparison.

HAWKINS LEVERED the crowbar into place beside the dead bolt and wrenched it open. The metal-and-mesh outer security door popped open and swung wide. Sidestepping it like a dancing partner, Hawkins moved forward and reinserted the crowbar into the doorjamb.

The Texan's shoulders flexed hard against the resistance, and in an instant the dead bolt was ripped out of its mooring. He stepped to the side and threw the crowbar down. Rafael Encizo, AKS-74U Kalashnikov carbine held at port arms, ran forward and kicked the door out of the way.

He darted into the building, sweeping his muzzle down. Calvin James followed in close behind him, his own AKS carbine covering a complementary zone vector. Directly behind them Manning and McCarter folded into the assault line, weapons up in mirror positions.

Freeing up a Russian AK-47 RAK .12-gauge automatic shotgun, Hawkins stepped into position and began covering the team's rear security as they penetrated the building.

Across the street from his elevated vantage Lyons spoke into his sat-com, "Phoenix is hot inside. Phoenix is hot inside."

A second later Barbara Price acknowledged him. "Copy."

Both Blancanales and Schwarz made additional sweeps of their zones. The streets remained deserted, buildings dark and silent. Inside the target building Phoenix Force rushed down starkly illuminated hallways and up dim staircases.

From the outside Lyons played the scope of his 7.62 mm SVD along the windows of the target floor. As he swept the crosshairs past a window it suddenly exploded with light as heavy drapes were thrust aside by a swarthy man in a muscle shirt.

Instantly, Lyons reorientated his weapon. His focus narrowed down, and the man's face leaped into sight with superb clarity. Lyons felt the corners of his mouth tug upward in a grin. Ziad Jarrah-el-asshole, Lyons thought to himself. Merry Christmas to me.

He initiated radio contact. "Be advised," he warned. "Be advised. I have eyes on Primary. Primary confirmation."

"Phoenix copy," McCarter responded. "We are at the door now."

"Understood," Lyons replied.

He tightened the focus on his sniper scope. Lighting a cigarette, Ziad Jarrah moved out of the way, revealing an angle into the room. Lyons's optic reticule filled with the image of a second man seated on a kitchen chair. The ex-LAPD detective felt his eyes widen in the sudden shock of recognition. Suddenly a balaclava-clad man in a business suit appeared in the window and snapped the curtains shut.

Lyons held back on his shot, trying desperately to work his com link in time. "Phoenix!"

On the other end of the com link McCarter was

giving Hawkins a nod. The ex-Ranger stepped forward and swung up the RAK 12 and placed the big vented muzzle of the shotgun next to the doorknob and lock housing. The .12-gauge roared as the breeching round tore through the mechanism like a fastball burning past a stupefied batter.

Hawkins folded back as the massive shape of Gary Manning stepped forward, sweeping up a solid leg into a tight curl. He exploded outward in a heel-driven front snap kick that burst the already damaged door inward.

Rafael Encizo shot through the opening and peeled left, AKS-74U up and tracking as Calvin James peeled off to the right. As McCarter, followed by Hawkins and Manning, sprinted into the room Encizo killed a man armed with a Skorpion submachine gun. Men started cursing.

"Phoenix! Phoenix suicide bomber—" Lyons's voice was loud and frantic in Phoenix Force's earbud.

The warning came too late to stop the assault force's forward momentum. McCarter swung around, searching for the threat. He saw Ziad Jarrah throw himself through the air, leaping away from a terrified teenager strapped down with a tan vest festooned with blocks of Semtex and bundles of wires.

"Bomb!" McCarter screamed.

Bullets burned across the room as the situation descended into a slow-motion montage. Manning struck Calvin James with a brutal shoulder block, knocking the ex-SEAL back into McCarter and toward the door.

Skorpion-wielding men in business suits spun and began trying to track targets. McCarter was driven backward as his eyes found the bomber's. The kid's gaze had glazed over, his mouth hanging slack. From out of his peripheral vision the Phoenix Force leader saw the other members of his team crowding in as he fell through the door.

Over their shoulders he saw the teenager squeeze his hand into a desperate fist, thumb hunting for the ignition. We're not going to make it, he thought.

Outside the building a wave of fire suddenly erupted into the night, filling the optic of both Lyons and Blancanales.

"Phoenix! Phoenix!" Lyons shouted into his throat mike.

There was no answer.

Black smoke roiled up into the air as orange flames licked at the inside of the building. Lyons popped up, breaking down the SVD sniper rifle with quick motions. He quickly slung the carryall over his shoulder and stepped to the edge of the building, where he snapped his rappel rope into the D-ring carabiners of his slide harness.

He went over the edge and dropped six stories to the street. Lights were coming on in buildings up and down the street. Lyons came out and saw Blancanales already on the ground and sprinting for the van where Hermann Schwarz was at the wheel.

Suddenly, David McCarter's voice was audible. "Be advised," McCarter growled. "We are up and we are bloody leaving."

The relief in Barbara Price's voice was obvious even over the sat link. "Good copy, Phoenix."

Sliding into the van's passenger seat, Lyons turned toward Schwarz as Blancanales jumped into the back. "Let's make sure all five of our birdies make it into their rig and then make a rapid strategic advance to the rear."

"Are we calling this a success?" Schwarz asked.

"Close enough for government work," Lyons replied.

INSIDE THE BUILDING Phoenix Force picked themselves up off the floor in the hallway. Their ears rang from the sharp crack of the explosion, and dark smoke obscured the interior ceiling above their heads.

"Let's go, people," McCarter said.

Hawkins looked around. The door to the target apartment had been blown off by the suicide vest blast and he could see that the outside wall on that side of the building had been blown outward, leaving a sagging ceiling and a gaping hole exposing empty space out over the street below. Fire burned in lively pockets.

"Jesus," Encizo suddenly cursed. "The stairs we came up hugged that wall—there's like a fifteen-foot gap here!"

Around them in the building Phoenix could hear people stirring, calling out in panic and milling in confusion. The building was rife with extremist foot soldiers. McCarter instantly went on alert, his weapon up.

"Gary," he ordered, "check the staircase down the hall."

"I'm on it," Manning answered, moving out. He ran down the hall, bent low to avoid the thickest part of the smoke, and kicked open a door at the opposite end of the corridor. "It's good!"

"You heard him," Calvin James barked. "Let's move, people."

McCarter spun and covered the hall as his men ran down the passage and entered the stairwell. "Go!" he snapped. "I've got security!"

The other four members of Phoenix rushed through the doorway just as the first of the enemy combatants exploded into the hall. The man, bearded and dressed only in pants with a automatic pistol in his fist, shouted an angry warning and lifted his weapon.

McCarter killed him but there was a chorus of answering shouts. A volley of fire erupted outside the hall, initiating a storm of lead that tore into the corridor. More glass from the few unbroken windows shattered, falling inward, and the wood paneling was shredded. After his initial burst McCarter threw himself to the floor, directing his momentum over a shoulder, and rolled clear of the hall, keeping below the hail of gunfire.

McCarter spotted a big man armed with a black machine pistol appear from the door of a room directly across the hall from the suicide bomber. The giant shouted an order and peeled back from the doorway. A second man ran forward, Kalashnikov assault rifle slung over his shoulder and across his back.

McCarter swore. The man went to one knee and leveled an RPG-7 at the end of the hall. Rising, McCarter turned and sprinted. The 84 mm warhead could penetrate twelve inches of steel armor; it would blow through even a reinforced door with ease. McCarter scrambled across the floor and leaped up into the air.

McCarter struck the floor and slid across as a fireball blew through the door where he had been and rolled into the already devastated room like a freight train. Shrapnel and jagged chunks of wood lanced through the air.

McCarter's ears still rang from the explosive con-

cussion and his face bled from a dozen minor lacera-
tions, but his hand was steady on the trigger as Pakistani
gunmen rushed through the front door.

CHAPTER THREE

The first shooter breached the door, AKM assault rifle up and at the ready. McCarter put him down with a burst from his submachine gun. The combatant hit the burning floor like a bag of wet cement. The man running in behind him looked down as the point man hit the floor. He looked back up, searching for a target, and McCarter blew off the left side of his face.

The third man in the line tripped over the second man's falling corpse. McCarter used a burst to scythe the man to the ground and then put a single shot into the top of his skull. Through the swirling smoke and angry screams McCarter saw a black metal canister arc into the room.

McCarter recognized the threat instantly as an RG-42 antipersonnel hand grenade. He popped up off his belly onto his hands and knees as the grenade hit the floor inside the hall and bounced toward him. Leaving the AKS where it lay, McCarter dived forward, scooping up the bouncing hand grenade, and wrapping his hands around the black cylinder.

He hit the floor hard from his short hop, absorbing the impact with his elbows. He rolled over onto one shoulder and thrust out his arm, sending the grenade shooting away from him. It cleared the corpses in the entranceway and bounced up and out the hall doorway on the far side. McCarter heard a sudden outburst of curses and buried his head in his arms.

The grenade detonated and another cloud of smoke billowed in through the doorway on the heels of the concussive force.

McCarter came to his feet, scooping up the AKS submachine gun. He shuffled backward and crouched next to the wall, heading for the door to the staircase down to the street level. McCarter caught a flash of movement and spun toward the blown-out doors of two apartments across from their original target.

"David!" Encizo's voice blared in McCarter's earbud. "We're coming, brother!"

"Negative!" McCarter shouted.

He saw two men in khaki jackets rush up to the shattered windows, AKM rifles clutched in their hands. McCarter dropped to one knee beside the wall and brought up the AKS. He beat the men to the trigger and his submachine gun spit flame. It recoiled sharply in his hands and shell casings arced out to spill across the floor.

"The stair is too narrow. I'm coming to you!"

McCarter put two rounds into the face of the first man. Bloody holes the size of dimes appeared, slapping the man's head back. Blood sprayed in a mist behind his head and he slumped to the ground, his weapon clattering at his feet.

McCarter shifted smoothly, like ball bearings in a sling swivel, toward the second gunman. They fired simultaneously. The muzzle-flash of the man's weapon burst into a flaming star pattern. The sound of the heavier assault rifle firing was thunderous compared to the more subdued sound of McCarter's 9 mm subgun.

The 7.62 mm caliber rounds tore into the molding of

the wall just to McCarter's right. The rounds punched
through the building material, tearing fist-size chunks
from the wall and door frame, spilling white plumes
of chalky plaster dust into the air.

McCarter's burst hit the man in a tight pattern. The
bullets drilled into the receiver of the AKM, tearing
it from the stunned gunner's hands. Two more rounds
punched into his chest three inches above the first, staggering him backward.

McCarter came to his feet, the AKS held up and
ready. He triggered two rounds into the stunned gunman
and took him down, blowing out the back of his neck.
McCarter danced to the side and, still facing the front
of the hall, held the AKS up and ready in one hand. He
stepped back into stairway door.

A gunman came around the corner of one of the
rooms, Kalashnikov firing. McCarter put a burst into
his knee and thigh, knocking the screaming man to the
floor. He put a double tap through the top of his head.
Brain matter and bits of skull splattered outward.

McCarter moved in a shuffle back toward the stair,
realizing that what had been billed as a safehouse by
intelligence had actually been more along the lines of
a barracks—a significant and unsubtle difference. He
took fire from the open door and swiveled to meet the
threat as another pair of gunmen rounded the corner
from the front hall. McCarter threw himself belly down,
his legs trailing out behind him down the stairs, angling
his body so he was out of sight from the shooters in the
hall.

McCarter swept his submachine gun in a wide loose
arc, spraying bullets at the gunman firing through the
shattered hall. One of the men's weapons suddenly
swung up toward the ceiling and McCarter caught

a glimpse of him staggering backward into the dark though he never saw his own rounds impact.

He lay on the stairs, only his arms and shoulders emerging from the door to the stairwell. He rotated up onto his right shoulder to get an angle of fire on the entranceway. He saw one of the terrorist gunmen rushing forward and shot the man's ankles, bringing him to the floor. McCarter fired another burst into the prone man, finishing him off, only to have his bolt lock open as his magazine ran dry.

McCarter let the AKS dangle across his chest as a second terrorist leaped over the body of the first and charged forward. The skeletal folding stock of his AKS-74U pressed tight into his shoulder and he fired the weapon as he bounded forward.

McCarter put his hands against the floor and snapped up, clearing the edge of the doorway. Bullets tore into the floor where his head had just been. He twisted on the stair and jumped downward. He landed at the bottom, his legs bending to absorb the impact, just as he had been taught during paratrooper training. He took the recoil, felt it surge up through his heels, and rolled off to the side. He turned in the direction of the side door to the lower level of the building. He got up and ran down to the ground floor, men screaming above him.

A burst of gunfire echoed in the stairwell and 5.45 mm rounds tore into the floor where McCarter had landed. He went up against the wall at his back and pulled a 9 mm Glock 17 from its holster. He heard boots thundering on the stairwell and he bent, swiveled and thrust his gun arm around the corner. He triggered four shots without exposing himself.

There was a satisfying thump as the gunman pitched

forward and bounced down the stairs. He spilled out at the bottom of the stairs, sprawling in front of McCarter, and his weapon skidded out from his hands. The ex-SAS trooper triggered a round into the back of the man's head and snatched up his fallen weapon.

Another figure appeared at the top of the stairs and took a shot at him. McCarter leaped back out of view of the stairwell, grabbing up the AKS-74U by its shoulder sling. Bullets struck the corpse of the dead Pakistani terrorist. McCarter caught a motion from his right side in time to see a khaki-clothed figure come through an interior door.

McCarter fumbled to bring the AKS to bear but didn't have time. He let it dangle from the strap and brought up his 9 mm pistol as he dropped to one knee. Instead of firing from the hip, his adversary brought the AKS up to his shoulder for a more accurate shot.

McCarter's shot took him in the throat. From the door to the alley outside, Hawkins fired a second burst, dashing the thug's brains out. McCarter immediately spun in a tight crouch and fired blindly up the stairwell for the second time. There was an answering burst of automatic gunfire, but no sound of bodies hitting the floor.

McCarter holstered his pistol and took up the AKS. He quickly ducked his head into the stairwell before thrusting his carbine around the corner to trigger a burst. Using the covering fire to keep the enemy back, McCarter snagged the dead man at the bottom of the stairs over to him by his belt.

"Can we go, boss?" Hawkins shouted. "Engines running!"

"Too hot!"

McCarter pulled a Soviet-era RGD-5 antipersonnel

hand grenade from the dead terrorist's belt. Like the RG-42, it had a blast radius of slightly more than seventy-five feet. He held his AKS by the pistol grip and stuck out his thumb. He used his free hand to help hook the pin around his extended thumb. He made a tight fist around the pistol grip of the AKS and pulled with his other hand, releasing the spring on the grenade.

McCarter let the spoon fly. He turned and put a warning burst up the staircase to buy time. He counted down three seconds and then chucked the grenade around the corner and up the stairs. He turned away from the opening as the blast was funneled by the walls up and down the staircase, spraying shrapnel in twin columns.

Ears ringing, McCarter made for the door to the building down the short entrance hall. He came up to it, AKS held at the ready. The door hung open, broken. From outside he heard gunfire as the Phoenix Force commandos engaged targets firing from the windows above them. A figure darted past the open door and McCarter gunned him down as Hawkins backed toward the running vehicle, directing rounds at targets above him.

A terrorist jumped into the hall and flopped down onto his belly, throwing a bipod-mounted RPK 7.62 mm machine gun down in front of him. McCarter jerked back outside the doorway as the machine gunner opened up with the weapon, sending a virtual firestorm in McCarter's direction.

McCarter's heart pounded as he moved, beating wildly in his chest. His perception of time seemed to slow as adrenaline speeded up his senses to preternatural levels of awareness. His mind clicked through options like a supercomputer running algorithms. His head swiveled like a gun turret, the muzzle of his weapon tracking in perfect synchronicity.

He saw no movement other than his team down the alley. Inside the hallway he saw woodchips fly off in great, ragged splinters from the withering machine-gun fire. He heard the staccato beat of the weapon discharging. He sensed something and twisted toward the staircase. A khaki-clad man with a beard rushed off the stairs.

McCarter had the drop on him and gunned him down. The AKS bucked hard in the big Briton's hands and he stitched a line of slugs across the Pakistani gunman's chest. Geysers of blood erupted from the man's torso and throat as the kinetic energy from McCarter's rounds drove him backward. The man's heel caught on the outflung arm of his compatriot and he tumbled over, dead before he struck the ground.

McCarter scrambled back out the door. He saw a flash from the stairs and felt the air split as rounds blew by his face. He fired wildly behind him for cover as he rolled up and across the alley. He swung back around and covered the staircase and the side door, prepared to send a volley in either direction. His finger tensed on the smooth metal curve of the trigger.

There was a lull in the firing for a moment and McCarter heard Manning screaming instructions. Cold anger burned deep inside of the Phoenix Force leader. A haze of smoke hung in the hall and the stench of cordite was an opiate to McCarter's hyperstimulated senses. A burst of fire broke out from behind him.

"Let's go! Let's go!" James shouted.

McCarter stood, weapon up, and made to turn toward the vehicle. A final, crazed jihadist burst out the door as more weapons fire burned down from above. The

Briton's 5-round burst tore out the man's throat as the van pulled up next to him. Hawkins leaped in the back and spun, spraying covering fire.

McCarter turned, pumped his legs and dived in the back. He landed hard on the vehicle floor and heard the sound of squealing rubber over the din of weapons fire. He tried to get to a knee but Manning jerked the wheel hard as they took the corner and he was thrown into James.

"Are we calling this a win?" the ex-SEAL asked, voice dry.

"Let's call it a push," McCarter replied.

Burj Dubai Tower, Dubai
United Arabic emirates

THE EMIR LOVED the old ways.

He loved having sixteen wives, riding his Arabian stallions through the desert, drinking tiny cups of strong black coffee in the company of wise men, smoking his tobacco from a hookah. Despite this love of all things archaic, the emir was a pragmatist. He knew his ability to enjoy those wives and high-blooded horses came from the seemingly endless supply of oil, the petroleum sold to the infidel in volumes so staggering it was impossible to imagine it ending.

So the emir wore his traditional dress as he stood staring out the floor-to-ceiling windows in a penthouse suite of the Burj Dubai, the tallest man-made structure in the world and a wonder of modern engineering. It was a luxurious building he'd arrived at via jet-helicopter from his home city of Riyadh.

Among all its other wonders, Dubai also offered the finest in Filipina child prostitutes.

The emir turned away from the massive bed where the silent, hollow-eyed girl sat motionless, curled up on herself. He felt exhilarated and when he stared out the tinted windows into the uniquely blue waters of the Persian Gulf he felt like a master of the very universe.

From behind him he heard a discreet throat clearing and recognized the voice of his majordomo immediately.

"Yes, Abdulla," the emir said without turning. "Take her away, pay her purveyor and tell him I wish three more for this evening after our meeting with survey committee of the Bank of Kuwait and the Exxon-Mobil geologists."

"Sir…" Abdulla hesitated.

"Yes? What is it?" the emir snapped.

"It's about your son…Ziad?"

The emir turned, regarded the slightly built man who, despite appearances, was irreplaceable in running his holdings. "Ziad? He is here? I thought he was spreading the jihad in Islamabad among those barbarians and American foot-lickers, the Pakis."

Abdulla turned toward the child and clapped his hands fast three times before making a hissing sound. The child rolled out of bed and scurried toward the door to the suite. Bruises lined her skinny thighs in vivid relief.

"What? What is it?"

"It's about your son," Abdulla said.

Just like that the emir knew. Forty-five minutes later he began to use his billions of dollars in oil money to fund his vengeance against the largest consumer of that product: the United States of America.

CHAPTER FOUR

Sadr City, Baghdad

The Blackhawks came thumping over the horizon.

Baghdad lay spread out below them, the sprawling slum of Sadr City emerging from the amorphous squalor. The Shiite stronghold was block after block of slammed-together buildings, jigsaw structures, twisting alleys stacked on asymmetrical courtyards and narrow, crowded streets.

In the northern district of the massive Sadr City slum the U.S. military had run into a problem as the beleaguered country lurched toward stability. The Sixth Infantry Division remained engaged in house-to-house combat with splinter-element insurgents of Muqtada al-Sadr's Iranian-backed Mahdi army. The ground forces had established a perimeter encircling the combat zone along with elements of the Iraqi National Army.

Fighting remained fierce in the face of the ratification of certain documents of nationalism by the Iraqi government, but five years of preparation had turned the urban terrain into a labyrinthine fortress extending from the tops of buildings to the sewers and basements below street level. An army of well-armed zealots manned the battlements.

At the center of the combat perched Abu Hafiza, al Qaeda torture master, cell leader and consultant strategist behind the Madrid, Spain, bombings. Hafiza waited, entrenched and surrounded by a hard-core bodyguard unit willing to die for jihad and the liberation of the Shiite people.

For obvious political reasons the U.S. had opted for a surgical strike rather than the use of massive force. Going into the snake pit to get Abu Hafiza was a suicide mission.

At the request of Brigadier General Kubrick, relayed through Brognola, Phoenix Force had deployed to Iraq.

American forces were arrayed around the landing strip, guns orientated outward, enforcing the security perimeter as the Blackhawk helicopters settled into position. Immediately a colonel, the division executive officer, moved forward into the brunt of the rotor wash to greet the arrivals.

The cargo door on the Blackhawk slid open under the spinning blades and five figures emerged from the helicopter transport. Dressed in black fatigues with faces covered by balaclava hoods, the men moved easily under a burden of upgraded body armor and unorthodox weaponry, the colonel noted.

The first man to reach the American officer stuck out his hand and shook with a hard, dry clench. When he spoke, a British accent was evident.

"You here to get us up to speed?" David McCarter asked.

The colonel nodded. "Have your men follow me," he said.

With the rest of Phoenix Force following, McCarter fell into step with the colonel. "Has the situation changed at all?" he asked.

"Just as we left," the colonel replied. "The Iraqi

National Army moved into Sadr City to quell violent demonstrations. They ran into heavy resistance and our reinforcement brigade was called in. We rolled forward and discovered Abu Hafiza has prepped this slum the way Hezbollah did southern Lebanon for the Israelis back in 2007. It's just a mess. But we've beaten them back to their final redoubt." The colonel indicated a Stryker vehicle with its ramp down. "But it's a hell of a redoubt," he added as they climbed into the APC. "We can either bring in the bunker busters or throw away hundreds of men in a frontal assault. Neither of which is going to look too goddamn good on twenty-four-hour cable news feed."

"Or you can call us," T. J. Hawkins noted dryly.

"Yes." The colonel nodded. "Whoever the hell 'you' happen to be."

"We do like our little mysteries," Calvin James acknowledged from behind his balaclava.

"You somehow manage to pull the rabbit out of this hat and I'll call you mommy if that's what you want."

"That won't be necessary," McCarter assured the man as the Stryker ramp buttoned up and they rolled deeper into the city. "Just don't call us late for dinner."

THE BLAST from a helicopter missile had knocked a hole in the street. The explosion ripped up the asphalt and punched a hole in the ground deep enough to reveal the sewer line. Workers had managed to clear enough rubble out of the crater to keep the sewage stream flowing, but there had not been enough security or money for complete repairs. A line of rubble like a gravel-covered hillside led up out of the sewer to the street.

While the rest of Phoenix Force crouched in the shadows, Calvin James eased his way up the uncertain slope to reconnoiter the area. He crawled carefully, using his elbows and knees with his weapon cradled in the crook of his arms. As tense as the situation was, there was a large part of him that was grateful to escape the stinking claustrophobia of the pit. Just blocks over, combined Iraqi and American forces hammered the Shiite positions to provide cover and distraction for the inserting special operators.

James eased his way to the lip of the blast crater and carefully raised his head over the edge. The Sadr City neighborhood appeared deserted at the late hour. Tenement buildings rose up above street level shops, the structures book-ending right up against each other. Rusted iron fire escapes adorned the fronts of the old buildings. Brightly colored laundry hung from windows and clotheslines. The roofs were a forest of old-fashioned wire antennae. The street was lined with battered old cars, some of them up on concrete blocks and obviously unusable. Across the street feral dogs rooted through an overflowing garbage bin.

Carefully, James extended his weapon and scanned the neighborhood street through his scope. He detected no movement, saw no faces in windows and doorways, no figures silhouetted on the fire escapes and rooftops. He looked down to the end of the street and saw nothing stirring, then turned and checked the other direction with the same result.

Satisfied, he looked down. He gave a short low whistle and instantly McCarter appeared at the foot of the rubble incline.

"All clear. Come have a look," James whispered.

McCarter nodded once in reply and re-slung his M-4 carbine before scrambling quickly up the rubble. He slid into place next to Hawkins and carefully scanned the street, as well.

"There," he said. "That building." He indicated a burned-out six-story apartment complex with a thrust of his sharp chin. "That's the building. That'll give us the entry point into the compound."

"Sounds good," McCarter agreed. "We'll run this exactly like we did our insertion in the Basra operation a while ago."

"Only without the sewer crawl."

"Which is nice."

Eighteen months before the building had been assaulted by an Iraqi National Army unit with American Special Forces advisers after intelligence had revealed it served as an armory and bomb-making factory for the local Shiite militias.

"I haven't noticed any sentries yet," James said. His gaze remained suctioned to the sniper scope as he scanned the building.

"They're there," McCarter said. "That's the back door to the militia complex."

"Heads up," James suddenly hissed.

Instantly, McCarter attempted to identify the threat. Up the street a Toyota pickup turned onto the avenue and began cruising toward their position. The back of the vehicle held a squad of gunmen and there were three men in the vehicle cab.

McCarter and James froze, nestling themselves in among the broken masonry of the bomb crater. Advancing slowly, the vehicle cruised up the street. Moving carefully, McCarter eased his head down below the lip of the crater and transferred his carbine into a more accessible position.

Beside him James seemed to evaporate, blending

into the background as the pickup inched its way down the street. The former Navy SEAL commando watched the enemy patrol with eyes narrowed, his finger held lightly on the trigger of his weapon.

The vehicle rolled closer and now both Phoenix Force members could hear the murmur of voices in casual conversation. James watched as a pockmarked Iraqi in the back took a final drag of his cigarette and then flicked it away.

The still smoking butt arced up and landed next to the prone Phoenix Force sniper with a small shower of sparks that stung his exposed face. The cigarette bounced and rolled down the incline to come to rest against McCarter's leg.

A gunman in the back of the vehicle said something and the others laughed as the pickup cruised past the two hidden men headed toward the fighting. Playing a hunch, James risked moving to scan the burned-out building across the street with his scope. His gamble paid off as a man armed with a SVD Soviet-era Dragunov sniper rifle appeared briefly in a third-story window to acknowledge the patrol rolling past his position.

James grinned. The pickup reached the end of the street and disappeared around a corner. "Got you, asshole," he whispered. "I got a security element on the third floor," he told McCarter.

"Does he interfere with movement?" McCarter scooped loose dirt over the burning cigarette, extinguishing it.

"He's back in the shadow now. I might have a shot with IR," Hawkins explained. "But he's definitely doing overwatch on this street."

"He the only one?"

"Only one I saw," James said. "But he could have a spotter or radio guy sitting next to him who'll sound the alarm if I put the sniper down."

"What's our other option?"

"I guess send the team across and hope he doesn't notice until we can be sure of how many we're dealing with."

"The clock is ticking," McCarter pointed out.

"Then I say let me take him."

"Encizo and I will cross the street and try to secure the ground floor before the rest of you come over."

"It's your call," James said simply. He clicked over the amplifier apparatus on his night scope and scanned the windows. A red silhouette appeared in the gloom of the third-story window. "I got him. No other figures present themselves from this angle."

"That'll have to do," McCarter said.

James held down on his target as McCarter called Encizo up and the two men slowly climbed into position. Encizo had left his Hawk MM-1 behind with Hawkins and held his silenced H&K MP-7 at the ready. McCarter slid his M-4/M-203 around to hang from his back and had pulled his own sound-suppressed weapon, the Browning Hi-Power, from its holster.

James settled snugly into his position as Phoenix Force gathered around him. His finger took up the slack on the curve of his trigger and he settled the fiber-optic crosshairs on the silhouette in the window.

The Mk 11 sniper rifle discharged smoothly, the muzzle lifting slightly with the recoil and pushing back into the hollow of James's shoulder. The report was muted in the hot desert air and the subsonic round cut across the space and tore through the open window.

In his scope James saw the figure's head jerk like a

boxer taking an inside uppercut. There was an instant of red smear in his sight as blood splashed, then the enemy sniper spun in a half circle and fell over.

"Go," James said.

McCarter was instantly up and sprinting. Behind him Encizo scrambled over the edge of the hole and raced after him. Both men crossed the street in a dead run, weapons up and ready as James began shifting his weapon back and forth in tight vectors to cover the building front.

McCarter crossed the open street and spun to throw his back into the wall beside the front door of the building. Half a second later Encizo repeated the motion, his MP-7 pointed down the street.

McCarter checked once before proceeding through the gaping doorway. He charged into the room, turning left and trying to move along the wall. Encizo came in and peeled right, coming to one knee and checking the room with his muzzle leading the way. Both men scanned the darkened chamber through their low-light goggles.

The front doors to the building had been blown out during the Iraqi raid and the room saturated with grenades and automatic-weapons fire. The two Phoenix warriors found themselves in a small lobby with a cracked and collapsed desk, a line of busted and dented mailboxes, a pitted and pocked elevator and two fire-scarred doorways. One of the interior doors had been blown off its hinges, revealing a staircase leading upward. The second sagged in place, as perforated as a cheese grater.

McCarter carefully moved forward and checked both doorways before turning and giving Encizo the thumbs-up signal. The combat swimmer turned and went to the doorway so that James could see him. He lifted a finger and spoke into his throat mike.

"Come across," he said. "We'll clear upward."

"Acknowledged," James replied.

Encizo turned back into the room just as he heard footsteps on the staircase. Booted feet pounded the wooden steps as someone jogged downward making no effort to conceal his movement. Encizo blinked and McCarter disappeared, moving smoothly to rematerialize next to the stairway access, back to the wall and sound-suppressed Browning pistol up.

Wearing a headscarf and American Army chocolate-chip-pattern camouflage uniform, a Shiite militia member with an AKM came out of the stairway and strolled casually into the room. On one knee Encizo centered his machine pistol on the irregular.

Oblivious to the shadows in the room, the man started walking across the floor toward the street. McCarter straightened his arm out. The Browning was a bulky silhouette in his hand, the cylinder of the suppressor a blunt oval in the gloom.

There was a whispered thwat-thwat and the front of the Iraqi's forehead came away in jigsaw chunks. The man dropped straight down to his knees, then tumbled forward onto his face with a wet sound.

Encizo kept the muzzle of his machine pistol trained on the doorway in case the man wasn't alone, but there was no sign of motion from the staircase as McCarter shifted his aim and cleared the second door.

Behind Encizo, Hawkins entered the room and peeled off to the left to take cover, followed closely by Manning and then Calvin James. Each member of the unit looked down at the dead Iraqi, his spilling blood clearly visible.

"We take the stairs," McCarter said in a low voice. "There's no way to clear a building this size with our manpower so it's hey-diddle-diddle, right-up-the-middle till we reach the roof, then over and in. Stay with silenced weapons for as long as we can."

The ex-SAS trooper swept up his Browning Hi-Power and advanced through the doorway as the rest of Phoenix Force fell into line behind him in an impromptu entry file. Hawkins took up the final position with his silenced Mk 11, replacing Gary Manning as rear security.

Weapons up, Phoenix Force continued infiltrating Baghdad.

RAFAEL ENCIZO opened his hand.

Greasy hair slid through his loosened fingers as he plucked the blade of his Cold Steel Tanto from the Iraqi militia member's neck. Blood gushed down the front of the man's chest in a hot, slick rush, and the gunman gurgled wetly in his throat.

Standing beside Encizo Calvin James snatched the man's rifle up as it started to fall. The eyepieces of the two commandos' night optics shone a dull, nonreflective green as they watched the man fall to his knees. Encizo lifted his foot and used the thick tread of his combat boot to push the dying Iraqi over.

The final Shiite soldier on the building roof struck the tarpaper and gravel as the last beats of his pounding heart pushed a gallon of blood out across the ground. As James set the scoped SVD sniper rifle down, Encizo knelt and cleaned his blade off on the man's jeans before sliding it home in its belt sheath.

Seeing the sentry down, McCarter led the rest of the team out of the stairwell and onto the roof. Phoenix

Force crouched next to a 60 mm mortar position beside the parapet and overlooked the cluster of buildings in the Baghdad slum. Below them, in the shadow of the militia sentry building, a large flat-roofed home stretched out behind an adobe-style wall. Armed guards walked openly or stood sentinel at doorways. In the courtyard near the front gate a Dzik-3 with Iraqi police markings stood, engine idling.

Hawkins took up a knee and began using the night scope on his Mk 11 to scan nearby buildings for additional security forces. As David McCarter took up his field radio Manning knelt behind him and began to loosen the nineteen-pound grappling gun from the Briton's rucksack.

"Super Stud to Egghead," McCarter said.

"That's so very funny," Akira Tokaido replied, voice droll.

"You have eyes on us?"

"Copy that," Tokaido confirmed.

At the moment the Predator drone launched by Jack Grimaldi from the Coalition-controlled Iraqi airport floated at such an altitude that it was invisible to either Phoenix Force or, more importantly, to the Iraqi Special Groups HQ below. Despite that, the powerful optics in the nose of the UAV readily revealed the heat-signature silhouettes of Phoenix to Akira Tokaido in his remote cockpit as they crouched on the Baghdad rooftop.

It was a little known fact that most of the larger drone aircraft seeing action in Afghanistan, and to a lesser extent Iraq, were piloted by operators at McCarren Air Force Base in Las Vegas, Nevada.

As soon as Kurtzman and Price had seen the remote pilot setup used by both the Air Force and the CIA they had gone to Brognola with a request for the Farm to field the same capabilities using the Stony Man cyberteam as operators.

Both Kurtzman and Carmen Delahunt had proved skilled and agile remote pilots, but it had been the good Professor Huntington Wethers who'd proved the most adept at maneuvering the UAV drones and he had consistently outflown the other two in training.

But Akira Tokaido, child prodigy of the videogame age, had taken the professor to school. The Japanese-American joystick jockey had exhibited a genius touch for the operations, and Kurtzman had put the youngest member of the team as primary drone pilot for the Farm.

Now Tokaido sat in the remote cockpit unit, or RCU, and controlled a MQ-1c Warrior from twenty-five thousand feet above Baghdad. He had four AGM-114 Hellfire missiles and a sensory/optics package in the nose transplanted from the U.S. Air Force RQ-4 Global Hawk, known as the Hughes Integrated Surveillance And Reconnaissance—HISAR—sensor system.

From a maximum ceiling of twenty-nine thousand feet, Tokaido could read the license plate of a speeding car. And then put a Hellfire missile in the tailpipe.

Having seen the effects of the coordinated air strikes during training with the FBI's hostage-rescue team at a gunnery range next to the Groom Lake facility known as the Ranch, David McCarter was more than happy to have the air support.

The ex-SAS leader of Phoenix Force touched his earbud and spoke into his throat mike. "You see the wheeled APC at the front gate?" he asked.

"Copy."

"That goes. I want a nice big fireball to draw eyes away from us while we come in the back door."

"That should obstruct the main entrance to the property," Tokaido allowed, voice calm. "That changes the original exit strategy Barb briefed me on."

"Acknowledged," McCarter responded. "But the truth on the ground has changed. Adapt, improvise, overcome."

"Your call, Phoenix," Tokaido confirmed. "I'll put the knock-knock anywhere you want."

"Good copy, that. Put one in the armored car and shut down the gate. You get a good cluster of bad guys outside in the street use Hellfires two and three at your discretion. Just save number four for my word."

"Understood." Tokaido paused. "You realize that if you're inside that structure when I let numbers two and three go you'll be extremely danger close, correct?"

"Stony Bird," McCarter said, "you just bring the heat. We'll stay in the kitchen."

"Understood. I'll drop altitude and start the show."

"Phoenix out." McCarter turned toward the rest of the team. "You blokes caught all that, right?" Each man nodded in turn. "Good. Hawkins, you remain in position. Clean up the courtyard and stay on lookout for Hajji snipers outside the compound."

Hawkins reached out and folded down the bipod on his Mk 11. "I'll reach out and touch a few people on behalf of the citizens of the United States of America." The Texan shrugged and grinned. "It's just a customer service I provide. Satisfaction guaranteed."

"Just try to stay awake up here, hotshot," McCarter said. "I'll put the zip-line on target. The rest of you get your Flying Fox attachments ready."

"I'm going first," Manning said. "You hit the mark with the grappling gun but we'll use me to test the weight."

"Negative, I'm point," James said. "The plan calls for me to slide first."

Manning shook his head. "That was before we got burned. Those assholes down there know we're coming. We'll only get the one line. I should go first." He stopped and grinned. "Besides, Doc, if you fall, who'll patch you up?"

McCarter lifted a hand. "He's right, Cal. We'll send Gary down first."

The ex-SWAT sniper took up his SPAS-15. "Doesn't seem right, a Canadian going before a SEAL, but I'll make an exception this time." He reached out a fist and he and the grinning Manning touched knuckles.

"Get set," McCarter warned.

CHAPTER FIVE

McCarter lifted the launcher of the T-PLS pneumatic tactical line-throwing system to his shoulder. The device sported 120 feet of 7 mm Kevlar line and launched the spear grapnel with enough force to penetrate concrete. Despite himself McCarter paused for a moment to savor the situation.

He felt adrenaline pump through his system like a bullet train on greased wheels. He knew that he was not only among the most competent warriors on the face of the earth, but also he was their leader. He could sense them around him now, reacting not with fear but with the eagerness of dedicated professionals.

They had the brutal acumen of men about to face impossible odds and achieve success. McCarter smiled to himself in cold satisfaction as he recalled the motto of the SAS—Who Dares Wins.

As his men, other than Hawkins, slid on their protective masks, McCarter's finger took up the slack in the grappling gun.

There was a harsh tunk sound as the weapon discharged, followed by the metallic whizzing of the line playing out. The sound of the impact six stories below was drowned out by the sound of Akira Tokaido's Hellfire taking out the Dzik-3 APC. A ball of fire and oily black smoke rose up like an erupting volcano. The blazing hulk leaped into the air and dropped back down with a heavy metal crunch that cracked the cobblestone court.

"Now we're on," Encizo declared, and Phoenix sprang into action.

THE MEN SLOWLY CHEWED their food as they watched the body hanging from chains set into the wall. The imam had dared to speak out against the random violence that claimed the lives of Baghdad's women and children, preaching in front of the prayer mats in the mosque that the Koran did not direct the slaughter of Muslim innocents in the name of Allah.

On his way to the market an Iraqi police car had stopped and two officers had thrown a sack over the imam's head and pushed him into the vehicle. When his hood had been ripped off, the cleric found himself chained to the wall and in the hands of the very extremists he had railed against.

Then he saw two men, one in the uniform of the Baghdad police, calmly eating. The two men continued eating as other men caught his tongue in a pair of pliers and cut it off with a bayonet. They had continued eating as the torturers had taken a ball-peen hammer to first his fingers and then his toes. Then, when his naked body was slick with his own blood, they had driven the slender shaft of an ice pick into his guts, perforating the large intestine and allowing his own fecal matter to flood into his system, causing sepsis.

From outside of the building the militia of the faithful held the Iraqi National Army bootlickers and their American allies at bay. The troops around the man now were those returning from the line to grab a meal and resupply. Despite their exhaustion and wounds the

Shiite extremists remained upbeat—happy with their performance.

Then a vengeful god rained fire from the sky.

Abu Hafiza jumped out of his chair at the sound of the explosion. Around him his men scrambled to respond and he looked across the table to the Iraqi police officer Saheed el-Jaga.

"It's *them!*" he hissed, stunned.

"Ridiculous. They never could have gotten close. It must be an air strike. I told you to leave the city," Saheed el-Jaga snapped back.

Abu Hafiza thought about Ziad Jarrah sitting in Dubai like a spider at the center of his web. He thought of telling the crown prince how he had failed, how the Americans had driven him from the Shia stronghold in Baghdad.

"No," the Shiite terrorist said simply. "I'm safer here."

"I'm not!"

Then they heard the gunfire burning out around them and they knew it was more than an air strike. They knew then that against all odds the unknown commandos had made it into the Shiite slum, had come for them. They both realized that whoever these clandestine operators were they would never give up.

Instantly they rose up and ran to rally their men.

"Fall in around me!" Saheed el-Jaga snarled.

"To the roof and perimeter!" Abu Hafiza said in turn.

Men were scrambling into positions and snatching up weapons.

THE LINE DIPPED under Manning's weight as he rode the Flying Fox cable car down the Kevlar zip-line. He sailed down the six stories and applied the hand brake at the last possible moment. He pivoted his feet up and struck the roof of the building on the soles of his combat boots.

Because of the size of his primary weapon, the cut-down M-60E, he couldn't roll with the impact and instead bled off his momentum by sliding across the roof like a batter stealing second. With the last of his forward energy the big Canadian sat up and took a knee, swinging his machine gun into position and clicking off the safety.

Behind him he heard the sound as Calvin James hit the roof and rolled across one shoulder to come up with SPAS-15 ready. Above them they heard the muffled snaps as Hawkins cut loose with the silenced Mk 11 from his overwatch position. Below them in the courtyard around the sprawling house they heard men scream as the 7.62 mm rounds struck them.

Covering the exposed roof, Manning turned in a wide arc as Rafael Encizo slid down to the roof, putting his feet down and his shoulder against the line to arrest his forward motion. The Cuban combat swimmer came off his Flying Fox and tore his Hawk MM-1 from where it rested against the front of his torso.

McCarter landed right behind Encizo and rushed across the roof, M-4/M-203 up and in his hand. Gunfire burst out of a window in a mosque across the road. Manning shifted and triggered a burst of harassment fire from the hip. His rounds arced out across the space and slammed into the building, cracking the wall and shattering the lattice of a window. Red tracer fire skipped off the roof and bounced deeper into the city.

Above the heads of Phoenix Force in their black rubber protective masks, T. J. Hawkins shifted the muzzle of his weapon on its bipod and engaged the sniper. He touched a dial on his scope and the shooter suddenly appeared in the crosshairs of the reticule on his optics.

The man had popped up again after Manning's burst had tapered off and was attempting to bring a 4-power scope on top of an M-16 A2 to bear on the exposed Americans.

Hawkins found the trigger slack and took it up. He let his breath escape through his nose as he centered the crosshairs on the sniper's eyes. For a brief strange second, it was as if the two men stared into each other's eyes. The Iraqi pressed his face into the eyepiece on the assault rifle. The man shifted the barrel as he tried for a shot.

The silenced Mk 11 rocked back against Hawkins's shoulder. The smoking 7.62 mm shell tumbled out of the ejection port and bounced across the tarpaper-and-gravel roof. In the image of his scope the Iraqi sniper's left eye became a bloody cavity. The man's head jerked and a bloody mist appeared behind him as he sagged and fell.

Autofire began hammering the side of the building below Hawkins's position. He rolled over on his back, snatching up his sniper rifle. He scrambled up, staying low, and crawled through the doorway of the roof access stair. He intended to shift positions and engage from one of the windows overlooking the compound in the building's top floor.

Below his position McCarter found what he was looking for. He pulled up short and shoved a stiffened forefinger downward, pointing at an enclosed glass sky-light that served to open up and illuminate the breakfast area. The opening had appeared as a black rectangle on the images downloaded from the Farm's Keyhole satellite, and from the first McCarter had seized on the architectural luxury as his means of ingress.

"We have control," Manning barked, and from half a world away Barbara Price and the Farm's cyberteam watched from the UAV's cameras. "We have control," McCarter repeated.

To create a distraction on the hard entry Gary Manning had prepared explosive charges. Being unable to precisely locate their target before the strike, nonlethal measures had been implemented. Working with Stony Man armorer John "Cowboy" Kissinger, the Canadian demolitions expert had prepped a series of flash-bang charges using stun grenades designed to incapacitate enemy combatants in airplane hangars, factories or warehouses. In addition to the massive SWAT noise-distraction device Manning and Kissinger had layered in several devices from ALS Technologies that contained additional payloads of CS gas.

McCarter slipped into his own SAS model protective mask, then gave Calvin James a thumbs-up signal. "Five, four, three, two, one."

The ex-SEAL jogged forward and pointed the SPAS-15 at the skylight. The semiautomatic shotgun boomed and eight .38-caliber slugs smashed through the reinforced commercial-grade window.

"Execute, execute, execute!" McCarter ordered.

Instantly, Manning stepped up and threw his satchel charge into the hole. As it plunged through the opening, the entry team turned their backs from the breach, shielding their eyes and ears. Instantly the booming explosion came. Smoke poured out of the opening like the chimney of a volcano.

James spun and stepped up to the ledge before

dropping through the hole. He struck the ground and rolled to his left out along the side of his body, absorbing the impact from the ten-foot fall. He came up, the SPAS-15 tracking for a target in the smoke and confusion.

A running body slammed into him, sending them both spinning. Ignoring the combat shotgun on its sling, James reached out with his left hand and tore the AKM from the figure's grip, tossing it aside as he rolled to his feet. His Beretta appeared in his fist. He pulled the guy closer but didn't recognize the stunned terrorist and put two 9 mm bullets through his slack-jawed face.

David McCarter dropped down through the breach into chaos.

He saw James drop a body and spin, his pistol up. Around him the whitish clouds of CS gas hung in patches but the interior space was large enough that the dispersal allowed line-of-sight identification.

The Briton was violently thrown into a momentary flashback to his experience in the assault on London's Iranian embassy after Arab separatists had taken it hostage. He saw a coughing, blinded gunman in an Iraqi police uniform stumble by and shot him at point-blank range with the M-4.

The man was thrown down like a trip-hammered steer in a Chicago stockyard. McCarter went back down to a knee and twisted in a tight circle, muzzle tracking for targets. Behind him a third body dropped like a stone through the skylight breach.

Rafael Encizo landed flat-footed then dropped to a single knee, his fireplug frame absorbing the stress of the ten-foot fall. His MM-1 was secured, muzzle up, tightly against the body armor on his chest and his MP-7 machine pistol was gripped in two hands.

Through the lens of his protective mask Enzcio saw two AKM-wielding men in headdresses and robes stumble past. The Cuban lifted his weapon and pulled the trigger, firing on full automatic from arm's length. He hosed the men ruthlessly, sending them spinning into each other like comedic actors in a British farce. He turned, saw an Iraqi policeman leveling a folding-stock AKM at him and somersaulted forward, firing as he came up. His rounds cracked the man's sternum, struck him under the chin and cored out his skull. The corrupt Iraqi dropped to the ground, limbs loose and weapon tumbling.

Gary Manning dropped through the breach, caught himself on the lip of the skylight with his gloved hands and hung for a heartbeat before dropping down. He landed hard with his heavier body weight and went to both knees. He grunted at the impact on his kneepads and orientated himself to the other three Phoenix members, completing their defensive circle as he brought up the cut-down M-60E.

Without orders the team fell into their established enclosed-space clearing pattern. Manning came up and charged toward the nearest wall, clearing left along the perimeter of the room while James followed closely behind him, then turned right. Encizo tucked in behind Manning as he turned left, and McCarter, also charged with coordination, followed James.

Manning kicked a chair out of the way and raced down the left wall of the room. Weapons began firing in the space and he saw muzzle-flashes flare in the swirling CS gas. He passed a dead man hanging by chains from the wall. A close-range gunshot had cracked the bearded man's skull and splashed his brains on the wall behind his head.

Manning suddenly saw a police officer standing with a pistol, three men with Kalashnikovs in a semicircle in front of him. The Canadian special forces veteran triggered the M-60E in a tight burst, and the 7.62 mm rounds tore the first police bodyguard away as he rushed forward. From behind him Encizo used the MP-7 to cut down the left flank bodyguard before the Iraqi police officer could bring his weapon around.

Manning took two steps forward and shoved the muzzle of his machine gun into the throat of the final bodyguard as Encizo swarmed around him. The Iraqi stumbled backward, at the blunt-tipped spearing movement, his hands dropping his weapon and flying to his throat. As he staggered back, Manning lifted a powerful leg and completed a hard front snap kick into the man's chest, driving him farther backward and into the police officer.

Both men fell as Encizo reached forward and thrust the muzzle of his smoking-hot machine gun into the coughing and half-blinded Saheed el-Jaga's face, pinning him to the floor. With his other hand Encizo broke the man's wrist, sending his pistol sliding away.

Hot shell casings rained down on Encizo as Manning cracked open the bodyguard's chest with a 5-round burst from the M-60. Blood splashed Saheed el-Jaga's face as he grimaced in pain, and the stunned and terrified traitor squeezed his eyes tightly shut.

Manning halted his advance and swung the machine gun up to cover them as Encizo flipped the Iraqi over onto his stomach and used a white plastic riot cuff to bind his hands. Saheed el-Jaga screamed in pain as the shattered bones of his wrists were ground against their broken ends by the Phoenix commando's rough treatment.

A block of light appeared in the gas-choked gloom. A knot of well-armed reinforcements surged through the open door from the outside. Manning shifted on a knee, swinging around the M-60. He saw one of the reinforcements fall, the side of his head vaporizing, then a second fell and Manning realized Hawkins had found his range even at this acute angle.

Manning pulled back on the trigger of his machine gun and the weapon went rock and roll in his grip. He scythed down the confused Iraqi terrorists, cutting into their ranks with his big 7.62 mm slugs. The men screamed and triggered their weapons into the ground as they were knocked backward. He let the recoil against his hand on the pistol grip push the muzzle up, and his rounds cut into the terrorists' bodies like buzz saws.

"Phoenix, we have company," Tokaido warned over the team's earbuds. "Hellfire number two is away. Danger close."

Calvin James spun, bringing up the SPAS-15.

The combat shotgun boomed like a cannon in his hands and steel shot scythed through the CS-tinged air to strike two AKM-wielding figures. The Iraqi terrorists were thrown backward and spun apart, arms flying in the air, weapons tossed aside by the force of the blasts.

One of them tripped over a wastepaper basket and went down hard. The second bounced off a wall and tumbled into a chair. James moved between them, double checking as he went. The one on the floor was leaking red by the gallon from a chewed-up throat and torn-open chest. The second was missing enough of his face that the ex-SWAT officer could see his brains exposed.

There was a burst of rifle fire and the SPAS-15 was

knocked from James's hands. Heavy slugs slammed into the ceramic chest plates of his Kevlar body armor. He staggered backward and grunted. His shoulder hit the wall and he went to one knee. Reflexively his hands flew to his Beretta. As he drew the handgun David McCarter lunged past, the M-4 carbine up and locked into his shoulder, the muzzle erupting in a star pattern blast.

He saw the figure wearing an expensive black silk *thobe* at the last moment and pulled his shot. The 5.56 mm rounds struck the man in his legs and swept him to the floor of the building. Bright patches of blood splashed in scarlet blossom on the figure's thighs.

Behind them the front of the building exploded as Tokaido's Hellfire struck.

CHAPTER SIX

McCarter was thrown to his knees. He grunted with the impact as something heavy and wet struck him between the shoulder blades, then he looked down and saw a severed arm lying on the floor. He felt the heat of the raging blaze behind him.

He struggled to his feet.

"Talk to me, people!" Akira Tokaido shouted over the line. "Talk to me!"

McCarter didn't answer but lunged forward. Abu Hafiza was screaming from his shattered thighs but was pulling a Jordanian JAWS pistol from out of his robes. McCarter slashed out with his M-4. His bayonet caught the man across the forearm, slicing a long ugly gash. The Iranian screamed again as he dropped the pistol.

Still on all fours McCarter scrambled forward, wielding the M-4 in one fist. The blade of the wicked M9 bayonet jabbed into the soft flesh of Abu Hafiza's throat and pushed the man backward.

"Freeze!" McCarter snarled in Arabic. "Move one fucking millimeter and I'll put your brains on the wall!" He lashed out with the bayonet again, lancing the tip into the meat of the Iranian's shoulder and opening a small wound.

"Speak to me, Phoenix!" Tokaido hollered again.

"Manning up," Gary Manning answered. "That

was very danger close, my man," the Canadian special forces veteran said.

"Pescado, is good," Encizo said. "I'm knee deep in tango guts, but that blast blew the front off the building."

"Copy that," Tokaido said. "They had two platoon-size elements as reinforcements at the door. Forty, fifty guys all bunched up at the entrance."

"McCarter up," McCarter said. "But Cal took a round and I have our boy." He paused. "If we're clear, I need help."

Instantly there was a reaction from behind him and the massive frame of Gary Manning appeared by his side as Encizo scrambled over to pull security near the prone Calvin James.

Encizo leaned in close, his eyes hunting for enemy motion from behind the lenses of his protective mask. "Speak to me," he demanded. "You okay, bro?"

James turned his head and opened his eyes. He opened his mouth to speak but no sound came out. Encizo, ears still ringing from the Hellfire blast, shook his head to clear his hearing.

"Speak, bro!" the Cuban demanded.

James lifted his head and muscles along his neck stood out with the effort. His lips formed the words under his protective mask and his eyes bulged with his effort under the lens but no sound came out. Finally there was a rush of air through the blunt nose filter.

"That *hurt*!" he wheezed. "Jesus, that hurt. I think I cracked my ribs."

"Is he good?" McCarter demanded over one shoulder. His weapon's muzzle never wavered from Abu Hafiza's face. "Is he good?"

Beside the Briton, Manning fired his M-60E in a

short 4-round burst. A crawling Iraqi terrorist shuddered under the impact of the 7.62 mm slugs and lay still. Encizo turned toward the Phoenix Force leader and shouted back.

"Yeah, he just had the wind knocked out of him. Maybe bruised ribs, maybe cracked—we don't know, but he's ambulatory."

"He's also right goddamn here," James snapped, sitting up. "He doesn't need you talking about him as if he were incapable of speech."

"Good," McCarter replied, his voice echoing weirdly under the mask. "I got our boy but he needs patching up before we yank him back to Wonderland." McCarter switched to his throat mike. "Akira, how we look out there?"

"You got vehicles coming up the street. You'll have more bad guys on site very shortly. I'm still sitting on Hellfire number three."

"Fine. Hit 'em at the gate and cause a further chokepoint but save number four for my direction."

"Understood."

McCarter pulled back as James moved forward, medic kit in hand. Abu Hafiza looked at the black man with real hatred as the ex-SEAL ripped open the *thobe* and began to treat the Iranian's wounds.

"Give him morphine," McCarter said as he rose. "We're going to have to carry him anyway with those leg wounds. It'll keep him docile."

"I'll be the one to play doctor here," James said.

"Fine, you're the medic—what do you want to do?"

"Probably going to give him a heavy dose of morphine to keep him docile."

"Whatever you think is best." McCarter shook his head.

Encizo spoke up. "What about the son of a bitch Saheed el-Jaga?"

McCarter looked over at the Cuban combat swimmer. "You guys tag and bag him?"

"Yep," Manning interrupted as he rose. "We got him against the wall." The big Canadian began to move down the length of the room toward the blazing hole in the building, checking each of the downed bodies as he did so.

"We aren't prepped to carry two deadweights out of here," McCarter pointed out.

"What's the penalty for treason?" Manning asked.

"Firing squad," Encizo said, an ugly smile splitting his face.

James looked up from bandaging the glowering Abu Hafiza. "Where will we find volunteers?"

McCarter turned, lifted his M-4 to his shoulder and pulled the trigger. Across the stretch of floor broken by the rapidly thinning clouds of CS gas the corrupt Iraqi police officer Saheed el-Jaga caught the 3-round burst in the side of the head.

Blood gushed like water from a broken hydrant and the blue-gray scrambled eggs of his brains splashed across the floor with bone white chips of skull in the soupy mess. McCarter lowered his smoking M-4.

The ex-SAS commando leaned down close to the wounded Iranian. "Abu Hafiza, you see I'm a serious bastard now?"

The al Qaeda commander paled under the scrutiny of the coldblooded killer. His eyes shifted away from the death mask McCarter's face had become. Then he jerked and winced as James unceremoniously gave him an intramuscular shot of morphine.

The black man smiled with ghastly intensity at the captured Iranian terror master. "Don't worry," he said. "If we shoot you, it'll only be in the gut."

Manning and Encizo reached down and jerked the now stoned Abu Hafiza to his feet. McCarter spoke into his throat mike. "Akira, how we look?"

"Clock's ticking. You got stubborn bad guys trying to dig their way through the burning barricade I made out of the first-wave vehicles. I'm still sitting on my last Hellfire."

"Good copy," McCarter said. "We'll be rolling out the back door in about ten seconds. Why don't you go ahead and blow me a hole out the back fence now?"

"One escape hatch coming up," Tokaido replied.

"Phoenix," McCarter said. "We are leaving."

En route to Bolivia

IN THE BACK OF THE Cessna executive turbojet Able Team prepared for their mission briefing. Scrambled with their preassembled kits directed by Barbara Price, the Stony Man direct-action unit had been wheels up and flying south even before Hal Brognola had finished being fully briefed by the President.

Now, via sat link the big Fed and director of the Justice Department's Sensitive Operations Group gave them a rundown on the situation.

"Currently FBI counterintelligence, counterterror and hostage-rescue units are scrambling to deal with a crisis. In Boliva, Juan Evo Morales holds power. A committed socialist and champion of the coca-leaf growers,

he is a strong ally of the Venezuelan strongman Hugo
Chavez, and no friend of the United States.

"A plane filled with U.S. citizens has been taken
hostage in the eastern lowlands where thick tracts of
Amazonian rainforest carpet the topography. Officially
the Morales government is helping the U.S. with the situation. Behind the scenes the government is restricting
the movement, investigation and resource deployment
of the FBI field team in order to maintain 'sovereign
integrity.'

"NSA has managed to discover that covertly, the
Bolivian special forces, the Polivalente, are running a
joint operation with Venezuela's DISIP, or Directorate
of Intelligence and Prevention Services. Faced with this
obstruction we need you to run a simultaneous black
operation to locate and free the kidnapped hostages
independent from the official FBI efforts. You must
infiltrate the country, acquire intelligence, perform tactical reconnaissance and execute the rescue." Brognola
paused. "Tactical specifics will be given to you once
you arrive in Bolivia."

Schwarz cocked an eyebrow and turned toward
Blancanales. "Is it me or does the old man seem to be
getting even more blasé as we pull off one impossible
stunt after the other?"

Blancanales shrugged. "What am I going to do at
my age? Start over and teach school?"

Lyons leaned forward and addressed Brognola
through the sat link system. "No worries. We're on
it."

La Paz, Bolivia

THE TAXI took Lyons away from the more affluent area
and into the poorer neighborhoods, far from the Hyatt

hotel, American consular branch office and the giant grocery store. Here Colombian refugees formed a strong minority, completely dominating some neighborhoods stacked with poorly constructed tenements and scattered with small shops.

This fact was punctuated to Lyons by his driver, named Jose, who spoke serviceable if broken English. At one point he noted to Lyons that they had entered an area exclusive to Colombians, a tent city from 1978 that had grown up into a labyrinth of winding, narrow streets separating concrete apartment buildings and one-room shops of every description.

After fifteen minutes of travel, the taxi entered another Colombian enclave and stopped in front of a four-story apartment building. Standing on the street, waiting for him, was Hermann Schwarz in street clothes. The American had allowed his beard to grow in under his thick mustache.

Lyons paid the driver and got out of the cab. Schwarz was holding open a steel door and he nodded and smiled in greeting.

"Que pasa, jefe?" he said, letting Lyons through the gate into a small courtyard, then directing him into the building itself. Lyons nodded a greeting and began to ask the Able Team commando a question, but Schwarz shook his head and whispered, "Upstairs."

Lyons followed Schwarz as they climbed four stories up a narrow, bare concrete staircase. At each landing there was a large square window open to the outside. On the fourth floor the two men entered a stark, poorly lit hallway. At the end of the hall Lyons saw a woman in a traditional dark dress duck into a doorway to avoid them.

Obviously waiting for them, Rosario Blancanales,

stubble-faced and dressed identically to Schwarz in street clothes, opened the door to their apartment. Lyons entered the room, shaking Blancanales's hand once he was inside. Schwarz shut the door behind them and flipped a series of dead bolts closed.

Immediately upon entering the apartment, Lyons saw that there was a short, alcove-style hall to the left leading to an open closet and the bathroom. A U.S. Claymore antipersonnel mine was set up in the entranceway, angled at the door so the back blast would be funneled into the alcove. The ignition cord trailed down the hall, taped to the ground to avoid tripping anyone, and leading around a corner.

"What's up?" Lyons asked. "Didn't want anyone hearing us speak English?"

"I want to avoid it as much as possible." Schwarz nodded. "Blancanales and I might fit in better than McCarter or Hawkins would, but nobody around here's really fooled. English is pretty common here but it shouts 'outsider' in a way that makes me nervous in these Colombian 'hoods."

"It's like in my old neighborhood when I was growing up," Rosario Blancanales added. "Everybody knows who belongs in the 'hood. Cops try to send in a plainclothes and he was always spotted. The gangs know if a guy comes from three streets over, let alone from out of town. We look like the Bolivian version of lost tourists come to the big city as long as we don't open our mouths."

"It's only going to get worse once we make our final approaches," Lyons observed.

Blancanales shrugged. "Like I said, Gadgets and I are better than McCarter or Hawkins and in crowded markets or just out and about we'll move easier. We knew it was going to be tough. You look like the giant gringo you are, my friend."

They led Lyons deeper into the cramped four-room apartment. The walls and floor were of the same bare concrete as the staircase. Lyons realized there would be no insulation, though the windows at least had glass in them.

"Plumbing okay?" he asked.

"Toilet and shower are weak but working. Don't drink the water," Blancanales answered.

"How's it going?" Lyons asked, meaning the surveillance operation.

Blancanales led him to the large common area at the rear of the apartment. Lyons saw a battered old futon next to a kerosene stove and several battery-operated lanterns. Schwarz and Blancanales had put down foam mattresses and sleeping bags on the concrete, with an additional one meant for Lyons.

A Soviet Dragunov 7.62 mm sniper rifle with the standard PSO-1 scope mount was set up on a bipod in the middle of the room. Against the wall were three AK-104 Kalashnikov carbines. On a card table near the couch and stacked weapons sat a VINCENT sat-com unit, a laptop, two Nikon cameras—one digital and one 35 mm—as well as a satellite phone.

"The Bureau set us up good," Blancanales said. "Your wish list for weapons and equipment was waiting for us when we got here. They got us Jordanian pistols instead of the more generic Makarovs, but since they're used by the Bolivian army I didn't bitch."

Lyons grunted. The Viper JAWS—Jordanian Arms & Weapon System—had a great reputation for a 9 mm pistol, especially when compared to the older Soviet Makarov and Tokarev, and was the product of a joint

American-Jordanian effort. He supposed that with the weapons going into service with the Royal Jordanian Army it was feasible that some would have made it out onto the black market. The fact that the Bolivian military services had all been outfitted with them only helped matters.

"Good enough. What about our good Juan Hernandez?" Lyons asked.

"Take a look for yourself," Schwarz said, and indicated where the Dragunov had been set up.

The designated infantry support weapon was set up on the ground on a foam shooter's pad. It was pointed out of a sliding-glass door that opened up on a railing around a patio that extended about six inches out. The glass door opened up on a narrow alley, and Blancanales and Schwarz had hung drapes, keeping them only open a few inches, to avoid being seen by anyone across the way.

Lyons settled into position. The PSO-1 scope was angled through the wide-set wrought-iron bars of the balcony and out toward the mouth of the alley, which opened up on a busy avenue. The crosshairs of the sniper rifle were focused on a balcony across that street, the fifth one up from the bottom and two over from the left edge of the target building. The balcony there was as narrow and unadorned as the one attached to Able Team's own safehouse.

Inside the apartment Lyons could clearly distinguish the front door through his sniper scope. A battered old television with a rabbit-ears antenna played what Lyons took to be a local soap opera. He had a clear image of the back of a large, balding head facing away from the open balcony.

"Looks like our guy," Lyons said. "I guess. The FBI

triangulated the communications of the Bolivian army commander in charge of the rescue to here?"

"Yep exactly. Akira did a computer enhancement match on photos we took. It came up on an NSA data file. The guy is a communications officer for Colombian intelligence. He's working as a scramble relay for Caracas."

"Ugly bastard," Lyons grunted.

"Got him?" Blancanales asked. "Good. Now come here. I want to show you our little glitch."

"Christ," Lyons muttered as he stood. "There's always a glitch."

Blancanales led Lyons to the edge of the drapes covering all but two inches of their apartment balcony. Lyons stood at the edge of the curtain and looked out. He heard the sounds of the street, smelled exhaust fumes from the cars. In the distance he could hear a radio blaring latino music through cheap loudspeakers. Heavy carpets aired out over balconies. Clotheslines filled the space above the street between buildings, draped with laundry.

On the street women in traditional blouses and skirts hustled by on errands while men in dirty jeans and battered old sandals rode in threes and fours in the open backs of pickup down the narrow avenue. He saw street vendors selling vegetables and cutting meat from hanging carcasses.

The unemployed lounged in little clusters and argued and laughed with animated hand gestures. School-age children kicked grimy soccer balls in the gutter. Rebar struts stuck from the unfinished corners of old buildings.

"Look down, against the wall, across the alley. See him?"

Lyons looked down. He saw what appeared to be a vagrant dressed in filthy Western shirt and pants under a grimy poncho. His beard was patchy, almost mangy, and the man's overall appearance was completely unkempt. Lyons narrowed his eyes. There were two empty bottles of the potent Bolivian beer called Orso lying empty beside the man who clutched a brown paper bag.

Lyons frowned. "A drunk? In the open?"

"Exactly. Here." Blancanales handed Lyons a compact pair of Zeiss binoculars. "Check out his right ear under the ball cap."

Lyons took the offered Zeiss binoculars and zeroed in on the lounging man. A small earpiece was fitted into the man's ear. Lyons grunted at the wireless communications tech. "Pretty upscale for a gutter drunk. Our boy Juan is being watched. I'm guessing not by Bolivian security, either, considering how the observer's screwing it up."

"Probably it's the Venezuleans doing overwatch on their boy. A secondary security operation," Schwarz said.

"Hell," Blancanales snorted. "Pretending to be a drunk, in Bolivia? I think that rules out any first-tier Western operators, as well."

Lyons narrowed his focus on the glasses. He took in how the man's hawk nose was more pronounced from having obviously been broken more than once. "You don't think he's on to us?" Lyons handed Blancanales back the Zeiss binoculars. "What happens when Juan leaves his apartment? That guy tail him?"

"No." Schwarz smiled. "Another guy, taller and thinner, tails him in a white Celica. They're definitely following our good Mr. Juan Hernandez. I followed him following Juan shopping one day. I could have sliced his throat at any time, he was positively asleep, real tunnel vision." The ex-Green Beret mimed drawing a finger across his neck. "I took some photos instead. Besides, what's the range on a wireless earpiece like that? Even with the receiver in the bag? We're clean for bugs in here and he'd be set up differently if he was using a parabolic mic. They must already have a bug in Hernandez's apartment."

"I assume you got film on that jackass down there, as well?" Lyons asked.

"Yep." Blancanales nodded. "Sent it off to Bear. He said he'll get back to us."

"We have to know who they are before we roll," Lyons said. "The Bolivians could have tipped someone or Venezuela could have sent a team hoping to ambush anyone who checks Juan Hernandez out. Whoever they are they've just made number one on our list of priorities," Lyons decided. "What happens at night?" he asked, pensive.

"Third man," Schwarz answered. "Juan isn't exactly a playboy. They keep the indigent in place until dark, then they have a nightshift guy, different than the daytime shadow, in a late-model Ford V-8 van. He parks in the alley crawls into the back and pulls the curtain. Must have a sibling transceiver to the one used by our Mr. Bum-by-day down there."

"He goes first, then," Lyons said.

CHAPTER SEVEN

Able Team settled in to wait.

Lyons took one of the 9 mm Viper JAWS pistols and kept it on him. He changed into street clothes and a poncho. With his darkly tanned complexion and two-day beard he didn't stand out awfully, but he knew better than to think he could pull off any complicated subterfuge.

They made strong coffee and took turns behind the PSO-1 scope, watching Juan Hernandez's apartment. The Venezuelan electronic intelligence specialist was a diligent man. The spook in the alley outside whiled away the time with a patience that Lyons had to admit was professional.

While Schwarz took a watch behind the sniper scope the sat-phone on the card table next to the laptop buzzed. Blancanales picked it up. "Go," he said.

He listened for a minute and Lyons heard the smile in his voice when he answered. "Nice, Bear, nice."

While Lyons watched, Blancanales moved to the laptop and nudged the finger-mouse pad to disrupt the screensaver. A rectangle graph showing an incoming download appeared. Once the download was complete, Blancanales said, "Got it. We'll call as we move forward. Out."

He hung up the phone and clicked on the download icon. Instantly classified photos with accompanying text appeared on the screen. Lyons came in close and studied the screen.

"Got a match on DEA international files. Cross-hit in Interpol. These guys are cartel mob freelancers," Lyons read.

"Venezuelans?" Blancanales mused. "We got cocaine cowboys pulling security on a Colombian intel op."

"Blackmail," Lyons grunted. "Maybe, anyway. But more likely there's a power struggle in Chavez's crews. The army doesn't trust intel, or intel the army, or something. So one side called in outside players they could trust. They're here because someone is afraid someone is running Juan Hernandez down. If they were a hit team they'd have taken him out by now."

"Christo," Schwarz agreed from behind the rifle. "They're Colombian. They would have blown up the whole damn building or gone in and chewed him up with a chain saw in front of his family by now if they'd been paid to take him out."

"So we take them out?" Blancanales asked Lyons.

"We can't have them at our six o'clock when we go in after Juan," Lyons said, thoughtful.

"We take them out, then whoever called in the shadow will know we're in Bolivia and onto Juan," Schwarz pointed out.

Lyons ticked off his points on his fingers, one by one. "This op is bloody wet already. Subterfuge will only take us so far. Speed and aggression is our key now, just like always. We hit them. We hit Juan. We hit the plane."

Schwarz and Blancanales nodded.

"So we take 'em out before we interview Juan," Blancanales stated.

"Yes," Lyons replied. "But I want to make sure I get every last one of them possible. Not just the point men."

"Find the nest?" Schwarz said.

"And clean it out," Lyons finished. "The clock is ticking. We need to interview Juan. We can't do it with that surveillance and I'm not predisposed to letting Colombian hitmen run around at will if I can have anything to do with it."

"I heard that," Schwarz said.

"I think we have an understanding," Blancanales said. "We go in, shoot and loot. At best we get some paperwork, a hard drive and/or some cell phones. Otherwise we simply put some bad operators out of business. Once our six o'clock is clear, we start stage two immediately."

"Win-win situation," Lyons said.

"THEY'RE ON THE FIFTH floor," Schwarz said. "Room 519. There's at least three of them in there but I think more like twice that."

"Building materials?" Blancanales asked.

"Reinforced concrete for load-bearing structural, but only Sheetrock covered by wood between rooms. The doors have a lock, a single dead bolt and a security chain."

"Windows?"

"Commercial variety. Set in the wall with no balcony. They open inward with a metal-clasp locking mechanism. The glass is set into four even quadrants of windowpane around standard molding and wood frames. High quality but not security level."

"Wall penetration will be a problem with our weapons. Even the nine millimeters," Lyons said.

"C-2 breaching charges on the door and shotguns with buckshot or breach-shot for the takedown?" Blancanales suggested.

"What's security like in the hotel?"

"They have a Bolivian police officer out front armed with a pistol and a submachine gun. He liaisons with hotel private security, who have a heavy presence in the lobby and restaurant area. They make hourly passes through the guestroom halls. They all carry 9 mm side arms," Schwarz answered. "I think we could get in and do the takedown. It's getting out without slugging through security forces I'm doubtful of."

"Position to snipe on the window?" Blancanales asked.

"Negative. The Inca Mall is across the street. Seventy-five thousand square feet. No defilade and no angle other than up-trajectory. Lousy for shooting."

"Yes, but does it have frozen yogurt? You know how I feel about my frozen yogurt." Blancanales laughed.

"That kind of exposure rules out rappelling down the outside, even if we could get to the roof." Lyons rubbed at his beard, thoughtful.

"Bait and switch followed by a bum rush?" Schwarz suggested.

"How do we get out?" Blancanales countered.

Lyons smiled. "Schwarz, I'll need you to find us a good covert LZ on the edge of the city, out toward the jungle, and pinpoint the GPS reading."

"That'll work. Depends on how fast Stony Man can get us a bird. This'll have to be black from JSOC, and even from FBI. And fast. Very goddamn fast," Blancanales said.

"Has Barb ever let us down yet?" Lyons asked.

SCHWARZ WALKED OUT of the hotel and dodged traffic as he crossed the busy street. Blancanales pulled out from the curb and met him as he crossed the median. Schwarz opened the passenger side door and slid into the seat.

"It's a go," he said.

"Good," Lyons replied from the backseat of the vehicle. "Let's do it."

Driving quickly, the Stony Man team circumnavigated the luxury hotel and pulled into the parking lot of the urban mall, quickly losing themselves among the acres of parking for up to 1,500 vehicles. A State Department courier with no association to the mission would pick up the vehicle ten minutes after Able Team left the area.

Over the horizon, in the hot Bolivian night, Jack Grimaldi was already inbound in an AH-6J Little Bird attack helicopter. The clock had started running on a tightly scheduled and overtly aggressive Able Team operation. Dressed in street clothes under colorful regional ponchos, the men moved quickly toward their objective.

The hotel loomed above them as they crossed the street. Lyons felt his frustration rising over the broken jigsaw that was the international web in play around the hostaged Americans. Terrorists were using violence to spread fear, and Bolivian officials tasked with helping those innocents had turned against the helpless and entered into a Faustian arrangement with other evil players on the world stage—the Venezuelan intelligence apparatus bolstered by narco-mercenaries.

With hopes of little more than causing embarrassment

to the U.S., two governments had become complicit in the murder of innocents for cheap political gains.

Now Lyons had an opportunity to do what he did best: go blood simple. He intended to seize the chance to vent his frustrations in righteous wrath against violent international criminals. It was a relief, a short-lived blessing.

Walking fast, Able Team moved onto the sidewalk behind the hotel. They sweated freely in the midnight air, dressed as they were with body armor and various weapons and tools for instant use once the dynamic entry began. The ornate wall ringing the hospitality structure was broken by a gate opening up on the loading dock where deliveries were made.

Bolivia was a security-conscious nation in a volatile region. Yet its problems were minor compared to other neighboring states, and the well-developed sense of paranoia evident in Colombia, Venezuela or even Panama was largely missing despite sporadic terrorist attacks and the heavy presence of narcotics trafficking. As such its security was as capable of being exploited as those in other, more violent nations.

They reached the back gate, hands sliding into black driving gloves of kid leather. As one, the three men reached up and swept their brightly colored ponchos off to one side, leaving them tumbled and forgotten on the ground. Black leather and canvas combat boots trampled the woven cloth as they sprang into action.

The black balaclavas were pulled into place, obscuring the Able Team commandos' faces from internal CCTV cameras. Schwarz pulled a pair of short-handled bolt cutters from off his vest as Blancanales grabbed the chain and padlock looped around the chain-link fence gate and offered it up.

Schwarz cut through the links in one easy motion. Blancanales pushed the fence gate open as Schwarz dropped the bolt cutters next to the forgotten ponchos on the ground. Able Team rushed through the opening, Schwarz taking the lead.

Each man carried a Viper JAWS 9 mm pistol at either shoulder or hip and all three wielded Saiga 12K Russian .12-gauge assault shotguns with folding stocks and shortened barrels. The 8-round box magazines went into a weapon designed on the AK-74M paratrooper carbine. Loaded with No. 1 buckshot of 16 pellets of .30-caliber diameter, the rounds were considered the most effective man-stoppers, even over double-aught buckshot loads. They were also considered generally more efficient at causing blunt trauma, even through protective vests, than the more widely touted antipersonnel fléchettes.

The first two rounds in Schwarz's Saiga 12K were breaching rounds designed to penetrate the civilian locks on interior doors. The outer fire door was made of metal, reducing the effectiveness of the rounds and potentially signaling the team's presence before they had fully exploited their advantage of surprise.

As they reached the fire door Blancanales allowed his combat shotgun to hang from its strap across his torso. He pulled up a two-foot-long titanium crowbar fitted with rubber grips at the end from a carabiner holster on his rappel harness. While Lyons and Schwarz covered him, shotguns at port arms, the ex-Special Forces member went to work.

Without preamble Blancanales wedged the comma-shaped end of the crowbar under the overlapping lip of the steel fire door. Throwing one big boot up on the other door, he grabbed the crowbar in both of his gloved hands and yanked back sharply.

There was a screech of metal and then a loud pop as the door snapped open. A fire alarm began to wail. Blancanales dropped the crowbar and grabbed the door with one hand as he scooped up the pistol grip of his Saiga with the other. Lyons went through the door, shotgun high, followed hard by Schwarz.

Once the other two were inside the hotel Blancanales stepped through, letting the fire door swing closed. Able Team took the stairs in a rapid leap-frog pattern. The stairs themselves were metal and set into the wall with a three-rail guard running along the outside edge. The staircase ran up in a squared spiral with a flat landing at each level where doors opened off onto the guest hallways. The cacophony of the midnight fire alarm was deafening.

Lyons bounded up to the second floor, then covered the area as Schwarz and Blancanales raced past him, the pounding of their boots echoing up and down the vertical shaft. At the third floor Schwarz provided rear-guard action as Blancanales and Lyons charged past him.

The skills of the commando or the paramilitary operative existed in a form like an inverted pyramid, with each layer of skills resting on the smaller, more fundamental level below it. Communications, medical, explosives, computer and other specialties like scuba, free-fall parachuting or piloting all depended on certain core abilities.

At the base of these ancillary abilities were physical fitness and personal weapon marksmanship.

Conditioning to the level of a professional athlete was the entry-level trait necessary for inclusion in the fraternity of special operations troops. Coupled with the ability to put bullets downrange at a superior level of accuracy, it formed the twin prongs of fundamental capability in any elite soldier.

The Able Team commandos were no different and their fitness routines were exacting. Loaded down by weapons and equipment, the three elite operators raced up the steep stairs with all the cardiovascular endurance of triathletes or Nordic Olympians.

Blancanales covered the landing on the fourth floor and Lyons followed Schwarz past the balaclava-covered ex-Green Beret. At the fifth floor Lyons stepped onto the landing and off to the left as Schwarz rushed forward and snatched open the door leading onto the guest floor hallway.

Lyons rushed through, weapon up and in place at his shoulder, the Able Team operators hard on his heels. A few hotel guests, eyes sleepy and hair mussed, had opened their doors and stuck their heads outside in response to the fire alarm. At the sight of the heavily armed and balaclava-masked intruders they screamed or shouted in terror and slammed their doors shut tight.

Lyons knew that security, already alerted by the fire alarm, would now have guest reports to guide their response protocols. He began to race faster down the hall. The decor was dark wood and thick, shag-rug-style carpeting with soft lighting and gilt-worked mirrors.

Able Team had come to a paradise for rent.

The occupants of room 519 hadn't opened their door in response to the alarm. Lyons streaked past their room, ducking under the spy hole set at eye level in the muted wood of the door. He spun around and put his back to the wall on the handle side of the room door, weapon up. Schwarz ran up and halted in the middle of the hall at a sharp angle to the door as Blancanales slid into position against the wall on the side of the door opposite from Lyons so that the two men flanked the structure.

Schwarz's shotgun roared. The breaching shot slammed into the door just behind the handle. A saucer-size crater punched through the solid building material. Schwarz shifted the semiautomatic combat shotgun's muzzle and fired his weapon again, blowing out the dead bolt.

Able had been inside the hotel for less than three minutes.

The door shivered under the twin impacts of the special shotgun rounds. The booming of the assault guns was sharp in the narrow hallway over the wailing fire alarm. The door shook open, trailing splinters of wood and loose pieces of stamped metal. Schwarz stepped forward and kicked the door wide before peeling back.

Blancanales pumped two loads of No. 1 buckshot around the corner, aiming high for covering fire as Lyons squatted and let his flash-bang roll through the threshold. The canister-shaped grenade bounced into the room as Lyons swung back and pressed himself up out of his crouch.

A flash of light like a star going nova followed the deafening concussion of the grenade's bang with a brilliant flash. Lyons swung through the door, Saiga shotgun held at his hip and ready. Rosario Blancanales followed hard behind him as Schwarz brought up the rear.

Lyons saw an opening to his left and covered it with his shotgun. It was a door to the room's bathroom and he caught a glimpse of a shoeless man in trousers and a white cotton muscle shirt staggering against the sink. A Skorpion machine pistol lay on the tile by the European-style toilet.

Lyons's flurry of .30-caliber pellets punched the Colombian mercenary in the chest and cracked open his sternum. The man was knocked across the bathroom counter, and blood splattered the dressing-room-style mirror and sizzled on the lightbulbs.

According to the hotel's Web site the room was a luxury suite laid out with two big bedrooms opening up on a common living area and bar. Blancanales, second in the file, raced past the engaged Lyons and peeled off to the left, followed hard by Schwarz, who stepped to the right.

A wet bar and service sink took up the front part of the suite while toward the far wall three couches had been set up in a U-shape around a large-screen television. Whoever was footing the bill for the Colombian cell's logistical support hadn't skimped. Three men in various stages of undress were in the room, attempting to scramble to their feet and recover various submachine guns.

Rosario Blancanales took the man on the left. The Colombian wore a huge gold hoop in his ear and his long hair was swept back in a tight ponytail. He wore silk boxers and a stunned expression on his face as he looked up into the cavernous muzzle of Blancanales's combat shotgun. Blancanales pulled the trigger and suddenly the man no longer possessed enough of a face to wear any kind of expression at all.

Still firing from the hip, Blancanales swiveled as the second man rose, fumbling to bring around an H&K MP-5. A trickle of blood flowed from the broken drum of his right ear and splashed the bare skin of his shoulder. Blancanales's point-blank shot knocked him to the carpet and tossed his jawbone into the television screen behind him.

The third Colombian in the room lifted his Skorpion and turned it toward the balaclava-covered killer who had just gunned down his cell members. Schwarz's hailstorm of buckshot hit the man with sledgehammer force in the neck and left shoulder, folding the gunner at the knees so that he flopped like a fish to the floor.

The muzzle of a second MP-5 thrust around the door of the left bedroom. Schwarz fired a blast from the hip, tearing through the wood jamb and trim around the door. Lyons sidestepped between Blancanales and Schwarz, firing a blast of harassing fire as he charged the bedroom. Blancanales moved to cover him as Lyons entered the room's doorway. The Saiga bucked hard in Lyons's hands as he stood in the entrance. He shifted and fired twice more into the room.

Behind Lyons, Schwarz moved quickly to the door of the second bedroom. He kicked the door open and entered the room. He fired a blast through the closet and then checked under the bed, finding nothing.

"Clear!" he shouted, using Spanish.

Since all three of the men shared different levels of fluency in that common language they had opted to use it on the ambush raid to confuse anyone overhearing them and to reduce any sense of an American footprint on the operation.

"Clear!" Lyons answered in the same language from the far side of the suite.

The Stony Man hit team folded back into the room. A haze of gun smoke hung in the air and trailed from the barrels of their shotguns. Cordite stink was a bitter perfume and the metallic scent of blood was pungent.

"Let's shake it down," Lyons said. "Gadgets—" he indicated Schwarz "—cover the door."

CHAPTER EIGHT

Schwarz was already in motion as Blancanales and Lyons began looking for paperwork, cell phones and laptops to scrutinize. They had discovered nothing other than two unattended cell phones when Schwarz alerted them from the room door.

"Company, security," he said. "Time to roll."

"Which side?" Lyons demanded.

Schwarz dropped his box magazine from the Saiga. "Elevators," he replied. "Two, with pistols and radios." He slammed a fresh 8-round magazine into the shotgun, this one with a short strip of green tape stuck to one side.

"We go out to the right. Let's roll," Lyons ordered as both he and Blancanales replaced the magazines in their own assault shotguns.

Schwarz thrust his Saiga 12K around the corner of the door and unleashed three blasts with his specialty ammunition. Hard-packed, nonlethal beanbags spread out down the hall and knocked the startled security officers to the carpet like drunks under a bouncer's haymaker.

Schwarz rolled back around the door and Blancanales stepped past him, tossing a concussion grenade. The bang as it went off rang even the Able Team commandos' ears inside the hotel suite. Schwarz turned the corner and entered the hallway. Lyons and Blancanales spilled out of the room, turning to their right as they raced for the staircase.

Lyons sprinted down the hallway, Blancanales hard on his heels. Behind him he heard Schwarz fire his shotgun twice more and he was able to pick out the brutal smack of the riot-load beanbags as they struck flesh, even over the blaring fire alarm.

Lyons kicked open the fire door and held it open against the wall as Blancanales went through. Schwarz caught up and all three of the team members raced up the staircase. Three stories up Lyons heard angry voices shout out from beneath them. He leaned over the railing and triggered a double blast of his shotgun, hoping the thunderous sound would spook anyone following them.

Schwarz yanked the pin on a flash-bang grenade and let it drop down the spiral well. It fell three floors and detonated, the echo-chamber effect of the stairwell amplifying its effect on the security forces below the Stony Man team.

They reached the top floor forty-five seconds later, breathing hard but not disabled. Lyons pulled a road flare from a cargo pocket as Schwarz dropped his shotgun's magazine for a second time. It clattered as it landed on the concrete landing in front of the roof access door.

Blancanales covered the stairwell as Schwarz triggered his shotgun, firing a breaching shot into the door. The team, moving with well-oiled precision, rushed through the door and out onto the roof of the hotel.

The nighttime lights of the city blazed around them and they could hear the cars and horns of late commuters. Police sirens rushed closer, sharper and more disconnected in rhythm than the blaring fire alarm.

Lyons popped his flare and tossed it through the air ahead of him.

It fell on the roof, burning intensely. Blancanales pulled a spring-loaded door wedge from a pocket and dropped it down in front of the access door. He kicked it into place and triggered the spring. Instantly a V-shaped wedge of hard rubber locked into place, jamming the door shut.

From overhead they heard the whump-whump-whump of a helicopter sweeping in toward them. They looked up as the Little Bird flared hard and settled down over them. A long, thick rope uncoiled and hit the ground. Loops of canvas had been sewn into the rope and the three commandos moved forward and hooked on at two points with their D-ring carabiners.

The technique was called SPIE, or Special Patrol Infiltration/Extraction, and was common among recon troops and special operations forces. Lyons gave the signal once Schwarz and Blancanales showed him thumbs-up, and the Little Bird shot straight up out of its hover. The three men went into the arms-spread position to avoid spinning.

The helicopter pilot, Stony Man's own Jack Grimaldi, swung the nose of the Little Bird around and pointed it northeast. The tail rotor elevated above the main blades as it sped off toward the LZ whose GPS coordinates had been programmed by Schwarz earlier. A vehicle and clothes waited the team there.

The raid had lasted seven minutes from the time they had cut the padlock on the fence to the time the Little Bird had pulled their SPIE rope off the hotel roof.

IN THE ALLEY behind their safehouse Able Team approached the late-model Ford van. Upstairs, forensics cleaners from the back rooms of the American consulate sanitized the apartment. Things were rolling, supporting the operation designed to rescue American citizens from the hands of vicious killers. Once the outward links had been sanitized Able Team would move to the airport to finish their tasking. Even as they operated now Stony Man pilot Jack Grimaldi was in the air above Bolivia, prepping the battlefield in an unconventional manner for Able Team's final assault.

Rosario Blancanales approached the van from the front while Lyons and Schwarz vectored in from the rear. All three men had dressed themselves up once again in street clothes and ponchos. A hard rain had begun to fall, thickening the darkness and subduing the lights of the city. Lyons walked up to the back bumper of the vehicle and stopped. He looked over at Schwarz, who nodded. He cocked an eyebrow toward Blancanales, who stood by the driver's door.

Lyons nodded at Schwarz, who then drifted up the side of the van and took up a position next to the passenger-side door. The electronics genius drew his Viper JAWS pistol. He could see the closed curtains separating the back of the van from the front cab. At the rear of the vehicle Lyons slid out at an angle to avoid opening himself up to cross fire from either Schwarz or Blancanales and covered the rear doors of the blocky vehicle.

Blancanales reached into his sleeve and removed the long, thin metal Slim Jim. Working smoothly, Blancanales inserted it between the window and the door and, with one swift pop, manipulated the control arm on the vehicle lock, forcing it open. Blancanales left the Slim Jim in place and used his left hand to open the van door as his right pulled the Viper from its hidden holster.

As the door swung open the black cylinder of an MP-5 equipped with an SD-3 sound suppressor slipped between the part in the curtain. Blancanales saw the action and rolled clear, at an angle too awkward to bring fire around the opening door. The silencer muzzle angled toward the ex-Green Beret with deadly promise.

Schwarz unloaded his weapon.

The Viper erupted in his hand and the muzzle-flash lit up the gloomy alley like a lightning storm, casting weird shadows on the smooth clay-brick walls around him. The van's passenger window exploded and glass splinters tinkled as they cascaded down the door and onto the ground. Five spent shell casings arced up into the air and tumbled down to bounce among the scattering of glass shards.

The black cloth of the curtain jumped and danced under the impacts as the 9 mm manglers slipped through the cloth like burning needles. The exposed sound suppressor of the silenced MP-5 jerked and pivoted up toward the roof. There was the thwat-thwat sound as two random bursts sent six subsonic rounds into the ceiling of the van. The metal roof tinged as the bullets clawed their way clear.

On the other side of the van Blancanales lunged through the open car door and snatched the curtain back. A Colombian hardass looked up at him with a stunned expression, blood leaking from a triumvirate of holes in his upper abdomen. A black receiver stuck from his ear under an unruly shock of wavy black hair.

The enforcer gasped for breath and his eyes narrowed as he tried to focus in on Rosario Blancanales. He made an ineffectual gesture with the MP-5, trying to bring the weapon up. Blancanales shot him once in the forehead and the Colombian hitter slumped over backward.

"Let's go," Lyons ordered in Spanish.

Blancanales slid into the van behind the wheel. Schwarz reached in through the shattered passenger window and popped the lock before opening his door. He clambered in and jumped over the front seat into the rear of the van. In the driver's seat Blancanales took out a flathead screwdriver and, without preamble, slammed it into the 1970 vehicle's ignition slot. He grunted with the effort, ignoring the ugly sound made by the invading metal.

Lyons jumped into the van on the passenger side and slammed the door closed. Blancanales turned the handle of the screwdriver and the van's V-8 engine roared to life. Blancanales flipped up the gearshift sticking out of the steering column, throwing it out of Park and into Drive.

Coolly, Blancanales eased the van out of the alley and into the street before turning left and heading away from the neighborhood of Juan Hernandez. Lyons turned around in the seat and swept the curtain back so he could get a look at Schwarz as the man searched the back of the vehicle.

"What'd he have?" Lyons asked.

"Wireless receiver. The bug must be in Juan's apartment for sure because he doesn't have a parabolic mic set up, either. Unlike the day man, this guy was set up to record. Got a plastic bottle half full of piss and a couple dozen skin magazines."

"Paranoia?" Lyons asked.

Schwarz shook his head. "Looks like it, simply

a set of eyes watching the set of eyes watching the watchmen."

"Typical fascist bullshit," Blancanales said, his voice grim.

"Let's dump this van and make contact with Juan," Lyons said. "We put Mr. Chavez's communications relay station out of business, isolate the hijackers from their command and control."

"Then take 'em down," Blancanales finished.

Fifteen minutes later Bolivian emergency services were rolling with sirens blaring to the address. Investigation later revealed that the fire in the apartment had been caused by precision placement of strategic amounts of Semtex plastic explosives. A single body was found in the smoldering ruin. There were three bullets in his head. The case remained officially unsolved.

IN THE LOWLANDS of Bolivia, where the country's borders overlapped the sprawling rainforests of the Amazon River Basin, precipitation was thick, humidity high and cloud cover often at rooftop level in the form of thick fog.

As a method of preparing their battlefield, Stony Man, using Hal Brognola's access to executive authority, had put Jack Grimaldi hard at work with a special flight crew from the United States Southern Command's unconventional-warfare unit. Even before Able Team had landed Grimaldi had been flying a B-2 Stealth bomber in tight grids over the geography of the area of operations.

Flying in tight geometric patterns while invisible to Bolivian radar, the Stealth bomber had been seeding the heavy cloud cover over the target area. Using massive quantities of silver iodide and flash-dried carbon

dioxide, the circling clandestine bomber thickened and
intensified the already present drizzle into a deluge that
threatened to cause rivers to overflow their banks.

On the ground, visibility was reduced to just a few
yards and heat signatures were reduced to blurry in-
significance. Inside the Tactical Operations Center of
the Bolivian response team, the FBI agents began their
designated subterfuge protocols.

The members of Able Team moved forward, soaked
by the massive rainfall. They crossed the tarmac like
ghosts toward the silent structure of the jet plane. Gray
streaks of rain hammered into the asphalt and made
the night inky-black. Bolivian security forces more
concerned on blocking outside observation than on
the hostaged airliner remained vigilant when orientated outward but followed lax procedures in the other
direction.

Inside the Bolivian TOC communications suddenly
failed, computer systems crashed and power units began
to behave erratically. Utilizing the precision-timed distraction Able Team used shallow wetlands along the in-
accessible side of the old airfield to penetrate the fence
and make their approach.

Underneath the wheel well of the aircraft Hermann
Schwarz initiated his surreptitious infiltration of the
passenger plane. Working quickly he used a titanium-
bladed engineering saw to cut through the hoses, creating enough room for him to disengage the coupling
housing and then access a maintenance panel.

Once the hatch had been removed it gave Schwarz
an opening to reach further panels lining the wheel
well, which, once removed, opened up on a crawl space
designed for emergency troubleshooting of the landing
gear by inflight engineers.

"We're in," Schwarz said.

Quickly the electronics genius pulled himself into the opening like a rabbit going down a hole. Without hesitation Lyons and Blancanales followed him into the plane. Once inside the aircraft the fire team worked quickly to follow the service crawl space to the forward cargo hold. They halted their progress once just long enough for Schwarz to tap into the plane's electrical grid using an engineer's diagnostic program on his CPDA. Splicing several wires and engaging a bypass system with alligator clips and industrial wiring, he taped the primary device to the bulkhead.

From there they quietly removed the hinges on the access panel to the flight attendant station at the rear of the plane that housed the kitchenette and storage areas. Hand wrapped around a silenced machine pistol, Lyons carefully pushed the hatch open a half inch and peered through the gap.

Slowly, Lyons lowered the hatch and nodded down to his team. All three of the men eased monocular night-vision devices into place and powered them up. Instantly the dark interior turned a monochromatic green and Able Team appeared in each other's sights as red-and-yellow outlines.

Lyons crawled into position and placed his hand on the hatch cover. "Do it," he whispered.

Schwarz took the prepared cell phone attached to his web gear suspender and in three button pushes sent the electronic signal back to his positioned and plugged-in CPDA. Instantly the plane went coffin dark.

Night goggles on, Lyons lifted the hatch cover. A hijacker with an AKS-74 Kalashnikov stood nervously smoking a cigarette outside one of the vertical coffins airlines passed off as a bathroom. Without hesitation

Lyons leveled his silenced pistol and stroked the trigger.

A bloody comma cracked the man's forehead and he crumpled like a folding chair to the floor of the aircraft. Lyons surged up out of the floorboard and shuffled forward, pistol up as he provided cover.

Blancanales emerged from behind him and shuffled in close. Schwarz brought up the rear as Lyons peeked his head around the corner and threw a flash-bang grenade into the passenger hold.

The bang was sharp and violent and the cargo hold filled with white smoke as the door was thrust forward off its hinges and cracked perfectly down the middle. The pieces of the hatch shot forward into the lower passenger section of the massive Boeing 777.

Blancanales swung around and brought his weapon to bear, lifting the H&K MP-7 and charging up the molded-metal scaffolding stair. He gained the doorway and pushed through, folding left and sweeping the muzzle of his submachine gun around. Directly behind him Carl Lyons sprinted through the opening and folded right.

Hermann Schwarz peeled off behind Blancanales as Blancanales copied Lyons's motions. The teammates found themselves in a narrow access hall leading to the sundries storage area behind the banquet dining compartment. It was crammed and narrow with wall-mounted hatches. White smoke from the breaching charge hung heavy in the air, and the cracked eggshell of a door lay in two smoldering pieces on the cross-checked rubber matting of the floor.

A shaggy figure rose up from the ground still stunned by the unexpected explosion, an Uzi submachine in his hands. Blancanales, keyed up in his dynamic entry, put a 3-round burst into him and knocked him to the floor.

Shuffling forward, Blancanales led Able Team out of the service area and into the banquet area. He rounded the service hallway corner and snapped his submachine gun into position. Behind him the muzzles of his teammates' weapons tracked for targets and Lyons pulled even with him.

CHAPTER NINE

Entering the lounge area, the Able Team warriors immediately stepped into a firestorm.

Men charged forward or twisted in seats, caught in complete surprise by the airborne assault. Passengers began screaming as terrorists clawed at handguns and Able Team poured out of the funnel of the access hallway. Support personnel caught in the cross fire scrambled and dived to get out of the killing field, but the air was thick with lead as Able Team bore down. Handpicked terror cell members attempted to react to the impossible ambush but the surprise was almost total and the terrorists paid with their lives. Blood splashed screaming women and children as Able Team put precise bullet after precise bullet into the snarling faces of the hijackers.

Hermann Schwarz leaned into his weapon and fired off a tight burst. The rounds sailed just past Rosario Blancanales at a tight angle and sliced into the terrorist guard struggling to rise from a coach class seat. The bullets punched into the narco-terrorist, mangling the flesh and cartilage of his throat and crushing his upper vertebrae. The soldier tipped backward as blood gushed, then he slowly spun and fell to the floor.

At that point the fundamental nature of the encounter changed.

They had been an elite unit storming an aircraft with

the advantage of complete surprise and the capability to decimate through extreme aggression. In an instant they were a grunt-line platoon, nose to nose with an entrenched and tenacious enemy.

Blancanales entered the middle section of the plane and realized in a horrifying moment that intelligence had been wrong. A squad of terrorists was actually a platoon and the reactions of the hijackers were well disciplined and instantaneous.

Blancanales did not falter.

Training, condition, courage was too strong, too ingrained. He darted forward, clearing the door. His weapon was up as he hugged the left side of the aisle of seats and he was firing.

His target acquisition was instantaneous despite the adrenaline that flooded his system like a superdrug. Precision had been drilled into him until it was a reflex, and in the face of withering fire he charged.

Behind him Carl Lyons entered the room, his own weapon blazing, followed by Schwarz. They raced hard into the aisle, each man taking down targets to either the left or the right.

They moved with fluid precision into a devastating killing spree, putting down terrorist gunman after terrorist gunman forever. Ahead of them the parallel rows of seats suddenly ended and gave way to a plush sitting area with low couches and desktop tables.

The inner circle of the clandestine hijackers scrambled to throw themselves away from the man as the bodyguard unit was decimated. People died in classic triple taps of two to the body followed by a single shot to the head.

The terrorist leader was screaming, cowering in terror. He made no move to reach for the 9 mm SIG-Sauer pistol under his leather jacket. Everywhere he looked he saw blood splashed: across the crushed-velvet upholstery, the porthole windows, the smooth grain of the custom white oak tabletops. Mouths gaped in silent screams and eyes bulged blindly showing the whites, covered in the film of death. Tongues lolled and limbs were twisted in grotesque parodies of life.

The leader of the terror merchants looked up from the carnage and saw black-clad demons hurtling toward him, faces hidden and distorted by masks, bodies bulging with armor and weapons and the kind of dense, frightening sinews men couldn't earn in weight rooms.

He heard someone screaming, then realized it was himself. His bladder let go in a sudden liquid rush and he could smell himself. Two of the biggest men raced toward him and he cringed. They pummeled him hard, beating him mercilessly. He felt butt stocks strike his kidneys and he screamed only to be struck in the mouth hard enough to knock out his front teeth.

Fingers like steel claws intertwined themselves in his hair and yanked his head cruelly back. A dark, wild-eyed demon leaned in close, his voice a hoarse whisper. The terrorist leader moaned and his lips tried to form prayers.

"Your time has come," the faceless commando said.

Steel bracelets clicked into place around his wrists and ankles. The terrorist leader screamed as his shoulder was pulled out of it's socket to facilitate his being hogtied with the high-tensile handcuffs. He lay trussed up like a pig for the slaughter.

He saw a man with shoulders like a rockpile step forward, a pistol in his hand. The man leaned down and gently rested the muzzle against the terrorist leader's forehead right between his eyes.

There was a horrifically loud click as the hammer on the pistol was cocked back. The terrorist leader closed his eyes tight shut. Here it was—the end. He heard the hammer fall and he jerked.

"Bang!" the devil shouted, and the terrorist leader soiled himself for the second time.

I'm still alive, he thought. How? Why?

"You are under arrest," the man said in flawless unaccented English, and in an instant the terror leader understood how badly his superiors had underestimated the resolve of the United States.

Passengers were screaming, shouting and cowering in their seats as Lyons cuffed the terror leader quickly.

"Able is leaving the AO," Schwarz whispered into his throat mic.

"Copy," Price replied in his earbud.

Without preamble Able Team turned around and exited the plane. By the time the first of the passengers gathered courage enough to open the plane door the strike team had disappeared into the marshland on the edge of the airfield.

Stony Man Farm, Virginia

BARBARA PRICE SAT at her workstation and opened her computer. Sipping absently from a cup of coffee, she began clicking through her messages, working through the more mundane aspects of her position as mission controller for Stony Man.

Once certain bureaucratic and logistical functions had been completed she opened her e-mail from the secure server used to facilitate interagency communications between departments of the government.

Her in-box contained two AARs, or After Action Reports. One was from the FBI, forwarded to her by Carmen Delahunt, and the second from the intelligence and covert action review panel of the Pentagon. Her gaze moved rapidly across the computer screen absorbing the information and memorizing the facts and conclusions offered within the files.

After closing out the Pentagon's report on Phoenix Force's action in Baghdad, she opened the FBI AAR on Able Team's activities in Bolivia. As she burned through the dry, condensed facts outlined by the Justice Department analysts, her powerful intellect began making connections. When she was done she immediately picked up her secure transmission cell phone and dialed Hal Brognola.

"Hal here," Brognola growled.

"I've got the AARs for Phoenix and Able," Price informed him.

"Something out of place?"

"I have a coincidence," Price replied.

"No such thing," Brognola countered.

"Exactly," she agreed. "Listen to this—in the days prior to his capture Abu Hafiza opened a bank account in Damascus, Syria. Shortly afterward he received a wire transfer of several million dollars from a Cayman Islands bank. The FBI's background sift on the Bolivian commander suspected of controlling the narco-guerrillas utilized as mercenaries in the Bolivian episode received payments to a Swiss account originating from the same Cayman financial institution account."

Brognola let out a long, low whistle. "'What a tangled

web we weave…'" he quoted in a murmur to himself. "You put Bear and company on this?"

"Just giving you a heads-up," Price said. "I'm tasking Kurtzman as soon as I hang up."

"Good," Brognola said. "I'll hold off briefing the Man until we have a full picture. Let's make this priority one."

"I'll call you," Price said and hung up.

TWO HOURS LATER Barbara Price summoned David Mc-Carter and Carl Lyons to the War Room. The leaders of the Farm's two direct-action teams sat across the conference table from Price as Kurtzman gave the leadership cadre the rundown.

"The brilliant minds in the computer room have pulled on some loose threads and started unweaving a tangled skein."

Lyons looked over at Price, face deadpan. "What?"

"The technomancers have uncovered some clandestine conspiracies of nefarious nature, mate," McCarter told him.

Lyons looked over at Price, face deadpan. "What?"

"We discovered something suspicious relating to your operations," Price translated.

"Such as?" Lyons asked Kurtzman.

"Good stuff, Ironman, two main things that'll get you boys rolling wheels up when we finish," Kurtzman replied. "One, the same account used by Hafiza and the Bolivian was used to purchase a freighter in the West African country of Ivory Coast. Two, a second purchase was made of a small jungle island in the western Atlantic off the Venezuelan coast near Barbados. We were able to trace the account back to a holding company used by Qatar National Industries, which is owned by Sheikh Ahmad ibn Ali al-Thani."

"Al-Thani?" McCarter asked. "That name seems familiar. Has he been on our radar?"

"He should seem familiar," Price answered. "You killed his son in that Pakistani raid."

"Which is providing a motive for the emir to become a global supporter of al Qaeda in strikes against America," Kurtzman added.

"Too bad, so sad," Lyons grunted. "We kill sonny, now we kill pappy. Obvious the fruit didn't fall far from the tree…or the nut, whatever the case may be," he amended.

"What do you need us to do?" McCarter asked. "How do you want to capatailize on this screwup of al-Thani's?"

"We want Able on the island for a soft probe," Price replied.

"No problem," Lyons answered. "I'll pull up geo-graphical information with Pol and Gadgets and get an op-plan to you ASAP."

"What about Phoenix?" McCarter asked.

"More reconnaissance," Price answered. "But we need you to be in two places at once so you'll have to split the team as you see fit. We need to get some surveillance on al-Thani at his headquarters in Dubai and we need to find out what that freighter in Africa is up to."

"No problem," McCarter said. "Let me have the printouts and we'll have a plan presently."

Price stood. "Excellent. Let's roll, people."

ADAPT. IMPROVISE. OVERCOME. These were the watch-words of the field soldier, Barbara Price knew, but within thirty minutes of her initial briefing the slick genius Kurtzman had sifted through a thousand pieces of seemingly unrelated intelligence generated by those two AARs and connected a jigsaw puzzle of frightening countenance.

Hal Brognola was already in the air on his way back to D.C. when his secured cell phone began to ring. He pulled it out, saw that it was Price and immediately clicked the phone on.

"What have you got for me?" he demanded without preamble. "It can't be good. Is Striker in trouble?"

"No," Price answered. "Striker's fine but out of contact. I wish it wasn't so because we need every man I can get now."

"What do you have?"

"I have a situation report that changes all our plans." Price spoke in rapid, succinct sentences, and Brognola could hear the strain in her voice. "I have situations ready for direct action all over the world unfolding now. I have a Zulu Contingency situation."

"What?" Despite his years of experience in clandestine service, Brognola was surprised to find himself shocked.

Simply put, the Zulu Contingency had never been more than a war game thought problem, a hypothetical solution to a purely hypothetical problem. What it boiled down to was a ticking-time-bomb situation across multiple geographical locations, most involving nations not actively hostile to the U.S., if not outright allies.

It called for the dispersal of the Farm's direct-action units, Phoenix Force and Able Team, into subunits or even individual deployments apart from each other. Each member acting as an operative on his own in conjunction with multiple, simultaneous strikes across a global battlefield.

It was never supposed to really happen, Brognola thought. The Farm was used to run-and-gun plays, multiple strikes across oceans and countries, but usually even in those cases the units had time to move, fight and function in their organic cohorts.

"What could be so bad we need to coordinate eight separate missions?" Brognola asked. His voice sounded hoarse to his own ears.

"I'm calling David and Carl back now," Price answered, "but I'll give you the short version. Every one of Bear's crew needs a round of applause on this one. It was sheer voodoo they were able to shift the nuggets loose then connect the dots this quickly. This time around it was our current master of game theory, Professor Hunt, who was able to see the big picture."

"We'll give 'em a raise when this is over," Brognola growled. "Go on."

"I've got FARC mercenaries headed to a supposedly abandoned airfield in Colombia for transport to a Caribbean island. I've got satellite flyovers of that same island already showing construction and gunmen crawling all over it. I've got the number-one terror cell leader of al Qaeda in Africa hiding out on the Sudan border. I got more jihadists holed up ready to board a freighter in Ivory Coast. I've got everything pointing back to our friend the emir in Dubai with two heretofore unknown, quote 'commercial' unquote operations centers and a planned assault of the homeland mere days away."

"How do you want to execute the Zulu Contingency?"

"I tap the Agency for transportation and logistical support. These countries are all officially neutral or allied to the U.S. politically, so that leaves JSOC resources unavailable. I scramble everyone at once for either tactical surgical strikes or strategic field reconnaissance—simultaneously. Once their primary operations are conducted, I collapse all the members of the Farm's units back into an assault force to strike the island."

Brognola saw instantly where Price was going. "We cut off all the heads of the Hydra in a single night of the long knives, then attack the heart."

"Exactly, Hal," Price agreed. "That Caribbean island is in international waters and isolated from trade and tourist shipping and flight lanes. Its appeal to the emir's people is also its weakness. You tell the Man we could get the emir, an al Qaeda operations officer, the head of al Qaeda in Africa and at least a company of diehard jihadists."

"Set it up, Barb," Hal answered. "I'll get the green light from the Man if I have to hog-tie him." He paused. "We're going to need a goddamn score card to keep track of the action."

CHAPTER TEN

Abidjan, Ivory Coast

The night had grown darker as Calvin James surveyed the ship secured to the pier. The vessel was small as freighters went at 2,500 tons and running 200 feet prow to stern by 30 feet across the main deck. Carefully, James chose his route of infiltration.

He crossed the yard and hit the dock, moving quickly to crouch near a huge piling in the shadow of the ship. The smell of the quay was strong. The stink was salt and fish and mildew along with the odor of floating garbage and rotting wood. It hung over everything in a greasy film that clung unpleasantly in his nose.

Off to his left from the aft of the ship he saw a single wharf rat scramble across a thick mooring rope of woven hemp. From the side of the ship an automatic bilge pump began spilling yellowish water in a stream out of a small port.

James uunconsciously reached up and touched the pistol butt of his Beretta 92F where it rode in a holster under his arm. His eyes, narrowed to slits, scanned the ship. The captain of the ship had made James's job easier by choosing the sort of company he now kept. The mercenary mariner had handpicked a small cadre of former Liberian guerrillas. The men were linked to bands accused of the worst crimes: ethnic cleansing, torture, rape camps, the sniping of civilians and relief workers.

James would be showing them no mercy.

His gaze roamed over the deck and across the superstructure. The big windows fronting the bridge were dark and he could detect no motion. James remained motionless, patient as a hunter in ambush. There would be a guard. A man like the captain always had a guard.

Wearing a pea coat and watch cap, the Liberian gunman strolled out from around a metal storage container. The cherry of his cigarette was a bright spot against the shadows of his heavy brow and full beard. A Heckler & Koch MP-5, the weapon that had supplanted the Uzi as the world's most ubiquitous submachine gun, hung from a shoulder strap. Hidden in shadow, James watched the man walk up to the railing and take a last drag off his cigarette. The sentry flicked the cigarette out and it flew in an arc before falling into the cold, polluted water and extinguishing with a hiss.

The man spit after the cigarette butt then turned from the ship's railing and leisurely strolled away across the deck. James unfolded from the shadow. His hands found the two-inch-thick weave of one of the vessel's mooring ropes and locked his grip on it as he swung out over the water.

Like a kid on a set of monkey bars James swung hand-over-hand out about a yard or so, then lifted his legs up so that his heels could lock around the rope. He went still for a moment, reducing the momentum of his actions, then began to climb up the rope in an inchworm, accordion motion.

He worked hard, pulling himself rapidly up the rope to the gunwale. He slid over the edge and quickly drew the Beretta. He moved smoothly to the lee of the anchor windlass and crouched in its blocky shadow.

James surveyed his surroundings. He ignored the cargo hold entrances in favor of the deckhouse. About a hundred feet of open deck separated him from the aft superstructure. He did not like the exposure and he had lost sight of the deck sentry.

James scanned the dark but saw nothing. His ears detected the creaking of the mooring ropes and the gentle lap of waves on the hull beneath him. The Beretta was out and up and ready as he made his move.

He broke from the shadowed lee of the windlass, cut around the forward cargo hatch and sprinted toward the kingpost and crane assembly positioned between the holds. He went down to one knee, Beretta up so that the silencer was even with the hard plane of his cheekbone, his left hand resting on the cool metal of the deck. His heart bumped up against his sternum in a strong rhythm. His head swiveled on his neck like a gun turret tracking for a target. His eyes narrowed in concentration.

James heard the scrape of metal on striker and looked to his right. The lighter flared briefly in the gloomy dark as the sentry lit another cigarette from the starboard gunwale. James extended his arm and leveled the Beretta. It was a long shot for a silenced weapon.

The Italian pistol coughed and the slide worked once. The sentry crumpled over, the cigarette tumbling from slack lips. The lighter fell and bounced off the deck, followed a heartbeat later by the corpse of the gunman. Blood spilled out across the plate metal flooring in a spreading crimson stain.

James slid along to the port side and reached the aft superstructure, where he found a flight of stairs. He followed them to the bridge. The wheelhouse door was locked, but through a grimy window he saw the glow coming from a wide array of sophisticated, modern navigational controls.

He crossed in front of the bridge and began checking doors. He was the consummate stalking predator, silent, deadly. He descended to the second deck on the starboard stair and found an unlocked galley door.

James opened the heavy portal and stepped slowly inside.

The hallway interior was claustrophobically narrow and dark except for a single dim emergency lightbulb set into the bulkhead at the far end of the corridor. James moved carefully down the hall, trying doors and finding them unlocked.

Each room was a comfortable cabin, obviously designed for the ship's officers when the vessel was under way. James found the first two clean, made up and empty. When he opened the third door he was forced to kill again.

James pushed the cabin door in smoothly and the bodyguard rose from his bed, the glossy pages of a European porno magazine sliding out of his hand. There was a submachine gun on the bedside shelf that was a twin to the H&K MP-5 the other sentry had carried.

James leveled his machine pistol and went to bark a warning but the man was already in motion. James waited until the Liberian mercenary's hands found the weapon before pulling the trigger on his own.

The Beretta recoiled smoothly in his grip and blood splashed the twisted sheets beneath the bodyguard. There was a sharp, wet sound as the 9 mm Parabellum rounds slapped into the man's flesh and pinned him to the bed.

Reflexively, James put a third bullet into the man's forehead. The man lay very still and for a moment the only motion in the cabin was blood spilling from bullet wounds, then the Phoenix Force commando was gone.

James ducked through the metal frame of the cabin door and only had time to throw up one hand in desperate surprise.

The eight-pound head of the sledgehammer sailed toward his face as the man wielding it let out a snarl of effort. James's forearm caught the heavy tool on the haft of the sledge just below the head of the maul. His arm exploded in pain and then went numb a heartbeat later.

He managed to stop the killing strike but was driven backward under the force of the blow. He staggered up against the cabin doorjamb as the silenced Beretta went flying. James saw a wild-eyed man with skin like dull onyx bearing down on him in filthy dungarees and a dirty flannel shirt.

The man yanked the sledgehammer back and stepped in close to deliver another blow. The man's forearms and shoulders were thick with muscle, and the attacker was tall enough to see eye-to-eye with the six-foot-plus James. His face was covered in wiry stubble, and his big, square teeth were stained nicotine yellow.

James lashed out with his left hand as the man brought the sledgehammer back over his shoulder like some maritime version of folklore legend John Henry. James's thumb caught him square in a brown eye, and the man hissed with pain and tried to shake his head clear. James felt the peeled-grape texture of the eyeball squish under the flat plane of his thumb and knew he'd hurt the man.

James flexed the muscles of his back in the next instant and rebounded off the door frame and centered on his feet. Even as he repositioned, his left hand was drawing back and then lashing forward. His thumb found the man's neck just next to the ready target of his Adam's apple.

The blinded shipman suddenly gagged and his face distorted against the sudden bruising. James darted in and used his left hand to grasp the heavy maul by its handle. He locked his grip around it like a carpenter's vise and then slammed his forehead into the man's face. Snot and blood splattered like fruit as James mashed the man's nose flat and smeared it across his face.

The man buckled at the knees and toppled, leaving the still upraised sledgehammer firmly in James's grip. As he dropped, James jerked his leg up and drove the hard edge of his knee into the falling man's jaw.

James struck at precisely the correct angle and there was a sickening sound as the mandible was ripped from the skull at the hinge joint. The man slipped down to the corridor flooring and lay in a heap of slack, twisted limbs.

James set the sledgehammer down and retrieved his pistol. His heart was pounding in his ribs from adrenaline bleed-off and his arm was throbbing with an agonizing pain that put his teeth on edge. Holding his pistol in his left hand, he forced himself to work his right hand, wiggling each finger and making a fist to ensure the bones of his forearm had not been cracked by the heavy blow.

The hand was weak and he knew his forearm would be purple with a sheath of contusion markings, but he didn't think the bone had been more than bruised. He held the injured limb down by his waist and continued moving forward, weapon in his left hand now.

He cat-danced down the hallway to the final door on the deck. He couldn't imagine the captain staying in any of the smaller rooms belowdecks designed for the regular crewmen. From the position of the doorway James realized the cabin he stood in front of occupied a corner area, making it larger than the officer's quarters he'd just investigated.

He put out his shaking and pained hand and grasped the doorknob.

THE MARITIME BLUEPRINTS Carmen Delahunt had managed to track down had paid off. He had found the room he was looking for. He ran down a transparent wall separating the ship's CPU and blade server farm from the IT and navigational workstations. Inside the vault were several hard drives locked in transparent plastic cases and carefully stacked atop plasti-alloy filing cabinets. On the other side was a small, rectangular box of polished German oak.

The containment unit was surrounded by a cluster of sophisticated electronics: climate-control sensors, humidity readouts, seismograph, gas analyzer, barometer and temperature gauge. On the other side of the glass Calvin James used a sliver of thermite to burn out a security door lock.

The thump of the massive, idling engines blanketed the cramped quarters with white noise. James moved quickly to the appropriate station and inserted his flash drive. One of the blue-screened monitors jumped to life in response, and the ex-SEAL sat in front of the console using the workstation's mouse pad to initiate the massive Trojan program.

"Stony," he said into his throat mic. "I'm in."

"Stony, copy," Akira Tokaido immediately responded. "You have the flash drive initiated?"

"Copy. It's downloaded."

"Good. Go ahead and remove the flash and insert the connector cable to your CPDA."

"It's done," he said after a moment.

"Understood. I'm going hot with the sat link now. Stand by."

"Copy."

Twenty-six seconds later Tokaido said, "Phoenix, this is Stony. That's a wrap."

"Copy, Stony," James replied. "I'm making exit."

"Stay cool. Farm out."

Calvin James slipped into the darkness and made his escape.

Caribbean Island off Barbados

COMING OUT of the water in a low, thick wetland, Rosario Blancanales circumvented the compound and approached it from the rear. The going was tough. The woods were thick and the terrain steep. Inside the commercial sniper camouflage Blancanales sweated freely. A former member of the Unites States Army Special Forces, he had been in uncompromising physical condition before coming to Stony Man and still followed a grueling fitness program.

He scrambled up hillsides thick with brush and weeds, making his way around al-Thani's newest estate toward the rear. He swept up the incline, sticking to patches of deep woods and using animal trails so that as he made his final approach he was coming downhill toward al-Thani's property.

As he neared the back of the estate Blancanales was forced to slow his approach. From his earlier reconnaissance Blancanales knew that a line of wild brambles and blackberry shrubs marked the beginning of al-Thani's property line, set well in front of the wall that encircled the estate. The Able Team veteran made his approach toward the brambles with trepidation.

Just beyond the brambles al-Thani's security relied on an array of sensors that consisted of spike microphones. Anyone thrashing through the brambles would be picked up on the hidden mics, thus triggering an alarm response. Blancanales knew he would have to leave behind the relative invisibility offered by the ghillie suit.

Rosario Blancanales sank to the forest floor and quietly removed the camouflage. The loose patches and swathes of fabric that were so effective in breaking up the outline of a human body would only serve to snag and catch on the brambles and thorny vines.

Moving carefully, Blancanales wove his way into the thicket on his elbows and knees. He plucked thick vines up and slid under them, carefully dragging his weapon with the stock folded down behind him. He pulled a pair of garden clippers from a cargo pocket and carefully began to cut out a path.

Though he had purposely chosen a section of bramble thicket that was in his opinion less dense than some other areas, it was still painstaking work with every movement he made a potential giveaway to the electronic sensors positioned on the other side.

Sweat rolled down his features and cooled his feverish skin. He pressed down slowly and steadily with the clippers to avoid the snipping sound common to his activity. Beyond the thicket and across a strip of

tall swamp grass al-Thani's wall rose in an imposing
barrier.

One thing at a time, Blancanales told himself. One
thing at a time.

HERMANN SCHWARZ PURGED his regulator and slipped
back under the surface of the Caribbean without a
splash. The Dräger closed-system rebreather eliminated
the telltale exhaust noise and bubble trail left by conven-
tional scuba gear and provided for a more silent diving
experience. Schwarz was an experienced combat diver
who had operated underwater several times during his
time with Able Team.

He felt the current of the coastal surf sweep him
along toward his target as he descended into the balmy
darkness. His load-bearing harness was front-loaded,
and Schwarz compensated by adjusting buoyancy for
that and the gear attached in oilskin to his back. He
settled slowly down through the murky water and began
to check his analog and digital displays. He would use
the bottom to ensure depth consistency and a built-in
pace counter to indicate distance swum.

Schwarz kicked out gently with his swim fins, using
the tide to push him along and conserve energy. His
breath echoed slightly behind his mask and visibility
was less than arm's length in the midnight water.

Schwarz took in calm, even breaths, conserving his
energy and executing his movements with a maximum
of efficiency. Occasionally he was forced to dodge underwater obstacles like dead trees or bits of garbage or
sudden barriers of coral reef, which required his concentration to remain sharp. Beneath him the ground sloped
up and after several minutes he entered the mouth of
the small river feeding into the ocean from the island.

He checked his watch and cross indexed the time he had swum with the distance his pace indicator displayed as traveled. When he calculated with what he believed was the appropriate figure, Schwarz began to rise, kicking forcibly for the surface. It was imperative that he not overshoot his target and miss al-Thani's quay.

He rose up from the depths, death from below, and his head broke the surface of the water. He kicked against the current, slowing his drift with the river until he could get his bearings. Fifty yards down he saw the wall of boulders al-Thani had used to construct his pier in the swampy tributary just off the coast.

The yacht sat in the protective lee of the quay. It was almost eighty-five feet long, and Schwarz recognized it as a twenty-five-meter Princess powered by twin Caterpillar 1570-horsepower engines. Despite himself the Able Team electronics genius was envious. The emir had good taste.

The craft itself was a thing of perfection. Capable of being manned by two to five crew members, the Princess had port and starboard guest berths in addition to the owner's salon. When al-Thani cruised the sea he obviously did so in style.

Schwarz allowed himself to drift in toward the big yacht. His predator senses were alive. The desire to punish and to kill was growing in him like a sleeping dragon stirring with the dawn. The sensation felt like hunger.

CHAPTER ELEVEN

Schwarz floated into the wall of stacked boulders and grasped them firmly in his hands. He allowed the current to gently pull him along the wall of rock as he watched the boat for any sign of movement. The flying bridge, with its sweeping arch housing the communications antennaes, was empty.

Through the heavily tinted windows around the forward salon Schwarz could see the flickering distortion of what could only be a large-screen TV. Someone was on board. Schwarz submerged beneath the river surface and floated until he came to the end of the jetty wall.

He swam into the open mouth of the quay, which faced south, away from the river current. He kicked deeper and entered the pocket of water protected from the pull of the current. The water was still here, like a gloomy pool, and Schwarz floated softly up toward the surface.

He broke the surface at the rear of yacht as he had intended, very near the flat extension of the tender deck. A Yamaha wetbike was secured to one side of the dive platform. A swim ladder extended over the edge and dipped down into the water.

Schwarz's eyes searched the aft section of the boat. He could hear the sounds of the television coming muted through the closed doors. The yacht was immaculate and for the first time Schwarz could see the name on its side: *Djodan*.

Deep in his zone of predator awareness Schwarz reached out for the ladder and prepared to board the yacht of Sheikh Ahmad ibn Ali al-Thani.

ROSARIO BLANCANALES CUT his way through the last bit of bramble and vine separating him from the grass strip surrounding the northern estate wall. In the area beyond the thorny bushes cheat grass grew up, bending slightly in the breeze that came down off the mountain slope.

Blancanales halted and slowly scanned the topography around him. He saw the back gate to the estate set down off to his left. Despite the temptation offered by the dirt track leading up to the rear entrance, he had avoided the egress point for his approach as being a focal center for the security system.

There were trip indicators, cameras and armed guards. Trip indicators had been placed around the general perimeter with CCTV camera networks on the gates and building exteriors. A trip indicator would alert a system controller in the main house, who would then either maneuver the camera pods off the gates and toward the source of the trip or dispatch personnel to the site. Inside the wall guards patrolled at night and manned unobtrusive posts during the day.

By moving slowly and avoiding the CCTV camera pod clusters, Blancanales hoped to circumvent the eyes-on areas of the system. The problem was, al-Thani's trip indicators were good. Pedestrian compared to some of the laser fences utilized on facilities with less foot traffic, but dependable.

Moving carefully, Blancanales entered the saw grass and palmetto. He kept low, parting the tall grass with his hands, then slowly penetrated forward beyond the brambles into the field, which was filled with spike microphones. Every few yards Blancanales was forced into an awkward two-step to avoid a trip indicator. He was sure his sound signature was being picked up by the system controller but he hoped by moving slowly the disruption of rhythm would prompt the technician to dismiss the sound fluctuations as wind causing tall grass to rub on the microphones.

The ground-surveillance system had been created and initially utilized by military intelligence programs to help pinpoint unsuspecting troop movements along trails, and a lone operator already aware of the presence of the devices had a good chance of cat-dancing past the spike microphones.

Blancanales exercised his self-discipline, squashed the adrenaline fear he felt at being so exposed and forced himself to continue moving slowly. There would be little indication when the defenses hidden among the tall grass changed from passive to active. Alertness was paramount.

Rifle still slung over his shoulder, Rosario Blancanales sank to his knees. He slowly felt out in front of him, moving even slower now as his proximity to the wall increased. He kept his body held in close and his touches as he parted the grass now became gentle caresses.

His fingers found the trip wire.

Blancanales carefully raised his hand and focused his eyes on the threat. He followed the line of the wire to where it disappeared into the clumps of tall grass. Slowly he eased himself forward, following the trip line deeper into the minefield. Fifteen harrowing feet later Blancanales came up to the mine.

A circle of trip prongs stuck up from a metal bottle-neck buried in the ground. Blancanales recognized the mine as a PROM-1 bounding antipersonnel mine. The PROM-1 was a homegrown Yugoslavian product and had been used prolifically during the various Bosnian conflicts. After NATO had moved into those splintered republics, the weapons of those nations' factories had flooded the global market, showing up in Africa, the Middle East and now here.

When detonated the mine bounded into the air to a height of roughly twenty feet before it exploded, unleashing steel fragments in a 360-degree arc out to one hundred feet. The shrapnel was propelled by 425 grams of Composition B explosives, making the PROM-1 a highly effective man killer. Blancanales gave it the respect it deserved. First he snipped the wire, releasing the tension on the trigger, and then moved carefully around the antipersonnel mine.

Three more times he was forced to repeat his dangerous game until he reached the estate fence. Finally the ex-Green Beret was flush against the brick wall of the compound property. He rested momentarily, forcing his breathing back under control. He was so thoroughly soaked with sweat after his ordeal that he began to shiver in the muggy Caribbean air.

He felt thirsty but he was traveling light and there would be time enough for drinking when the operation was finished. Slowly, Blancanales rose out of his crouch. The wall was ten feet high and made of smooth-fitted redbrick.

Blancanales removed his APS-95 assault rifle from its position around his back and undid the black nylon sling from the buttstock attachment point, leaving it still secured at the muzzle under the front sight. Having prepared for this, Blancanales took a thick needle like the kind used by riggers to sew parachute harnesses out from where he had inserted it through the cloth on the cover flap of his cargo pocket.

The Able Team commando slid the free end of the nylon rifle sling under his belt and pushed the needle, point down, through the two folds of the sling, attaching the strap to himself quickly and efficiently. Without hesitation he placed the assault rifle against the estate wall and used it like a step ladder, exploiting momentum to keep the ad hoc platform in place.

His hands reached the top of the wall and he smoothly pulled himself into position, the assault rifle pulled up and dangling behind him. Once astride the brick wall he leaned low to avoid silhouetting himself and drew the rifle up by its sling and rolled over onto the lawn.

He landed cat quiet and pulled the needle from the sling, releasing the strap. He swept the rifle up and scanned the area quickly, finding no movement nor hearing any alarm raised. With deft fingers he secured the sling to the buttstock swivel and rose.

Like some malevolent ghost Rosario Blancanales penetrated farther into the al-Thani estate. For thirty minutes he ghosted through the compound, laying his own directional microphones, taking pictures and prepping the battlefield for the assault to follow.

When he was finished he went over the wall and melted into the swamp.

HERMANN SCHWARZ KICKED OFF his fins and let them drift away into the water before ducking under the surface and peeling off the Dräger rebreather kit. From beneath the water of the tiny estuary Schwarz grasped the yacht's swim ladder with one hand and pulled himself up.

As he rose the American commando removed one of Stony Man armorer John "Cowboy" Kissinger's little treasures. The upgraded PB/6P9 pistol had come out of the man's gunsmith lab but the pistol itself was a Russian Spetsnaz favorite.

The 6P9 was a direct descendant of the Makarov and designed specifically for use with a silencer, though it could be fired under emergency situations with the front half of the silencer removed. At close-quarters battle range the 9 mm round was more than sufficient for putting men down.

Schwarz came out of the water smoothly and slid across the tender deck. He kept the 6P9 poised as he stalked through the outdoor lounging area with its white couches and toward the door leading into the aft salon. The sound of the television grew louder as Schwarz approached.

He heard rapid bursts of what he thought was German, followed by grunts and high-pitched squeals coming from the surround sound system. He moved through the aft deck in a slight crouch, attempting to present as low a profile as he could manage to avoid being silhouetted through the tinted windows of the passenger salon.

He reached the door and quietly pulled it open. Immediately the level of noise from the television rose, no longer muffled by the closed door. The porno orgy raged on a plasma-screen TV cranked to a generous volume.

Between the rear of the salon and the plasma-screen wall mount sat a plush couch of brown leather. Beyond the salon a large galley and dining area were situated before the floor plan tapered up into the helm.

Schwarz had pulled the blueprints for the Princess yacht up from online while waiting for McCarter to join them in Zagreb. He knew exactly which door led to the staterooms housed below this deck and he kept one eye cocked toward the door and the curved stair leading down from the flying bridge as he ghosted farther into the yacht salon.

He tracked slowly with the silenced 6P9 as he moved through the room. He felt confident that if a sentry had been on the flying bridge he would have seen him from the water, so Schwarz kept most of his senses keyed toward the door leading to the staterooms.

Beyond the couch a heavy coffee table commanded the center of the generous room. On the floor beyond it was a pair of black thong women's panties, wadded up and forgotten. On the coffee table a Monet in a heavy gilded frame had been placed, glass face up. On the protective glass sat several conical heaps of white powder Schwarz recognized as not cocaine, but the newer form of heroin that could be snorted. A woman's silver lipstick case sat next to the picture, a matching silver razor blade placed beside it.

He peered into the shadows beyond the galley area to try to pick out a shape or motion from the helm concave but found nothing there. He rounded the edge of the couch facing the plasma screen and looked to see if one of al-Thani's employees was laid out on the lavish piece of furniture.

In a single heartbeat anticipation was fulfilled.

The door leading up from the staterooms burst open and Schwarz shifted, snapping the silenced 6P9 around in a two-handed grip. The dark paneled door bounced off the inside wall and a couple stumbled through it, tangled up in each other's arms. The man wore a rumpled and unzipped pair of the blue coveralls Schwarz recognized as al-Thani's generic security uniform. The man, a dark-skinned African Schwarz assumed was one of the Liberian mercenaries, held a giggling brunette in one hand and an open magnum of champagne in the other. Huge tuffs of black chest hair spilled out of the partially open zipper, making a thick gold chain glitter in the tangled nest. Around his waist the terror gunman wore a black pistol belt holding a Glock 18 handgun.

The girl wore a flimsy but expensive kimono-style bathrobe strained to the limit by fake breasts of a size every bit as improbable as those of the porn stars on the television screen. She was laughing wildly and her dark, Slavic features were drawn to an anorexic tightness. She had one hand clamped to the crotch of her lover's pants, and the other held a champagne flute half filled with the ginger-ale-colored bubbly.

A second pair of black male hands emerged from the staircase behind her and began to squeeze at the taut nipples of her industrial-size breasts. The girl shrieked in laughter and fell against the first mercenary terrorist, making him spill his own champagne as he tried to fill his glass from the magnum bottle. She looked up, saw the masked Schwarz with pistol drawn and screamed.

The first Liberian snapped his head up, his laughter dying. He saw the dark figure of death standing in front of him. Behind the intruder mechanical sex pumped out on the plasma screen, punctuated by shrieks and gasps. The man dropped his champagne flute and the magnum bottle as he went for his holstered pistol.

The glass magnum struck the carpet and bounced. Champagne bubbled out furiously, like white-water rapids spilling over rocks. The girl screamed again and the man cursed. Schwarz's hands were stone steady on the trigger of the Russian pistol.

The 6P9 spit twice with subdued pops as the silencer's muzzle brakes bled off the sonic vibrations. The first mercenary lost a left eye and an untidy comma cracked his forehead open. The man went rigid and gouts of scarlet splashed the screaming girl.

Still shrieking, she was brutally shoved aside as the second man pushed past her, pulling his Glock 18 free from its holster. Schwarz gunned him down with a double tap to the head, and the man dropped to the carpet, dead. He lay there, cheek caressed by the spilling champagne, his eyes staring wide open and fixed.

The girl turned and saw the second terrorist fall dead at her feet and she started shrieking again. Her hands flew to her blood-splattered face and she sank, still screaming, to her knees.

Schwarz leaped forward. He was brutal and efficient, operating without pity. He pulled the girl up by her wrist, desperate to stop her screeching before she alerted anyone on the pier to his presence. She came up easily and he figured she must have weighed all of 115 pounds.

He released her and she stumbled back against the bulkhead but stayed on her feet. Schwarz's eyes surveyed her anatomy with precise intentions. The carotid sinus was a network of nerves running along the side of the neck just under the ear. Schwarz lifted the 6P9 up and chopped the butt of the pistol into the nerve cluster along the woman's throat.

Her central nervous system short circuited. Her eyes rolled up, showing whites, and she folded like a house of cards, unconscious. Schwarz let her fall and dropped to his knees beside her as he drew his dive knife from his calf.

He quickly cut the laces out of the dead security tech's boots. Sheathing the knife, Schwarz bound the girl's hands and feet behind her, then used her own kimono to hood and gag her, tying it off with her silk belt. He picked her up and threw her on the couch, ignoring the naked flesh.

Tired of the noise, Schwarz turned and punched off the power button on the plasma screen with one gloved finger, killing the graphic sex flick. He hoped the girl had enough alcohol and heroin in her system to keep her out, but for all he knew she'd been taking some form of uppers. He picked up the 6P9 and cleared the rest of the yacht in as expedient a manner as possible.

Coming up out of the staterooms, Schwarz checked in once more on the woman. The party girl remained unconscious but breathing, and Schwarz quickly mounted the stairs to the flying bridge. It was cool outside after the climate-controlled warmth of the yacht and it felt good to Schwarz inside his drysuit.

With his listening devices in place the Able Team electronics genius eyed the woman. He brought out his secure sat-phone and made the connection.

"Stony, Gadgets here," he said without preamble. "I ran into a glitch. I'm scrubbing the rest of the recon. Prep for extraction."

Schwarz cursed as he cut the connection. The Stony Man timetable had just been cut. It did not bode well for the upcoming operation.

CHAPTER TWELVE

Al-Thani compound, Dubai

Working solo, David McCarter had chosen Phoenix Force's most dangerous mission for himself. His surreptitious entry of al-Thani's forward operating business office had been a manifestation of perfect covert-entry technique. Now, deep within the building that housed the nerve center of the emir's activities, he prepared to enter the sanctum sanctorum.

McCarter eased the door from the service hallway open and stepped into the kitchen of the exclusive penthouse. He ran his eyes along the doorjamb, saw the magnetic connector switch alarm apparatus recessed into the door.

He guessed the model and supplier from visual clues and nodded to himself. The alarm was top of the line, but commercial. McCarter closed the door to the kitchen behind him softly and entered the bodyguard's quarters.

"Guess who's coming to dinner, asshole," he muttered under his breath.

McCarter moved through the house. The decor was obviously Western Asiatic, even mosque-ish in influence, blended with an obvious penchant for technology. Looking for an office or master bedroom, and fear-ing that time was tight, he cut down hallways, crossed rooms, checked behind doors.

Quickly, McCarter found the emir's home office. It was of a masculine design, the six-by-eight-yard room boasting a huge desk, conference phones, personal computer and a globe made out of semiprecious stones. McCarter ignored the computer. In the field it was too dangerous to attempt to access files from a protected PC. If the infiltration had been accompanied by proper Stony cyberteam backup he would have proceeded differently.

As it was, any attempts to insert hacking software into the CPU without the Farm's supercomputer as backup could cause a multitude of protection programs to destroy internal software. A laboratory setting was the only risk-acceptable method with an operator of the emir's ability, and McCarter wasn't prepared to isolate, power down and then physically remove the CPU at this point.

McCarter began shaking the room down, careless of making a mess. He had no intention of trying to keep the entry hidden from the emir. It would be nearly impossible anyway and time was the biggest factor at this point. McCarter pulled tables out, moved paintings, pulled up carpet edges. Finally, behind a row of Collector's Edition Encyclopedia Britannica volumes, McCarter found the safe.

He swept the books aside, knocking them to the floor. Without taking his eyes off the safe McCarter shrugged his black knapsack free and opened it. The safe was a Mass Hamilton high-security model with keypad access instead of tumbler. McCarter removed several items from the knapsack and placed them on the shelf like a surgical tech laying out tools for a physician.

First he put a small, unmarked aerosol can down, then a pair of VisiTech night-vision goggles followed by a small screwdriver, a cable attached to a compact black box and finally one of the Farm's Combat Personal Data Assistants.

McCarter keyed up the program and then set the handheld device on the shelf. Picking up the aerosol canister, McCarter triggered it and lightly misted the keypad. He slipped the VisiTech goggles into place and turned them on.

The aerosol spray contained a bonding solution that caused it to adhere to human skin oils. Once bonded, enzymes in the spray interacted chemically with compounds in the oils and showed up on ultraviolet spectrums. McCarter shifted the VisiTech goggles from infrared to ultraviolet vision modes.

On the keypad the cluster of numbers showing fingerprints stood out in vivid relief. McCarter entered the grouping of numbers into the CPDA. He hit the button to activate the number-crunching program and pulled off his goggles. He put his equipment away while the device's analog program calculated all the number combinations possible from the digits he'd inputted into its memory.

He slid the edge of his screwdriver into the seam where the case housing for the keypad was recessed into the front of the safe. He dug in and snapped the screwdriver down, popping the faceplate off. He picked up the black plastic box frame and slid it into place over the now exposed keypad.

He checked the CPDA and saw that it had finished running the probability calculation program. Taking the loose end of the cable, McCarter inserted it into the device's input jack and then hit the Enter key.

The CPDA immediately began running sequences of numbers and instantaneously transmitting them to the Field Electronic Interdiction and Disruption Device. The FEIDD manipulated the keypad faster than a human could, clearing the instrument after each usage so that a total sequential access attempt record would not trigger a failsafe. The black plastic box hummed slightly and from inside of it McCarter heard a rapid clicking of keys, like a court reporter working a stenograph.

In under three minutes the CPDA display froze on a numeric sequence and the safe popped open as the locking mechanism was disabled. McCarter quickly broke down the CPDA and FEIDD, replacing them in the knapsack. He reached up and opened the safe.

Inside, the commercial security container was stuffed full of items. There were several passports and ID cards under various names, all with the emir's picture. McCarter found this strange. Such a man flew in private jets, he didn't surreptitiously navigate customs like a spy or criminal. There was a 9 mm Heckler & Koch VP-70M sitting on top of an accountant's ledger and stacks of money in dollars, yen and marks, as well as several piles of rubles. In the back there was single black video cassette devoid of markings.

The VP-70M pistol was built around the main unit of the MP-5 submachine gun used by West German police. Outside of the continental United States it was possible to procure a pistol capable of firing 3-round bursts. The bodyguard had used black electrician's tape to depress the pistol's fire selector switch. Normally the switch was only manipulated when the shoulder stock attachment was in place on the pistol. All of these items were stacked on top of a business-size manila envelope sealed with security-clearance tape.

A tight smile played across McCarter's face as he reached in and pulled the thick envelope out. McCarter opened the package and poured the contents onto the shelf. He looked quickly through the mess, searching for familiar names or locations. From the clearance codes stamped across the files and documents, it was obvious that the bodyguard was bringing a lot more home from work than he should have.

As McCarter scanned the papers, two important points jumped out at him. The emir was in deep, and he was an arrogant son of a bitch. It didn't matter what Able and Phoenix did—he had a plan and he was going to execute it. Excerpts and titles flashed out at McCarter like lightbulbs exploding in his face. It was all right there like a recipe or a grocery list. Cold anger burned inside of McCarter, followed by a hate as vicious as any he'd felt.

One paper titled "Buenos Aires Assets" included the line, "All African base assets primed for transport."

The paper also listed more than a dozen names under a heading of "Somalian/Sudan: Paramilitary Capable Assets." The emir had done more than build himself a little squad of door kickers and shooters—he had gathered himself a battalion of fanatics.

McCarter rifled through the pages. He came across one document with the heading "Veracity Adjustment Operation. Re: Sanders & Sable." On it was a timetable of purchasing items. He realized that much of the paperwork was written in English, which could only mean that a large coalition of international players had been assembled. Vast enough that English—and apparently French, from what he saw—was a viable option for disseminating information.

The operations center for the group, tagged "Task

Force Arabia Allah Akbar," was listed with the GPS coordinates to the island Able Team was investigating. At the bottom, hastily scribbled in a bold hand was the annotation, "Several suspicious indicators have appeared on the periphery. Involvement suggests Western intelligence."

"Do you think?" McCarter grunted.

"Everything is to be fast tracked. Speed will trump suspicion."

"Why are these communiqués in English?" he muttered to himself.

McCarter began stuffing the papers into his knapsack. The emir had more assets listed as opposition, but McCarter didn't have time to decipher everything. He also seized a memory stick that promised valuable intel.

From behind him, at the front of the house, he heard a door open and then slam shut.

McCarter cursed silently to himself as the slamming door reverberated through the penthouse. Reaching up to his knit cap, McCarter pulled it down over his face so the balaclava obscured his features. The emir wasn't the kind to give his security codes out to his cleaning woman. If it wasn't the man himself, then it could only be his majordomo, Abdulla.

McCarter swung the backpack onto his shoulders and shrugged it into position. He crossed the room toward the door, moving fast. His mind was racing as he ticked off options.

McCarter reached out and grabbed the handle of the office door. He twisted the knob slowly and then, when it unlatched, lifted up slightly as he swung it open, preventing the hinges from squeaking.

The door swung open easily. McCarter straightened,

shifting his body position. When it was about half-way open, the door suddenly exploded inward toward him.

McCarter was knocked back by the force of the blow. He staggered, arms windmilling to catch his balance. The emir's primary bodyguard and majordomo, Abdulla, burst through the entryway hard on the heels of the swinging door. Unafraid, he charged straight into McCarter, pressing his attack. The man was big and fast for his size. He rushed in using a shuffling side step but throwing haymakers and pressing his advantage.

McCarter retreated before the onslaught, hands up and head ducked into his arms. The bodyguard's big fists hammered through his guard or struck his hands and drove them up against his lowered face. McCarter rocked from the impact of the big punches, reeling under their force, staggering backward.

He came up against the desk and was bent over backward under the bodyguard's onslaught. The change of position left him vulnerable but also changed his elevation, forcing the bodyguard to reorient himself to continue his attack.

Abdulla turned to face McCarter fully and thrust himself up and forward, leading with a big right-handed hammer blow.

The expression on the bodyguard's face was oddly detached, like a man performing some slightly odious but necessary task. It was red from his exertion but betrayed no emotion whatsoever. His hair was perfectly coiffed and his Vandyke had been groomed recently. Shoved up this close to the man's bulk and mammoth power, McCarter realized the bodyguard must have been pushing over 260 pounds and was heavily muscled under a misleading layer of cosmopolitan fat.

Abdulla leaned in over the awkwardly positioned McCarter and brought his right hand down like a railroad maul toward the ex-SAS member's unprotected face. McCarter made no attempt to block the powerful blow. As the arm came down McCarter turned his head to the side and lifted his left shoulder up toward the strike while wrapping his arms around the descending fist in a hugging maneuver.

McCarter winced as the strike hammered home into his shoulder and neck hard enough to rattle his teeth before he snapped his trap closed. McCarter's right hand captured the bodyguard's arm at the wrist while his left arm snapped up and bent back to grab the same wrist, pressing his elbow and forearm in a parallel position with the bodyguard's own grasping arm.

Joint lock in place, McCarter grasped as hard as he could and twisted like a snake around Abdulla's grip. His long legs came up and wrapped themselves around the bodyguard's upper arm, sinking in a brutally tight lock at the bigger man's wrist and elbow. One foot pushed hard into the bodyguard's face while the second foot found position under the bigger man's extended arm.

McCarter threw himself over, holding the bodyguard's entrapped arm tightly to his torso. The bodyguard grunted with the sudden pain and was thrown off his feet beside the desk. Now on top of the hyperextended arm, McCarter threw himself backward off the desk. This time Abdulla screamed.

The sound of the elbow popping was sharp, while the sound of the shoulder coming out of socket was sloshy and more muted. Both men sprawled to the floor of the office and the bodyguard screamed again.

Abdulla was frantic to shake McCarter loose, but

couldn't shift his bulk quickly enough to rise up. McCarter, refusing to let go of the bodyguard's now mangled arm, began to hammer a heel into the big man's face.

The bodyguard's head rocked with each impact, but McCarter felt as if he were putting his boots to a stone. The flesh of Abdulla's right ear tore, and blood soaked the side of his face, running freely down into his sporty mustache and beard. Bruises like horseshoes blossomed on the bodyguard's cheek and face. The tread of McCarter's boot tore an ugly gash in the bodyguard's forehead above his bushy eyebrows.

The bodyguard swung his bulk around until he was facing McCarter. With his free hand he began shoving at the legs entangled around his injured arm. McCarter felt the big man's weight shift and rolled sharply with the changing leverage. McCarter spun with the trapped arm in the opposite direction, brutally reversing angles.

Abdulla screamed again and was driven over McCarter's turning body. He planted his nose hard into the carpet. Now on his belly, facing away from the bodyguard with the man's arm trapped beneath him, McCarter started using his heel stomp again.

Face a bloody mask, the bodyguard managed to grasp hold of McCarter's ankle and slow the force of the kicks down. Blind with pain now and beaten to a mess, the big man managed to get his legs underneath him and rise. McCarter was stunned at the amount of damage the bodyguard was able to absorb. The man rose to his feet, threatening to upend McCarter in the process.

McCarter quickly changed positions. He released the man's arm just as the bodyguard reared up and sought to lift McCarter from the floor. Abdulla went stumbling backward, his balance completely compromised. He slammed hard into the bookshelf and sent leather-bound volumes spilling out across the floor. McCarter leaped to his feet and started toward the Saudi Arabian.

The bodyguard swept the heavy globe of semiprecious stones off the edge of the desk and sent it hurtling into the rushing McCarter. McCarter twisted to avoid the projectile and the bodyguard lunged toward the open safe. McCarter knocked the globe aside and leaped toward the bodyguard, remembering the Heckler & Koch automatic pistol hidden in the safe.

McCarter smashed into Abdulla, driving him up against the bookcase before the other man could access the contents of the wall model safety container. The bodyguard grunted in pain as his mauled shoulder struck the unforgiving wall.

McCarter lifted the bodyguard up and then began rocking blows toward the big man's head. The bodyguard swept his good arm back, driving the elbow into McCarter's head. McCarter rocked back, staggered. Abdulla twisted sideways and used the little space he had created to lash out with a side kick.

The bodyguard's foot strike hit McCarter on his thigh as he stumbled and pushed McCarter farther back. McCarter spun, absorbing the force of the blow, and reset himself. The bodyguard turned back toward the safe, plunging his good hand inside the safe, scrambling for the Heckler & Koch pistol.

Even as he moved, McCarter knew he was too late.

Abdulla whirled, gun in hand. Loose papers, documents and money spilled out of the open wall safe. Snarling, the big man brought up his pistol. His right arm useless, the bodyguard had grabbed the weapon with his left hand, which was all that saved McCarter. The pistol exploded as McCarter dived forward.

McCarter felt the impact like a hammer blow low in his gut, just high enough that his vest still took the bullet and stopped the round. Two more rounds spun out, missing as recoil carried the bodyguard's pistol muzzle off target.

McCarter changed tactics instinctively, throwing himself backward, and leaped for the protection of the massive desk. Shooting with his off hand, Abdulla fired another triburst at the diving blur McCarter had become. McCarter hit the big desk and slid across it to the other side. The bodyguard's bullets slapped into his study wall.

McCarter pulled the mini-Uzi machine pistol free. Unsure of Abdulla's tactics, he fired up at an angle in case the bodyguard had followed him over the top of the desk. Still firing, McCarter reached up over the edge of the desk and angled the Uzi, triggering a longer blast. Finally he popped up behind the firing weapon and sprayed the room.

The door to the hall hung open and 9 mm rounds from McCarter's weapon punched into the wall outside the office door. McCarter picked himself up, holding the smoking Uzi at the ready. Spent shell casings rolled across the desk and spilled onto the floor.

McCarter squinted through gun smoke toward the open door. Abdulla's beefy hand came around the edge of the door and he triggered his pistol. McCarter ducked behind the desk again and then answered with a burst that chewed up the hand-crafted frame of the wooden door.

McCarter rolled out from behind the desk, coming

to his feet and bringing the mini-Uzi machine pistol up. In the hallway McCarter heard an empty magazine strike the floor, followed by the metallic click of a round being chambered. Then he heard nothing else.

CHAPTER THIRTEEN

McCarter's ears rang from the deafening gunfire in such an enclosed space. He rolled over on one shoulder behind the desk in the other direction. He came up against the wall on the same side of the room the door opened up on. This angle gave him a drop of seconds should the bodyguard choose to rush the room.

Weapon up, McCarter padded forward to the door. He heard nothing. Now was not the time for half measures. Covert action and subtle maneuvers were no longer an option. This was, by God, a firefight.

McCarter burst into violent action. He thrust the mini-Uzi around the corner and opened fire. Still firing, he pivoted himself around the fulcrum of his weapon and threw his back up against the wall on the opposite side of the door, giving himself a narrow view of the hallway.

He saw a corner of the kitchen down the short hall and could make out a piece of the dark marble-topped island in the center of the room. McCarter ducked back from the opening and dropped the spent magazine from his mini-Uzi. He slammed home a fresh one and released the bolt on the Uzi, priming the weapon for use. A haze of gun smoke hung in the air.

McCarter swept the barrel up and stepped out into the hallway, keeping to a tight crouch. His finger was taut on the trigger as he moved down the hall. Three steps down from the office door more of the kitchen revealed itself. Tensed, McCarter pushed forward.

Abdulla popped up from behind the kitchen island, triggering his H&K pistol. The machine pistol fired a triple burst of 9 mm rounds. McCarter threw himself backward. A ragged fusillade of rounds tore down the kill zone of the residential hallway. McCarter went to a knee and triggered the mini-Uzi, answering the bodyguard vicious burst for burst. The little stutter gun unleashed a torrent of rounds into the kitchen.

Sparks flew off pots and pans hanging from a rack suspended above the island, and the utensils rang like church bells. Glass shattered in the windows behind the bodyguard and the cabinetwork was reduced to splinters. Skid marks streaked across the marble top of the counter and bullets ricocheted wildly.

The bodyguard shouted something foul in Arabic, then came around the side of the counter island, popping out like some oversize, malignant jack-in-the-box and triggering double 3-round bursts under McCarter's arc of fire. McCarter threw himself up against the inner wall of the hallway to avoid the furious spray of bullets. A third burst cut the air through the hall, pinning McCarter back.

McCarter slid to one knee, still hugging the wall. Once he changed elevation McCarter dived forward, thrusting the mini-Uzi out and up in front of him. He fired a burst as he dived forward, took the force of his landing on his elbows and recentered his aim as he absorbed the shock of impact.

McCarter heard the reverberation of the slam as the door struck the wall next to it. Instantly he realized what the bodyguard had done. McCarter high crawled forward and peeked quickly around the corner. He saw the side door he had used to breach the penthouse standing open and knew the bodyguard was making for the elevator bank or some other area he could defend while attempting to contact backup.

McCarter hopped up, Uzi machine pistol at the ready. He orientated himself correctly and then rushed forward, chasing the bodyguard. As McCarter came into the kitchen proper of the penthouse, he caught a dark flash as the bodyguard threw himself through the door to the hallway. Firing through the door, McCarter pulled hard and just missed the man. Then he heard more voices yelling in anger and knew he was screwed.

ONCE AGAIN McCarter had tasted the wine of violence.

He was a jungle cat. He was a fistload of lethal hate in a hard right hand. He was rough like a chisel and relentless as a jackhammer, tearing away at the fabric of reality. He was silk-smooth and razor-sharp, running hell-bent for leather.

McCarter was two hundred pounds of raw power and suppressed violence wrapped up in a six-foot-two-inch frame. The automatic pistol in his fist was a natural extension of his body and the dangerous gleam in his eyes spoke of his willingness to use it.

He had the body of a professional soldier and the steel-trap mind of a street runner. He operated in that land of split-second decisions that bullfighters called the moment of truth and he excelled there, in that most hostile of environments.

The hounds were baying at his trail, his blood scent in their noses and his body count in their eyes. Seven hardmen after one fugitive. Seven hungry pack hounds trying to run a lone wolf to ground.

The linoleum floors shone harshly under the artificial glare of the ceiling fixtures. The rubberized soles of his shoes slapped rhythmically as McCarter ran for his life. He clutched the mini-Uzi in his clenched fist, the pistol his ticket to freedom. In his backpack he carried a ticket of a different sort: a memory stick containing the contact information used by the emir's network to conduct his business.

On it was the electronic trail that would lead McCarter straight to the heart of the emir's plan.

Behind him McCarter could hear the emir's bodyguards closing in. His adrenaline-enhanced senses picked up their movements like blips on a psychic radar. A bullet screamed past his ear and smacked into the wall next to him, forming a crater-like impact point in the Sheetrock. A heartbeat later he heard the sharp bark of the pistol.

McCarter turned a corner in the hallway and bypassed the elevator banks in favor of the fire stairs. It hadn't been Abdulla who had fired, he knew. Abdulla wouldn't have missed.

McCarter burst through the fire door and sprinted at breakneck speed down the stairs of the high-rise building, stopping at each landing to vault the safety railing down to the next level of stairs. He had purposefully chosen the east wing of the building for his escape, knowing it would be deserted, giving less chance that innocents would be caught in any cross fire. Now as he attempted to outmaneuver Abdulla he began to question his noble but potentially foolish sentiments.

The staircase ran in a squared-off spiral with each landing providing a fresh set of steps running at a ninety-degree angle on every floor. McCarter was three floors down by the time the emir's personal death squad of hired muscle and terrorist bodyguards hit the stairwell. One of the men leaned over the railing and let go with a 3-round burst from his HS-2000 automatic pistol at McCarter's retreating shadow.

Abdulla barked an angry warning to his subordinate and reached out to pull him back from the railing. The man came away easily, his head jerking sharply from an unseen impact. The back of his skull erupted outward, spraying the other six gunmen with blood and brain and bits of bone.

"Fool!" Abdulla snarled.

Furious, Abdulla jumped past the corpse of his soldier, the other bloodhounds following behind him. Their speed, while no less, was now marked with a certain caution that bordered on outright hesitancy.

THREE FLOORS BENEATH them McCarter ran on. The time would come to kill Abdulla, but for now he had to escape, to advance his operation. There was nothing else but to extract justice and he had his eyes set on something bigger than the emir's operational front no matter how thick it was with international influence, he had his sights set on the Caribbean connection and the possibility of an army off America's shores.

McCarter barreled down the stairs. The landing marker read Fifth Floor and at that level McCarter bypassed the stairwell in favor of the door leading into the warren of halls that the blueprint schematic indicated typified the east wing of the great structure.

The building itself had served the emir with a veneer of legitimacy. It housed the offices of his credit union, construction contracts management firm, as well as his shipping and air freight operations. The building had been long deserted that night when McCarter had managed his clandestine entry.

Halfway down the hall McCarter came to a four-way intersection. He paused, certain he would kill some of these gangster gunmen before he left. McCarter smiled; Abdulla was vain. He thought he knew all the tricks but Abdulla was just a pup for all of his violent accomplishments. It was the Phoenix Force leader who was the master of hounds.

ABDULLA WASN'T THE FIRST gunman through the door.

Omar and Arafat entered first. Omar came in high and on the right, swinging forward with his HS-2000 pistol and using the compact Croatian handgun to lay down a hailstorm of covering fire. The weapon jumped and kicked in his hand, scattering hot shell casings onto the floor.

Arafat was the low man, his own pistol poised to send additional 9 mm slugs hurtling down the wall in support of Omar's fire. A thunderous silence echoed down the acoustic chamber of a passage as their prey neglected to return fire.

"He's gone rabbit!" Arafat said in rapid-fire Arabic.

He pointed a forefinger down the corridor toward the intersection of hallways.

Omar's face split into a smile, his teeth blunt and very white against the darker complexion of his skin. He put a finger to his lips to silence his partner and pointed. Abdulla came through the doorway and peered over Omar's shoulder. He looked down the hall to where the subordinate was indicating.

"You better be right," he whispered, lips close to the man's ear. "Now slide on up to that corner and take a look, little sister."

Omar bristled at Abdulla's mocking tone. The emir's lieutenant was always testing the crew, establishing his dominance in little ways, pushing them to see if they would snap or if he could provoke emotion. It didn't matter to him that each man had made his bones with various organizations from Hezbollah to Abu Sayef a dozen times over before being promoted to the emir's personal bodyguard. Abdulla was never satisfied and Omar knew it wasn't likely to get any better.

Omar sighed and began to move forward, clearing the corner with Arafat, using rudimentary but practical tactics. Unlike Abdulla, who had served as a Saudi royal commando, none of the other hitters had formalized military training, only street experience. Still, the men had picked up a lot being on the receiving end of Israeli and American tactics.

Omar's head exploded like an overripe melon.

Zahid and Montenegro died in the next second. Arafat screamed in fear and flung himself down to his belly on the blood-slicked linoleum floor. Behind him Abdulla grabbed up Omar's falling corpse and swung it around to use as a shield.

A hitter named Fareed had time to turn, dropping low in a combat crouch and swinging around on one knee, his HS-2000 pistol outfitted with a laser sight that burned down the hall, tracking for a target.

Fareed saw the black-clad form of the crazy bastard who'd dared slip into the emir's inner sanctum. The Saudi gunman lined up the sights of his handgun and his finger flexed around the plastic-alloy curve of his Croatian pistol. He *had* the bastard.

One shot and the night fighter was gone, leaving Abdulla with another corpse in his decimated crew, an untidy third eye in Fareed's forehead.

Arafat was sweating, pressed flat against the floor and panting in fear. The bastard is rolling thunder, he marveled. In two and a half seconds he had gunned down four experienced killers.

For the first time since the wild hunt had begun Arafat thought about just running. He no longer cared if the kill was personal. Screw avenging the emir's honor, screw pride, screw his oath and screw the foreigner. He wanted to live.

"Get up!" Abdulla snarled at the prostrate man.

Arafat looked up and Abdulla pushed the bullet-riddled corpse of Omar away from him. It fell to the linoleum floor with a wet slap like a bag of loose meat. Arafat realized that as terrified as he was of the apparition that had brought hell to this place, he was still frightened of his emir's lieutenant, as well.

He scrambled to his feet, following Abdulla down the hall, trusting the ex-commando's instincts. Arafat had never seen anything like the ambush before in his life, not ever and not even close. Even the Punjabis didn't kill like that and they were fucking crazy.

McCARTER MOVED more cautiously now that Abdulla wasn't hindered by others. The background check Stony Man had run on the Saudi enforcer had been extensive. If half of what McCarter had read was true then he'd likely never hear Abdulla coming if he wasn't cautious.

He had to move carefully if he wanted to get out of the office high-rise alive.

McCarter feared no man, but he wasn't a reckless fool, either.

Abdulla should have been dead already anyway. McCarter had hit him during the fusillade of his mini-ambush, but in the heat of the moment he'd taken the easy shot and now Abdulla was carrying around a 9 mm slug in his body armor.

McCarter felt for the package he'd ripped out of the emir's safe. It represented an electronic trail that would lead him straight toward a final resolution in the Caribbean; it was exactly what Stony Man had sent him for.

Yet he knew now that he had Abdulla's measure it wouldn't be enough.

THE ELEVATOR stood silent.

Arafat turned toward Abdulla, his heavy unibrow cocked up on one side in a silent question.

"Those are service elevators. They'll take him all the way down into the underground parking lot or even the storage basement. He may have gone there," Abdulla explained. He looked around, his confiscated HS-2000 pistol up and ready. "Or he could still be on this floor. We should split up."

"Ah," Arafat began, "maybe it would be better if—"

Abdulla looked at the other man, cutting him off midstammer. "You take the elevator. I'll check out this level."

Arafat swallowed, trying to get hold of himself. He was a professional, had survived some hairy plays, including pulling Kalashnikovs for opium deals with the crazy Chechens. He could be cool. It just wasn't every day he saw five top gunners go down. It wasn't every day he went on the warpath against a force of nature.

"Right," he forced himself to say, and nodded.

Arafat ejected his old magazine and slapped a fresh one home. He turned toward the elevator, well aware the mystery killer in black could be in there, waiting.

He resisted the urge to tell Abdulla to cover him; it was obvious the man would, he hoped. Arafat was a pro at urban close-quarters battle, an experienced veteran of room-to-room combat. His knowledge had been earned right out on the Gaza streets against the might of the IDF.

Arafat slid up next to the elevator doors and pressed his back tightly against the wall. He looked across the lobby and saw Abdulla positioned directly opposite the elevator doors, down on one knee with his HS-2000 held steady in both hands.

Keeping his own Croatian pistol up at port arms, Arafat used the thumb of his left hand to punch the control button on the wall, opening the elevator doors. They slid open with a hydraulic hiss and he dived onto his shoulder, rolling across his back to land flat on his stomach in front of the opening. His HS-2000 was tensed in his hand, ready to explode in violent action.

Behind him Abdulla tensed so suddenly he almost seemed to flinch, coming very close to accidentally triggering his weapon.

The elevator car was empty.

Abdulla relaxed as Arafat came to his feet.

"All right," Abdulla growled. "Check out the basement below us. I'll call my guy on the force and get some cops who are part of our operation to respond. I'll look out up here—we've got to keep him in the building. Now go."

"You get that backup." Arafat nodded.

The terrorist stepped into the elevator. His last image before the doors sealed closed was of Abdulla's angular face, tightly smiling and impossible to read. Abdulla's a cobra, Arafat realized. Just a poisonous reptile.

CHAPTER FOURTEEN

In the darkness McCarter crouched, again the jungle cat stalking its prey. The ceiling of the elevator car vibrated beneath his feet as it descended toward the basement of the office building.

Silently, McCarter reached out and slid aside the compartment door of the maintenance hatch.

ARAFAT DIDN'T SEE the hatch on the elevator ceiling slide open.

As keyed up as his senses were he didn't feel the dark eyes of the malevolent entity upon him. He didn't hear the slight popping of joints as his executioner straightened his arm, deadly pistol in a steady hand.

Arafat moved to one side and pressed himself flat against the side of the elevator, his pistol up and ready in hands slick with sweat. He wasn't about to be caught like a rabbit out of its hole when those doors slid open.

The elevator bell rang as it settled. There was the familiar but slight hiss of compressed air as the doors unsealed and slid open. The discreet cough of the silencer was lost in those sounds.

Arafat's head smacked up against the elevator wall, a ragged hole appeared in his temple and the other side of his head cracked open and sprayed his brains out. The jihadist gunner slid to crumple on the floor, leaving a slug trail of crimson smeared behind him. The Croatian pistol fell out of his slack fingers and bounced off the floor.

David McCarter had just done what the Israelis had never been able to do.

McCarter's muscles strained and jumped beneath his skin as he climbed hand-over-hand up the elevator shaft, clinging to the thick cables like a spider to its web. He'd sent the elevator up a few floors, pressing multiple buttons so that the passenger car would stop at every floor in between. Once the elevator was in motion McCarter had pried open the shaft doors and begun his journey upward. He hoped the ruse would give him enough time to hunt down and catch an angle on Abdulla.

Abdulla stood in the shadows and watched the elevator going up, plotting its progress by the lighted numerals above the doors. The lift had stopped on his floor; the doors sliding open to reveal nothing more than the crumpled form of Arafat's bloody corpse. The doors slid shut again and the elevator rose. When it finally halted, Abdulla had recalled it and, stepping inside, had quickly pushed the button to send the elevator all the way back down before stepping out.

All the way down to the basement.

He snickered. If the mystery gunman was doing what Abdulla suspected he was doing, then he'd be squashed flatter than a bug under the ex-commando's heel. That is a sign of old age, Abdulla thought, predictability. In their business, the business of professional killers, that was a fatal thaw. In the future Abdulla intended to make sure he didn't make the same mistakes.

McCarter looked up as he heard the elevator kick into life and he knew he had mistimed his trick. It was a potentially fatal mistake, but he'd known the risk when he played his gambit and he was prepared to live or die by his instincts.

He scrambled up the service ladder set into the shaft. Above him the bottom of the elevator smoothly powered down toward him; he was in a race. He had been climbing against the clock and time had run out. He'd tried to play Abdulla for a fool and had been off by a good thirty seconds.

That could prove to be a lifetime.

He reached up and his hand found some cold, slimy fluid dribbled along the metal rung. Perhaps it was maintenance oil or some other service fluid; in the dim light McCarter couldn't tell. His hand slid off the slick metal, surprising him and he overbalanced. His hands flung outward and one foot slipped off the rung below him. He scratched for purchase in desperate shock and his pistol fell away.

Darkness enveloped him and he fell as if through a womb. His body was jarred savagely by the impact as he bounced off the walls of the elevator shaft. His hands reached out to encircle the rungs of the service ladder. His downward momentum pushed him roughly up against the sheer metal wall again, forcing air from his lungs. His head slammed forward and his lip was split where it met the cold formed steel of the ladder.

The agony was a sharp, sudden shock and he cried out loud as his tenuous grip weakened and he slipped and fell backward down the shaft for a second time. His leg was jerked cruelly in its socket and he came to a brutally abrupt halt, his ankle twisted up in one of the rungs.

Hot spears of pain lanced through his leg, and he felt the muscles and tendons shriek in protest at the tension.

Above him the elevator raced down.

McCarter reached out with one strong hand and pulled himself back up. His face was sticky with blood and mucus from where his nose had crumpled on impact with the wall. His lips were a bloody mess of pulpy skin and reflex tears burned his cheeks as he fought to regain control of his breath.

You screwed up this time, he snarled to himself.

But there was a truth McCarter had always understood: what happened to a man was not important; what the man did after it happened to him was all that mattered.

To his ears over the sound of the dropping elevator he heard the distant clattering of his pistol as it struck the bottom of the shaft. McCarter fought himself up into a vertical position. Standing on the ladder, favoring the leg that hadn't nearly been wrenched from its socket, he stretched out a blood-smeared hand and prised his fingers into the rubber buffer curtain set between the floor-level doors.

The muscles along his back and shoulders bunched under the strain. He snarled in rage through a mask of dripping blood as the top half of the fingernail on his middle finger was ripped away, but the doors came open under his grip.

He looked up. The bottom of the elevator was in plain sight, rushing down toward his upturned face with impersonal but murderous potential. McCarter tensed then sprang off the ladder rung, reaching out for the opening. His fingers found purchase and he scrambled through the opening. The elevator filled the space directly above him.

Adrenaline shot through his body and McCarter found the desperate strength he needed to live.

Snarling like a wolf, he pulled himself through the opening just as the elevator dropped past him. He had made it.

ABDULLA STRUCK HIM like a runaway locomotive, driving McCarter back into the open shaft. Their momentum was greater than the elevator's and they hit the roof of the carrier hard. They fell like squabbling cats, punching and striking at each other as they dropped.

In the split second before they smashed into the elevator roof McCarter managed to twist his enemy beneath him so that he landed on top of the man.

The two killers rolled in frenzied combat. In his weakened condition McCarter was barely holding his own and he didn't have time to question why his adversary hadn't used his pistol instead of tackling him. Abdulla kicked McCarter from him, knocking him back across the elevator roof to the other side of the lift. McCarter rebounded off the wall of the shaft and bounced forward to his knees before coiling and leaping up to his feet.

Both men sprang for the other's throat. Locked together, they struggled as the elevator descended toward the basement of the building.

When McCarter had served in the British Army he'd undergone training in defense against attack dogs. The premise had been as simple as it was brutally effective. You gave the animal an arm, knowing it would be bitten, then the free arm came down like a bar and wrapped around the back of the head where the skull met the spine. The man then fell forward and the beast's neck snapped like a stick of rotten wood.

McCarter's arms broke the clinch and encircled Abdulla's head in a jujitsu neck crank. His forearm pressed hard against the Saudi's face. His other slid into place behind the man's neck, right where the skull met the spine. He began to push.

Abdulla could feel his neck begin to break. Terror lent him a superhuman strength. To no avail. His huge fists hammered into McCarter's midriff, and his knee attempted to maul McCarter's crotch.

But, blood mad, McCarter ignored the blows, the damage, the pain.

The elevator settled into position on the ground with a subtle lurch, just enough to cause McCarter's injured leg to buckle. He tripped back and fell through the open maintenance hatch, dropping straight down through to the elevator compartment below.

His purchase suddenly gone, Abdulla tumbled forward, as well, his momentum carrying him down through the elevator hatch to land on top of McCarter. A backward elbow caught the bodyguard in the face, stunning him for a second as McCarter lunged for the pistol lying on the floor next to Arafat's limp hand.

McCarter lifted the pistol just as the elevator doors slid open and Abdulla's heel cracked hard against his wrist, sending the handgun spinning off out of the compartment. McCarter twisted back toward the terrorist enforcer and saw him clawing his own HS-2000 out of a shoulder sling. McCarter brought a hammer-hard fist up from the hip and smashed it into Abdulla's temple, staggering the man as he tried to rise up to his knees.

McCarter's other hand lanced out and tried to take the pistol from Abdulla. The two men struggled for control of the weapon. McCarter drew back his left hand to strike the other man again.

Abdulla squeezed the trigger, sending the handgun off in a quick succession of explosions. A stream of 9 mm rounds jumped from the end of the muzzle, riddling the roof and walls of the elevator as he continued jerking the trigger. The pistol bucked and kicked in their hands as McCarter tried to wrestle it free, slugs stitching a crooked line across the wall toward the control panel.

Three soft-nosed slugs smacked into the delicate electronics and chewed their way through the thin outer casing. The elevator doors finished sliding open as sparks flew in rooster tails. The lights went out the instant Abdulla pulled the trigger on the final bullet in the handgun.

ONCE AGAIN darkness enveloped McCarter.

Abdulla swung wildly in the dark, his knuckles clipping McCarter on the chin. His head snapped back under the blow and he rolled with the force, letting the momentum carry him back away from the Saudi terrorist.

As he finished his backward somersault he felt the worn carpet of the elevator give way to the cool hardness of a concrete floor. He had cleared the elevator. The basement was as dark as a tomb and for one moment he realized Abdulla might actually be good enough to kill him, to bring his decades-long battles for justice to an end. He remembered the information he carried in his backpack, the knowledge that would advance Stony Man's operation against the Caribbean connection. He realized it didn't matter that there could be a thousand exits around him in the dark, he would still need to kill Abdulla.

A criminal this competent, this accomplished, could not be allowed to continue. The ex-Saudi commando turned royal bodyguard had proved to be everything Stony Man intelligence had claimed and then some. McCarter had to turn the tables, seize the initiative and finish the terrorist.

He rose and reached out a hand to either side of him in the pitch darkness. He walked quickly forward, lifting his feet high and putting them down flat to avoid tripping in the dark. Despite his precaution he nearly tripped over some invisible obstacle and he used the noise to dodge hard to the left, coming up against a wall.

He pressed his back against the structure, his ears straining to catch any sound. Silence was the key. When you fought with one sense gone the surest way to victory was to deprive your opponent of his other senses.

He stood motionless, fighting to gain his breath back, painfully aware of how loud his ragged, gasping breath must seem. After what felt an eternity he regained control of his body.

Holding his breath, McCarter strained to listen in the darkness.

Soon the sound of his own blood rushing in his ears deafened him to the point that he was defeating his original purpose. Slowly he bled the air out of his lungs, struggling to keep the escaping breath silent.

Then he heard it. He was sure of it. He heard Abdulla breathe. He couldn't be sure, not when the basement was as large as this one seemed, but it had seemed, in that instant, that Abdulla was no more than a few yards from him. McCarter began to move.

He stood with his back flat against the wall, hands reaching out far to the sides of him to feel for obstacles.

He moved slowly, crossing one leg over the other. He swallowed tightly; with each movement he made he was sure Abdulla was pinpointing his exact location.

Five steps and then he halted. He could hear no sound. Tension gripped him in an ironclad hold. If he couldn't hear Abdulla, then how could he be sure he had heard him in the first place?

McCarter had spent too many years on the hell grounds to be killed by indecision. For good or for bad he would act.

Blind fighting was a skill like any other. It existed with its own rules and dogma to be followed. In a darkened room the combatant relied upon his hearing, sticking close to walls to gauge the perimeter of the room and for defense. In the center of a chamber you could be attacked from all sides. With your back from the wall, you could only be attacked from straight ahead.

McCarter frowned to himself. He swallowed tightly and then stepped away from the safety of the wall. He couldn't hear Abdulla moving and he froze. After a short while he heard the strained outlet of escaping breath and realized Abdulla had been listening for him.

In the deep darkness of the basement McCarter had his enemy pinpointed. He stepped forward and reached a sprint in three quick strides. Only guessing how far from the wall he was, McCarter leaped into the air, thrusting out both feet in front of him.

His injured leg struck Abdulla in the gut, driving the younger man's arm into his own stomach and forcing the air from him. McCarter's other leg struck the cinder-block wall Abdulla had been standing against and buckled under the force of impact.

McCarter bounced away, striking the floor on his

rebound. Abdulla fell beside him and McCarter rose up, smashing his fist down. He cried out in pain as his already ravaged knuckles struck the concrete floor and his arm went instantly numb.

He heard a sharp crack and instinctively threw up his good arm to ward off the invisible blow. His forearm jerked under the force of some club, probably a snapped-off broom handle.

Intuiting Abdulla's position by the angle of the blow, McCarter whipped his legs around and felt the bodyguard topple. McCarter heard Abdulla's club clatter away as he slammed to the floor and he used the sound to snatch it up for himself.

McCarter didn't hesitate. He rose on one knee and brought the stolen stick crushing down, snarling with satisfaction as he felt the stick splinter along its length from the force of the blow on Abdulla's body.

Abdulla responded like a fighter, lashing out quickly with surprisingly fast reflexes. The ball of his foot slapped into McCarter's face, driving him backward with the blunt force of a sledgehammer.

CHAPTER FIFTEEN

Blood splashed hot in his mouth as McCarter's bottom lip was impaled by his own teeth. Again he used the energy to roll with the blow and disengage. He gagged on his blood and his pain, flipping over backward and coming to his feet.

He swooned and fell back. He landed hard on his butt with a jar that seemed to loosen the teeth in his head. He blinked in surprise. He was sitting up higher than the floor. He reached questioningly behind him and was rewarded. He was on a flight of stairs.

McCarter turned and scrambled up them, racing so fast that his head butted against the door. With trembling fingers he yanked at the knob.

It was locked.

McCarter felt around the walls, found what he was looking for and the lights came on as he flicked the switch. McCarter blinked in the sudden illumination and looked behind him. Abdulla was at the bottom of the staircase, a jagged-ended broom handle in his fists. The left side of his face was a long purple bruise where McCarter had struck him with his own club, swelling the eye shut.

Abdulla began to slowly climb the steps. His eyes never left McCarter's for an instant. "You're mine now, infidel," he growled. "I'm gonna jam this stick up your ass."

"I don't speak Arabic," McCarter replied. "But that didn't sound good."

Abdulla raced up the last few steps and jabbed the splintered end of the stick forward in an attempt to stab McCarter. McCarter dodged to the side and kicked Abdulla in the face. Weakened, the man tumbled down the stairs rolling end over end.

The man bounced once at a wrong angle and McCarter heard the snap of the Saudi's neck as it broke. The terrorist lieutenant plopped into an unceremonious pile of tangled limbs at the bottom of the stairs.

McCarter blinked in surprise. The kill had been almost accidental; it was anticlimactic after the struggle he had endured. Sometimes death wasn't cinematic, he realized; sometimes you were just glad the son of a bitch was dead.

He turned and scrambled for the door. The clock was ticking fast now with his soft probe turned deadly. McCarter and the rest of Phoenix Force had an appointment on a Caribbean island.

Sudanese border, Libya

THE SUN WAS GOING DOWN on the brutal badlands. Pockets of rubble and bomb craters stretched from the bounty hunter's position toward the horizon. They stank from waiting in the heat and their sweat made them feel sticky and cranky.

Stony Man had followed one of the emir's intelligence leads to the home of a notorious al Qaeda cell. Now T. J. Hawkins and Stony Man pilot Charlie Mott wore Kevlar hauberks with ceramic plate inserts, making waiting in the blistering heat a hot, itchy hell. Hawkins looked around, sucking water from a clear plastic tube extending from a bladder on his back. The Kevlar was good stuff, police not military, but good enough.

Instead of the cut-down VTOL gunship JSOC had promised, however, they were sitting in a shitty little piece of history dating back to the first counterinsurgency actions. An OH-6A light observation helicopter, or "Loach," as Mott insisted on calling it. But under the circumstances, and given the last-minute nature of the deployment, they had taken what they could get.

Only thirty-feet long, the four-passenger helicopter had a payload of 415 kilos, a cruising speed of 240 kilometers per hour and was powered by a single Allison T63-A-5A turboshaft engine. Blah-blah-blah, Hawkins had thought. The relic had no indigenous weapons systems and Hawkins would be hanging out the door, one foot on the skid, and firing a squad automatic weapon hanging from a bungee cord. State of the fucking art, he thought.

It was then that the GPS trigger went off like a submarine klaxon and Mott started up the ancient helicopter.

THEY WERE FLYING knap of the earth, coming out of the volcanic rays of the setting sun. They wove in and out of the skeletons of buildings over piles of rubbles and past acres of mass graves where government-backed Islamic militias had slaughtered the nation's Christian minority and razed their villages and towns to the earth. The wind tearing at Hawkins's body was hot and dry, like the breath of a dragon, and left him sweating out precious moisture by the gallon.

Ahead of them he saw the off-road motorcycles burst out of the shadowed opening of an underground hangar and roar onto the wasteland. To a person the helmet-covered heads swiveled backward to look at the fast-moving Loach coming in behind them.

Foot planted firmly on the skid of the helicopter, Hawkins brought the SAW up to his shoulder. He kept both eyes open as he sighted and used the tracer rounds to walk his fire in. Puffs of dust sprang up in stereotypical imagery as he walked his rounds on target.

Operating under the protection of the local *janaweed* and backed by money coming from Saudi Arabia, the al Qaeda cell had outfitted itself with equipment enough to make its stronghold deep in ungoverned desert waste.

Two of the trailing motorcycles cut short and held up. The riders leaped off their machines and pulled long weapons from scabbards. In truth, this was the best way to deal with the airborne assault rather than attempting to outrun it or firing from a moving cycle.

In reality the bounty killers had the jump and they were too close to give the riders time to lay down a very effective field of fire. Hawkins saw the flame spit from the muzzles of their weapons but he felt no impact on the helicopter or heard any rounds close by.

He walked his fire straight down the broken pavement of road leading up to the duo and buried a 3-round burst into the left one's fuel cell. The explosion was immediate and bright. The concussion tossed both corpses spinning like pinwheels. Flaming fuel spread out like a napalm drop across the ground, but Mott was flying the helicopter out in a sweep, bringing them in from the flank on the riders' left side.

Hawkins felt the adrenaline coursing through his veins. He felt angry. He felt no remorse; in many ways he felt damn good as he triggered blast after blast from his weapon. Snatches of lyrics from hard-driving music he had listened to while pushing heavy weights flared through his head. The terrorists had tried to hide but he was showing them how pitifully they had failed.

Dimly he heard himself screaming. Mott was even more jazzed, flying the helicopter like a street-rod drag racer. The riders were looking for less broken terrain to split up and dive into the ruins in escape, but the Loach was as fast as they were, and Hawkins's bullets were even faster.

Mott swooped the Loach over to the right flank of the riders, giving Hawkins the best view for his fire platform. Hawkins didn't try to target any one rider at first. Instead he simply picked a pack member, laid down a stream of bullets in front of his racing cycle and let the outlaw terrorist drive into it. Sometimes it was the bullets that brought them down, sometimes the ignition of their fuel cells.

Hawkins scrunched the skeletal stock of his SAW tightly against his shoulder. He closed one eye and sighted in on the hip of the largest terrorist where he was running in the lead. The Egyptian man was a former professional wrestler turned jihadist and was massively built in a region where most males were only of medium build. Compared to Western standards he stood out like a giant. The cold-blooded killer had made a name for himself cutting the heads off captives on video camera with a Ghurka knife. The man was known throughout the continent by the moniker given him by the South African intelligence agencies: K-Max.

Keeping his sights glued to him, Hawkins squeezed his trigger. The rounds streamed out in a mechanical chatter. They tore down toward the running gang and struck the ground right behind the racing K-Max's rear tire. The rounds pounded into the road then slammed into the front wheel of a red-helmeted terrorist's cycle.

The speeding vehicle went end-over-end. The African terror soldier was tossed off like a rag doll and spun through the air in wild flips before striking the broken ground at a speed in excess of sixty miles per hour. The body bounced, struck, bounced again and rolled off to lie in a mangled heap.

Got ya, bitch, Hawkins thought.

Hawkins squeezed off two more long, ragged bursts from the automatic weapon, sending one motorcycle up in a cloud of oily black smoke and another tumbling off into a pile of rubble at breakneck speed.

They overflew the lone running K-Max now. Mott banked the Loach around hard, momentum trying to pull Hawkins back inside the helicopter as he found himself suddenly looking up straight into the sky. The little scout helicopter dropped down in a sudden plummet and Mott swung it around.

Below them K-Max had reached a straight, unbroken stretch of road and was gunning his big cycle flat out. Mott brought the bird around and picked up his tail. He put the nose of the bird down and gunned it forward, picking up speed quickly.

Using his weapon with a surprising amount of delicate restraint Hawkins began to pin the running cycle down with sharp staccato bursts, forcing the outlaw rider to weave in sudden reactions to his tight groupings. Behind him the Loach was catching up. In moments they would be directly over the racing man.

"Shoot him!" Mott screamed. "Come on, Hawk!"

Hawkins put his bursts all around K-Max but seemed incapable of hitting him. Just as the helicopter caught even with the motorcycle the outlaw pulled a near suicidal stunt—his only chance to turn the tables. He jacked his brakes and turned the bike up on its side in one smooth motion, leaving a patch of smoking black rubber yards long in his wake.

K-Max laid the sliding bike down gently as he skipped across the surface of the tarmac. He let go and lay back on his heavy leathers, sliding along as the bike pulled ahead of him. Reaching out in a cross holster snatch, he yanked twin machine pistols free.

As the helicopter tore down on him he brought his machine pistols up and triggered the weapons simultaneously. The stutter guns burped long jets of flame and shell casings arched out in a clattering rain. Bullets lanced up in deadly arcs and Hawkins ducked back inside the helicopter in an instinctive movement.

Like a fistful of gravel on a tin roof rounds tore into the Kevlar-lined belly of the Loach. The rounds were too light to affect the flight path of the racing bird but the whine and shriek of bullets cutting through the cabin between them caused both veteran fighters to hunch like frightened children.

For a moment the Loach veered wildly out of control and the helicopter tipped up on its side as Mott fought to regain the yoke. His feet worked the stabilizing pedals in a desperate tap dance. Hawkins was screaming. Having released the SAW, he was holding on to the edge of the passenger side opening with both hands, his leg thrust out in a vain attempt to stay stabilized against the skid as Mott fought to bring the bird under control.

The Stony Man pilot corrected and suddenly Hawkins found himself almost pitched out as the helicopter tipped in the other direction and he was looking out straight down on the ground racing by below. The weapon snapped on the end of its bungy cord and popped up. The hard metal of the stock struck Hawkins in the face, tore his helmet to the side and pushed his nose up hard against his face.

Hawkins's head snapped back in recoil and blood flew from his broken nose. Holding on to the "oh-shit handle" with one hand, he snatched at the bouncing weapon. Sulfite stink burned his nostrils as he tucked the weapon up against him and fought his helmet back into place.

Finally, Mott got the bucking bird back under control and the helicopter leveled out again and he swung it around. Hawkins secured his grip on the door gun and scanned the field of ruins and broken rubble for some sign of K-Max.

"Where is he?" he yelled.

"I don't know!" Mott yelled back. Then he yelled, "There! He ducked inside that building."

Hawkins followed the angle of Mott's outthrust arm and saw a free-standing building about four stories high perched like a lighthouse in a sea of rubbish and debris left in the wake of the *janjaweed* ethnic-cleansing campaign. The windows had been blown out and stared like dark, empty eye sockets. The adobe-style structure was scorched and stained by smoke. The door lay fallen in like broken teeth around a gaping mouth.

"We got him," Hawkins announced.

THEY CIRCLED the building like a vulture over a kill.

Mott kept the flying platform steady while Hawkins calmly went about his preparations. He secured the SAW in side-mounted brackets inside the helicopter cabin. From underneath his seat he pulled another piece of JSOC's surprisingly archaic black market arsenal.

The M-79 40 mm grenade launcher was a squat, ugly weapon weighing just over six pounds and looking like a bulky version of a single-barrel break-open shotgun. Hawkins snapped it open and fed a 40 mm projectile into the tube. He nodded to Mott and the pilot brought the helicopter into a hover just off the front of the building.

Hawkins lifted the M-79 and used the sliding front sights to target the doorway. He triggered his round and the weapon fired with its characteristic bloop. Hawkins absorbed the recoil into his shoulder and watched the gentle arc of the round as it traveled out. It flew through the open door and detonated with a tight explosion followed by the whoosh as over five hundred grams of white phosphorous ignited.

Three more times Hawkins fired the weapon while Mott held the helicopter stable, one round for each side of the building left. When they were finished the ground floor of the wood and stone structure was ablaze and black smoke rolled out through the busted windows and cracked frame.

"He's either going to make a break for it or he'll have to go in one direction," Hawkins said. "Up."

"So we wait for the fire to take him?" Mott asked.

"No." Hawkins shook his head. "Take me to the roof and then pull back for overwatch."

Mott started to argue but Hawkins cut him short with a curt chopping motion.

"I'm going in to get him. Just put me down on the goddamn roof."

Without further argument Mott swung the Loach over the rooftop of the building and lowered the helicopter down. When the skids were about ten feet from the top Hawkins tossed his gear out and, leaving the SAW behind, dropped down after it.

He landed flat-footed, absorbing the force of the fall, then gave a thumbs-up to Mott, who pulled the bird back. Hawkins reached behind and pulled his big automatic pistol from its holster in the small of his back. Reaching down, he slipped an arm through one of the shoulder straps and shrugged the frameless rucksack into position on his shoulder.

Moving with deliberate steps Hawkins crossed over to the door leading to the stairs inside the building. Pistol up, he reached out and grabbed the door where it leaned crazily on a single rusted hinge.

Without a moment's further hesitation he yanked the door open and descended into the burning building.

CHAPTER SIXTEEN

The interior of the building was dark. Below him Hawkins could hear the white phosphorous burning. In the background he could hear the soft whup-whup-whup of the helicopter as Mott circled the building. It sounded very far away and Hawkins felt very alone in the dark at that moment. He knew the flames would leave little choice for K-Max but to be driven upward and he began his descent.

Coming out of the roof access stairway he entered the cavelike stretch of corridors and rooms making up the fourth floor of the building. He was betting K-Max wouldn't have had enough time to have climbed this far yet and he moved slightly faster than he would have if he'd felt closer to his adversary.

It was dark here down the long stretch of straight hall, and he hadn't brought a night-vision device for the daytime operation. Softly closing the door behind him, Hawkins crept down the hall and then squatted, giving his eyes time to adjust. After long moments counted out in soft breaths and hammering heartbeats he rose and began to move down the hall again.

He moved slowly, placing each step carefully, brushing debris and broken glass aside before softly putting each foot down. The Ranger school instructors had called it cat-dancing, and the name seemed appropriate enough to Hawkins. He passed by several doors as he moved down the hall, heading for the one at the end that he estimated was the access to the building fire stairs.

His plan was simple and called for a steady nerve. He would descend one floor and then lie in wait for K-Max as the fire below forced him up. Then it would be time to use the heavy automatic he kept at port arms in front of him, its big muzzle pointing the way in front of him.

The .45-caliber M1911A1 was as old and sturdily dependable as Mott's choice in helicopters. It packed enough punch to hammer a grown man flat onto his back with only a grazing wound and regardless of any bulletproof vest. Even if K-Max was outfitted in top-of-the-line Kevlar and ceramic body armor the concussive force of the rounds would pummel him like swinging sledgehammers and give Hawkins time to direct bullets into his unarmored aspects. At the point-blank range of close-quarters battle it was exactly the kind of weapon the ex-Delta Force commando needed.

Kissinger, the Stony Man armorer, had modified the weapon to better suit Hawkins's needs. In his state-of-the-art shop on the Farm, Hawkins had watched him first reload twenty rounds of the .45 ACP ammunition with magnum loads. Next the armorer had fed them into a single, hand-crafted extended magazine. Setting the hot-loaded mag down, Kissinger had begun taking the pistol apart, filing down the catch pin until the weapon would cycle on full automatic.

Hawkins stopped moving. He was screwed.

He opened the door to the fire stair only to discover that there was no third floor in the building anymore. The door had shown a tattered stretch of steps sticking out from the landing and coming to a ragged, broken end over a yawning blackness.

Hawkins could see nothing in the darkness, no matter how much he strained his eyes. He knew there was another level below his because he could see the WP burning right below it through holes in the floor. If K-Max had been driven up from the ground, then he was down there waiting for him in that black, because there was no way the terrorist could make it up to the roof with an entire floor collapsed.

Hawkins leaned back from the edge to make sure he didn't skylight himself. His throat felt tight. This wasn't the way it was supposed to go down. He'd been thrown a curve ball. He closed his eyes and drew in deep breaths. He looked over the edge again, saw the yawning darkness.

Hawkins knew there was no way he wasn't going to go. He'd been entrusted with this mission, traveled across the world to exact vengeance on a man responsible for massacres and the spreading of terror against the helpless. Hawkins would finish the job, then provide undeniable confirmation.

He slipped his rucksack off his shoulder and opened it. Quickly he slid into the canvas harness he pulled from inside, jerked it tight around his shoulders and hips, snapped it close around the swell of his chest under the Kevlar hauberk.

Working with an economy of motion, Hawkins laid out two grenades on the floor beside his feet. He pulled the nylon rope free from the rucksack and secured one end around the metal handrail next to him on the landing. Once that was secure he clipped the ropes through the D-rings on his harness. He tucked the .45-caliber pistol into his harness at his waist.

Leaving the rope in a loose pile at his feet on the edge of the broken stair, he stooped and picked up the two grenades, moving with a concentration so total he was like an automaton. He thumbed down the timers on the two grenades, armed them. Preparing himself, he swallowed.

He tossed the grenades out into the dark and stepped back, turning his head to the side. There was an eternity of silence as they fell, then the detonations came.

They came hard, tripping one right after the other. He'd timed the first as an air trigger. There was a flash like primordial lightning and then the concussive thunder of the explosion as the first flash-bang went off. The second struck the floor and detonated a full second after the first, giving him a double hammer blow of shock and disorientation to operate behind.

Hawkins kicked the rope over the edge and stepped forward, drawing his pistol from his harness. He scooped up the loop of rope in his leather-gloved hands and pitched forward off the edge. He jumped, the rank, dead air of the old building pulling at his close-cropped hair as he fell.

He felt the rope sliding through his grip as he dropped, heard the whizz as it slid through the carabiners. He was rappelling into the dark headfirst, one hand guiding the rope through his harness rig across his chest while with his other he held the handgun out in front of him. Like a spider he dropped at the end of his nylon web, searching for his prey.

He counted the seconds of the drop with a cool detachment. Once in the action the time for self-doubt was past, and terror was suppressed with an iron will beneath the need to operate at the height of his abilities. When he was close to the bottom he slapped the hand holding the guide rope against his chest and brought himself up short.

His legs swung down underneath him as he was jerked short into an upright position. He didn't meet the floor but he was nearly helpless dangling there, so he released the rope, dropping straight down as if inserting into a hot LZ. He felt the floor beneath the Vibram soles of his boots and dropped down into a crouch to absorb the force of his short fall.

He held his pistol out in front of him and stepped back, using his free hand to disengage from the rope. He took a calculated risk and rolled back over one shoulder, came up and, using one hand to make three points of contact with the floor, crab-scuttled to the wall.

There he froze. He waited, tense, certain a hail of bullets would cut him down. Long moments stretched out into even longer components of time. He could smell the smoke now, rolling up from the fire below, could feel the heat like a blanket envelop him.

He'd need to take K-Max down as quickly as possible. But quick wasn't the way blind fighting worked. It was a game of nerves where the other senses struggled to make up for the lack of sight. Rushing in the dark caused noise, and noise was like a laser sight illuminating the target, bringing certain death.

His operating procedure would be textbook, as would K-Max's. He would move slowly after his initial burst of activity. He would put his back to the room wall so that he could only be attacked from a single direction and he would move slowly, hugging the wall and waiting for his enemy to make the mistake that would give his position away.

It was a game of animal patience, not a game of cat and mouse. Neither of the players was a mouse. It was feral, skilled cat against feral, skilled cat and the game wouldn't end until one of the players was dead.

Hawkins stayed motionless in the oppressive, tomb-like atmosphere. He strained for even the slightest hint of motion or sound above the trip-hammer thumping of his own heart in his ears. The floor was littered with debris and as uneven as a lava field from the wreckage of the collapsed floor. The ground was precarious with jutting timbers and piles of masonry. Artifacts of the building's former use were scattered like pieces of broken landscape among the rubble: overturned desks, bits of crockery, busted chairs and various other bric-a-brac. It was a treacherous hunting ground.

Acutely aware of breathing in deadly smoke, Hawkins fought against the feeling of slow asphyxiation and began moving.

The air choked him, forcing him to fight for every trace of oxygen his lungs could scrape up and threatening to send him into fits of coughing that would equate to a death warrant in such a situation. Add to that the growing amount of smoke, and he realized he faced the very real possibility of blacking out.

He kept his back as close to the room's wall as he could. He pivoted his head slowly, the muzzle of the pistol tracking in time to his slowly shifting eyes. He used one hand to press against the wall and steady himself. He crossed one leg in front of the other, shifted, stepped, stopped. Repeated his scan.

Over and over he did this as the minutes stretched into unbearable chunks of tension twisting his already frayed nerves. He was not attacked from out of the darkness but neither did he come across any evidence of his quarry.

The inevitable happened. Hunting among the dark

ruin he came upon a pile of rubble too big to cross safely. Like a peninsula of land the mound jutted from the wall. Hawkins lowered himself and reached his free hand out in front of him, taking up a position like a fullback crouching at the line of scrimmage.

Pistol up, he maintained his three points of contact and edged forward. Step. Listen. Step. Listen. Each moment stretched into the next like nails dragging on a chalkboard. His foot came down on a bit of debris and it made a sharp crunch. He dropped flat and froze.

From less than three feet away and directly in front of him K-Max triggered his machine pistols. The roar was a deafening, sudden avalanche of sound. Hawkins saw the big man silhouetted in the muzzle-flash and spun into action. Posting on his leading hand, he swung himself around in a tight semicircle.

He banged his shins into K-Max's legs and swept his feet out from under him. The African outlaw was thrown to the ground and at least one of his machine pistols clattered off across the rubble. Night vision ruined by the muzzle-flash, Hawkins used his adrenaline-enhanced proximity sense to complete his maneuver. He slid up onto the sprawled man and twisted over.

One hard, strong hand latched on to his enemy's throat and the other brought the cavernous muzzle of the modified .45-caliber pistol down into his face hard enough to crush the outlaw's nose. Dark blood gushed out.

Suddenly the heat and pressure from the burning fire below cracked the already damaged floor beside them. Like a volcano flame rushed up through the crack and shards of glowing wood exploded outward, spinning like boomerangs.

K-Max reached over and snatched up a burning torch. He lifted it in one smooth motion and stabbed at Hawkins's eye. Hawkins managed to turn his head just enough to take the blow on his forehead. He snarled at the sudden pain and fell back even as the terrorist tried to rise and grab the pistol from him.

Hawkins pulled the trigger, crazy with the pain of the flesh on his face searing. The modified pistol went off, and didn't stop firing as he fell back.

He emptied half the clip before he landed on his back. Almost a full two-thirds of the rounds he triggered missed the African terror leader completely. But at that range the ones that didn't miss tore the killer apart.

Chunks of loose flesh exploded from the outlaw's chest, throat and head. The heavy-caliber slugs burrowed in with a merciless force. Bones shattered, organs burst and blood splashed as if from a hose. Hawkins couldn't have done more damage with a machete and a sledgehammer.

Hawkins dropped the pistol and brought both hands up to his burning face. He was still fighting, the pain, which drove him mad in useless attempts to escape from it. He kicked backward, pushing himself across the floor. He tried to stand, fell, stood again. Still cursing in his agony, he stepped backward and spun. He hit a support beam and staggered back.

His foot came down on one of the dead man's outstretched legs. His ankle rolled and he went down, pitching over backward. He hit the ground and felt the heat rise up from it like an oven and knew it was on fire beneath him. He struggled to get up and heard the creak as the timber gave way.

Then he was falling.

Hawkins dropped ten feet and hit hard. The jolt stunned him hard enough to knock the pain back for a moment, and in a dull, stupid way he was able to think again after the all-encompassing pain of having his flesh seared. Thankfully the Kevlar hauberk soaked up some of the concussion.

He felt a burning sensation on his arm and snatched it to him. His sleeve was on fire and he slapped it out. Once it was extinguished he brought his arm up and sat.

Flames leaped around him. He inhaled deeply, fighting for breath, and felt his nausea increase. He fought for consciousness again, roused into action.

With consciousness came the pain.

He staggered to his feet and looked up. The hole in the ceiling was ten feet above him. He couldn't jump that far so he looked around him, desperation pushing on the pain. Panic threatened to grip him for a moment.

He saw what he needed and sprang into action. He grabbed the old kitchen table and heaved. It exploded from under the burning timber heaped on it, smoldering like a campfire itself. It was heavy and awkward but it came when Hawkins pulled.

The table slid across the burning, uneven floor and Hawkins heaved it up under the hole in the ceiling. He climbed up onto the table and looked up. It was still one hell of a jump.

He exploded upward, caught the hole by the edge and pulled himself up until he came over the edge and pushed clear of the hole. Rolling over onto his back, he gulped down huge drafts of air. It merely choked him, threatening to sear his lungs, but it was all the air he had.

He rolled over and came to his feet. He looked around. The walls and floor were starting to truly burn. He saw the corpse of the African terrorist. He turned and looked at the rappel rope.

This was a stupid, half-assed plan, he thought, and tore his body armor clear. He began to climb, stubbornly refusing to admit defeat. From across a great canyon he heard the helicopter hovering above the burning building, and he redoubled his efforts. Once he was back at the door to the fourth-floor corridor, it was a short sprint to the roof, where Mott held the Loach in a hover, poised to extract Hawkins as soon as he emerged.

Hawkins leaped and seized the landing skid as Mott pulled away from the burning building.

Mott was yelling, laughing as he flew them away. Below Hawkins smoke rolled from the building as if from an island volcano, and flame was claiming the entire structure. It's a funeral pyre, he thought.

CHAPTER SEVENTEEN

Caribbean Coastal Region, Colombia

Lyons walked around the edge of the terminal and crossed a muddy stretch of grass before walking into the tall grass bordering the airport. The surrounding area was mostly undulating plains filled with tall grass and short, brushlike trees.

The abandoned airport was dark and silent, forming the perfect prefabricated platform for clandestine movement of the FARC mercenaries.

Setting up behind a stand of short acacia, Lyons watched the area through a pair of Bushnell binoculars. He looked at his watch. It was time. Communication with Stony Man and the CIA pilot was based on a prearranged timetable. Everything would unfold as scheduled without further interaction unless something varied in an unforeseen manner. Unless Lyons made contact, the pilot would begin his approach in the Cessna Conquest I in ten minutes. Once he landed, the Agency pilot would turn the airplane around and point the nose straight back up one leg of the twin strips with engines idling, prepared for an immediate takeoff.

Lyons caught a flash of movement and turned. A Toyota SUV pulled off the highway and began to speed down the terminal access road toward the isolated Colombian airfield. Lyons zeroed in on the vehicle's windshield. He saw the square head of the man Stony Man intelligence had identified as the emir's liaison to the FARC mercenaries come into focus behind the wheel, a man named Kaseem. Lyons felt a grim smile tug at his face in satisfaction. Kaseem appeared to be grinning madly at some private joke. His lips moved as he said something to someone else in the Toyota.

Lyons frowned and refocused the binoculars. The rest of the SUV appeared empty. He zoomed in on the Arabian operative again. The man pursed his lips and blew a long breath out so hard his nostrils flared. Was he in pain? Lyons wondered. Dysentery was a very real threat, even for a man used to such hostile environments.

Suddenly a pile of black hair appeared between Kaseem and the steering wheel, from out of the mercenary's lap. Lyons swore in surprise and frustration. A teenage girl sat up and snuggled back into the comfortable passenger seat of the Toyota. Lyons turned his head and spit as the SUV pulled up to the airport terminal. He ground his teeth together in frustration.

He didn't know why Kaseem had brought the girl with him. Was she a prostitute, his mistress, a kidnap victim or—hell—even his wife? There was no way to tell but Lyons had just been thrown a very uncomfortable curve ball.

Like a portent the steady drizzle of the monsoon rains began to increase. The stiff breeze shifted slightly and the orange windsock on top of the abandoned airport terminal spun in a different direction. Lyons watched as the pair got out of the Toyota and entered the terminal. Lyons had minutes to figure out how to change his plans.

She's just a whore, Lyons tried to tell himself. He

didn't like how it sounded, even in his head. She had chosen her company and he couldn't be held responsible for that. His life and the lives of innocent Americans was on the line. Lyons frowned.

He sighed. It didn't matter; he wasn't going to do anything to harm the girl unless she directly attacked him.

Lyons looked down at his watch, then back up to the sky. Right on time Lyons's adrenaline-sensitive ears picked up the sounds of the Cessna Conquest's big, prop-driven engine. The pilot, a veteran Lyons only knew by his call sign of Buzzsaw, was approaching for his landing. Lyons reached for his sat-phone, prepared to scrub the mission. His eyes fell across his little cache. He saw the clackers for the Claymore mines he had set out along the runway where the helipad was located. It was more than enough to take out the Super Puma the emir had provided for transport as it landed, destroying Kaseem's transportation and neutralizing his eighteen-man strike force of narco-terrorists.

Claymores were indiscriminate killers and the back-blast area was significant. If Kaseem pulled the Toyota up next to the helipad to rendezvous with his team, the girl would be gravely injured. At best.

The CIA pilot brought the Cessna Conquest I down smoothly despite the heavy rain and crosswind. He began to brake the aircraft as he guided it toward the terminal. Its rear end skidded out to the side slightly as the landing gear slid in the mud on the runway. On board the plane was the rest of Lyons's equipment for the mission, including his long weapons. Lyons knew he needed those weapons. While he had wreaked considerable havoc before through the use of the Beretta and the .357 Magnum Colt Python, he was talking now about going into a complete war zone after he left the air terminal. It would be suicide to consider completing the operation armed as he was.

Lyons, his mind racing, debated with himself as Buzzsaw taxied the plane into position. At that moment, from over Lyons's shoulder, came the rhythmic thumping of a powerful helicopter approaching. Kaseem had managed to place his troops and equipment in the area of operations in just hours despite the heavy rains.

Lyons watched the terminal. Maybe Kaseem would leave his child-whore in the building when he came out to meet his men. Maybe, because of the rain, he would simply wait inside and Lyons could kill him afterward.

The lone Able Team leader swung his binoculars toward the observation window set in the rear wall of terminal, facing the landing strips.

Buzzsaw reached the end of the runway and turned the plane around smoothly, his tires leaving deep ruts in the muddy strip as he did so. From above Lyons's head the racket of the helicopter coming in obscured all other sounds. A doorway set next to the observation window in the terminal opened and Kaseem walked out, heading toward the helicopter pad.

Lyons gripped the binoculars. Stay inside, he willed silently at the Colombian girl. Just stay inside. The girl emerged from the terminal right behind Kaseem. Lyons's face twisted in a silent snarl of frustration.

The pair approached the landing pad as the helicopter hovered into position and the pilot began to lower the powerful chopper. Lyons had placed his Claymore antipersonnel mines on either side of the pad, away from the raised dirt mound, camouflaging them and the det-cord carefully so they were positioned in a V-pattern facing out from the rear of the helipad.

Lyons watched Kaseem and the girl walk to the edge of the landing pad. Kaseem gave the pilot a thumbs-up gesture through the windshield of the Super Puma helicopter as the skids touched down on the muddy soil. From his position Lyons could see the confused helicopter pilot gesture questioningly toward Buzzsaw's Cessna on the far side of the airport.

Lyons made up his mind. He was willing to risk detonating the Claymore on the far side.

He reached over and pulled the detonation clacker to him. He covered the edge up and double checked the electrical connection by looking for the blinking light in the small, recessed window of the detonator. The connection was good. Lyons looked up.

The pilot began to power the rotors down. Kaseem stepped away from the girl and approached the crew doors now sliding open on either side of the helicopter cargo bay. The emir's man was yelling something and pointing toward the Agency plane.

Beyond the helicopter landing pad Lyons saw the door set inside the frame of the Cessna Conquest I open up and Buzzsaw kick a short rope ladder out the side.

It was now or never. From this distance it was hard to see the set line of the girl's jaw, or her world-weary and jaded expression. She looked pretty in a brightly colored wrap. Lyons set his own jaw hard and squeezed the detonation clacker.

The Claymores positioned on the far side of the Super Puma helicopter went off with a sharp bang, and over 750 steel ball bearings per mine erupted, powered by thick blocks of C-4 plastic explosive, slamming into the side of the Puma with ruthless efficiency. The frame of the aircraft shrieked in protest and tempered glass shattered.

From his position Lyons couldn't see the FARC pilot but knew the man had taken a healthy dose of the shrapnel. The men clustered inside, preparing to spill out the doors, were knocked clear. On the side opposite Lyons bloody bodies dropped like overripe fruit from orchard trees. The explosion was murderously loud, but Lyons could hear the mercenaries' screams immediately.

Metal struts positioned at the point where the main rotor shaft met the roof of the helicopter shredded under the impact of the steel ball bearings and the still spinning blades drooped dangerously. Lyons realized that if he triggered the second Claymore the mortality rate would be final for the narco-mercenaries. He looked at the girl, hated her for being there, but couldn't bring himself to do the smart thing.

Kaseem had been thrown to the ground and behind him the girl cowered at the explosion. Kaseem rose as he pulled twin pistols from their nylon holsters. More wounded mercenaries stumbled out of the helicopter, holding injuries, their clothes soaked in blood. Blood pooled on the floor of the Super Puma and ran over the edge, spilling out onto the already muddy landing pad.

Lyons came up and cleared the Beretta 92F to the ready. He thumbed the selector switch to the semiautomatic setting and hooked the thumb of his free hand through the oversize trigger guard. He swiveled, running for the terminal from his concealed position.

Kaseem saw the motion and spun, his pistols coming up. Even across the distance Lyons could see the other man's eyes widen in the shock of the attack. The Saudi

Arabian's face hardened in determination and he triggered the twin pistols.

Lyons fired the Beretta rapidly, aiming low and letting recoil climb the muzzle up as six rounds spit out, speeding toward Kaseem. Lyons's rounds flew wide as Kaseem's own shots tore into the turf two steps behind the American. With each stride Lyons's feet jarred into the mud and falling rain slashed at his face, forcing him to squint against its force.

Behind Kaseem, Lyons saw the scrambling mercenaries working for cover, some helping their wounding comrades, others simply throwing themselves into mud puddles in an effort to escape the flying lead. Lyons triggered two more bursts, but Kaseem was already scrambling and the falling rain obscured the ex-LAPD detective's aim.

Lyons reached the corner of the terminal and raced around it. Mud splashed up his pant legs as he ran down the front of the building. Through the windows he saw the dark and empty shapes of the old airport terminal, the forgotten structure bearing witness to the desperate plight.

Once out of sight of Kaseem, Lyons continued sprinting down the length of the terminal. He came up to Kaseem's Toyota and pumped six rounds into the vehicle, puncturing the radiator and front passenger-side tire. Lyons risked a glance behind him as he neared the rear of the SUV, his hands dropping the magazine and punching a fresh one home.

Kaseem came around the corner low, his own pistols leading the way. Lyons twisted into a side shuffling gait and lowered the Beretta to his waist before triggering a quick spray of rounds at the crouching Saudi. The shots scored the side of the building, knocking chips of masonry flying and forcing Kaseem to duck back around the sharp corner.

Lyons ducked behind the back of the Toyota and went to one knee. Filthy water soaked the material of his jeans, chilling him unexpectedly. He took the Beretta up into two-handed grip and drew a bead on the edge of the terminal.

Kaseem did a quick sneak and peek around the lip of the building after changing his elevation in an attempt to try to throw Lyons's aim off. A gust of wind blew stinging drops of rain into Lyons's face. He triggered the Beretta, missing Kaseem but forcing him to duck back around the building edge once again.

Lyons popped up to his feet, weapon held in front of him, and shuffled back toward the corner of the build-ing opposite Kaseem. He fired the Beretta tight against the line of the terminal front wall to keep Kaseem's head down, then turned and sprinted the last few yards for the edge of the building.

Lyons twisted in midstride and muscled himself around the corner of the terminal. He put his head down and ran for the tail of the Cessna Conquest I even as he heard Buzzsaw revving the engines to a feverish pitch of mechanical intensity. Lyons hit the danger area between the cover of the building and the safety of the airplane at a dead sprint. He pumped his arms and raced flat-out toward the waiting airplane.

Lyons risked a look over his shoulder as he ran and saw confused narco-mercenaries fanning out for the cover on the edge of airport landing strips. Stony Man had known Kaseem was holding off armament until his crew was on the Caribbean island to facilitate quick hop times between intervening nations as the Super Puma flew into the costal region. Lyons had still been fearful that the men might have chosen to arm themselves with at least pistols in spite of Kaseem's orders, out of habit of a life spent carrying weapons.

This appeared not to be the case as Lyons raced toward Buzzsaw and the waiting Cessna Conquest I. He heard a burst of fire and knew Kaseem had doubled back around the terminal's far corner and he realized he was lucky to have gotten even as much of a lead as he'd pulled off so far. He needed to gain position and pull an angle to bring the emir's henchman down. He felt like cursing the rain and wind that had hampered his aim but held back as he knew it had hampered Kaseem's aim, as well.

He caught a glimpse of a limp arm hanging out the door of the Super Puma helicopter, trailing scarlet. He saw two men covered with their own blood lying unmoving and in the muck. Past them Lyons saw wounded men being helped by other mercenaries toward the edge of the airfield. He had hurt the Colombians. Not as badly as he'd hoped, but hurt them still and they were no longer players in the emir's game.

There was a twin barking of pistols and, despite the wind, Lyons felt the shock wave as Kaseem's rounds tore past him.

Lyons spun as he ran, sliding in the mud and throwing himself flat into the damp South American earth. He stretched out his pistol and fired back toward the terminal where Kaseem knelt by the corner, his back to Lyons's original observation post among the acacia trees. He fired again and Lyons heard the man's pistol rounds strike the fuselage of Buzzsaw's plane, dimpling the airframe.

Lyons pulled down and returned fire, squeezing off three careful shots. The girl stood on the ground between Lyons and Kaseem. She simply stood unmoving in the rain as both men tried to fire around her, frozen in her fear at the swirling violence. Lyons forced himself to look away and to concentrate on Kaseem, but the girl's eyes tracked him like lasers.

On his feet again, Lyons pulled his shot to the left of the girl, still trying to throw off Kaseem's aim. He whirled and raced for the plane. Lyons heard Kaseem's guns go off again and ahead of him Buzzsaw started the plane rolling.

Lyons shoved the Beretta into his shoulder sling and reached out for the rope ladder the Agency pilot had kicked over the lip of the aircraft door. He grabbed hold with first one strong hand and then the other. He could no longer hear Kaseem's firing over the plane's racing engines. Buzzsaw saw he was on the ladder and Lyons felt the plane pick up speed as he clung to the dangling rope structure.

Lyons hauled himself up the ladder as the Cessna Conquest I began to sprint down the muddy landing strip. Lyons looked back. He saw Kaseem racing after him now, both pistols blazing in the rain. The girl stood still, only her head turning as she tracked the fleeing plane's progress.

Lyons reached the top of the ladder as Buzzsaw pulled the nose of the plane airborne. The big ex-cop tumbled inside and yanked the ladder in after himself. He stood in the doorway and looked down as the airfield disappeared beneath him. The rain was falling too hard for him to see clearly and he was soaked to the bone.

He yanked his Colt Python from its nylon holster at his side and thumbed the hammer back. The massive side arm barked once, the report deafening in the confined space. The .357 Magnum bucked hard in his hand. Fifty yards away the scrambling Kaseem stopped cold, his head jerking to the side then he tumbled to the ground like a circus clown doing a pratfall.

Filled with grim satisfaction, Lyons grabbed up the door and slammed it shut with all his strength. The metal of the door reverberated in his hands.

He made his way toward the front of the plane.

"Give me the radio," he said. Time to let Stony Man know the FARC situation had been neutralized.

CHAPTER EIGHTEEN

Dubai City, Dubai

Earlier, Manning had pored over an architect's blue-prints of the structure procured for him by Carmen Delahunt at Stony Man Farm. Like most of the build-ings in the Dubai City industrial sector, the old building was aesthetically unappealing. Delahunt's research had managed to connect the building to emir al-Thani and to discover that it was being used not only as a Wah-habite *madrassa* for the recruitment and instruction of extremists but also as a way station for terrorists moving through the region.

The mosque was not a beautifully gilded or minaret-tipped building like those found in Mecca or Istanbul or even elsewhere in Dubai. It was too utilitarian in its function for such ostentatious displays. Only the placard sign announced in any obvious fashion what the squat and grimy brick building housed.

A red flag had risen immediately when ownership of the building was traced to a charity owned by emir al-Thani.

The mosque took up two floors of a four-story adobe-style building in the industrial Dubai neighborhood on the edge of the western desert far from the beautiful ocean vistas found on the east side of the city. On the street level there was a small family-owned grocery and the top floor housed five apartments rented to people, as far as Delahunt could find, who had no connection to the radical activities going on beneath their feet.

Manning looked at the dive watch on his wrist. It read 0148. Rafael Encizo, the Cuban-born Stony Man commando, would be in his overwatch position by now. Armed with communications gear and a precision sniper rifle with powerful scope, Encizo would provide his Canadian counterpart with security and liaise with the Navy Sea Stallion waiting just over the horizon.

Manning slid the earpiece into place so that the microphone was resting against the prominent jut of his cheekbone. He placed a single finger against the little device and powered it on.

"You ready?" he asked.

Encizo answered immediately, "Copy that, boss. I'm up. I've got eyes on your approach and the area. Radio chatter is good."

"Let's do it."

Manning eased open the door to his nondescript Toyota 4-Runner and stepped out into the street. There was dirty slush on the ground from a seasonal shower and everything lay cast in a gray pallor. Streetlights formed staggered ponds of nicotine-yellow illumination. In the building facing the street a single light burned in the window of the building's third floor.

Manning closed the door to the 4-Runner and fixed the stocking cap on his head before walking to the rear hatch of the vehicle. Despite the dampness in the air Manning left the zipper to his heavy leather jacket undone. The deadly Glock 18 hung in a shoulder holster designed to accommodate the silencer threaded onto its muzzle.

Manning opened the rear hatch and reached down

and pulled up the lid over the compartment that held his spare tire and jack. He moved it to the side and pulled out a hard plastic-alloy box of dark gray. His fingers quickly worked the combination locks and he looked up once before popping the case open.

Inside, snugly held in place by cut foam, was a Heckler & Koch MP-5 SD-3, the silenced version of the special operations standby weapon. Manning pulled the submachine gun out, inserted a magazine, chambered a 9 mm Parabellum round and then secured a nylon sling to the front sight and buttstock attachment points. He thumbed the selector switch to the 3-round-burst position. When he finished he shrugged his jacket off his right arm, slung the weapon over his shoulder so that it hung down by his side and then slipped the sleeve back into place.

Manning slammed the rear hatch down and looked around the quiet street. No one moved in the early morning hours. He could see a light, misty rain falling in the halos of streetlamps and feel the dank moisture on his face. It was an incongruous feeling in what was normally an overwhelmingly arid environment. He activated the alarm to the Toyota and shut the automatic locks as he crossed the street.

He wore dark jeans and heavy hiking boots with thick tread. He left waffle-pattern footprints in the grimy piles of dust turned to mud that gathered in the curve of the street curb.

He turned left, away from the mosque set above the small grocery. A used-furniture store sat next to the grocery and next to that was a rundown apartment building six stories high. On the other side of the tenement filled with Filipino foreign workers, next to the intersection, was a store dedicated to exporting rugs.

Manning turned down the sidewalk next to the apartment building and circled the tire store, entering a narrow alley running behind the businesses fronting Jaffa Street. He slowed his pace as he entered the alley, senses keyed up as he neared the target. There was a sheen to the grungy asphalt under the light of two naked bulbs burning over the back doors of the buildings. Large green garbage Dumpsters were set against the alley walls.

Manning kept his gaze roving as he moved closer to the back door of the mosque's building. A couple of empty bottles were littered around among wads of crumpled newspapers. It was too damp for there to be any significant smell. Gritty mud clung to the lee of brick walls in greater mounds than out on the open street, and several patches of the noxious clumps were stained sickly yellow. Halfway down the alley Manning drew even with the building housing the mosque.

Worshipers entered the stairway leading up to the temple through the rear entrance, avoiding the grocery altogether. An accordion-style metal gate was locked into place over a featureless wooden door, a Master lock gleamed gold in the dim light, obviously new. Manning shuffled closer to the security gate and drew a lock-pick gun from his jacket pocket.

He inserted the prong-blades into the lock mechanism and squeezed the lever, springing the dead-bolt. Manning reached up with his free hand and yanked the accordion gate open. The scissor-gate slid closed with a clatter that echoed in the silent, wet alley and he quickly inserted the lock-pick gun into the doorknob and worked the tool.

He heard the lock disengage with a greasy click and put the device back into his jacket pocket. He grasped the cold, smooth metal of the doorknob and it turned easily under his hand. He made to push the door inward but it refused to budge. Dead bolts.

Manning swore under his breath. He placed his left hand on the door and pressed inward. From the points of resistance he estimated there were at least three independent security locks attached to the inside of the door. He'd need a crowbar or a Hooligan tool to get in, and that would announce his presence too quickly.

His mind instantly ran the calculations for an explosive entry. He factored in the metal of the bolt shafts, their attachment points on the door frame and the density of the door itself. He was able to sum up exactly how much plastique he would need and ascertain the most efficient placement on the structure.

The exercise was purely theoretical, however, as Manning had no intention of blowing the door of a building in downtown Dubai. Not until he was exactly sure of what he would find inside. He was well versed in various forms of surreptitious entry and had been thoroughly schooled in the techniques of urban climbing, or buildering, as it was sometimes called.

Manning lifted his head and looked up. As per standard fire codes, a means of emergency egress has been placed on the outside of the building to aid occupants above the ground floors. The fire escape was directly above the back door and ended in an enclosed metal cage around the ladder on the second floor.

"Change of plans," Manning said into his throat mike. "I'm going up."

"Your call, boss," Encizo answered. "Everything's good at the moment."

Manning looked around the alley. He thought briefly of pushing one of the large green garbage bins over and climbing on top of it to reach the fire escape. He rejected the idea as potentially attracting too much attention. He looked around, evaluating the building like a rock climber sizing up a cliff face. Above the first floor five uniform windows ran the width of the building along each floor.

Manning made his decision and zipped up his jacket. It would keep him from getting to his concealed weapons quickly but it was a necessary risk if he was going to attempt this climb. He opened the scissor gate again and grasped it at the top. He stuck the toe of one boot into a diamond-shaped opening and lifted himself off the ground. He placed his other hand against the edge of the building, using the strength of his legs to support him as he released one handhold on the gate and reached for a gutter drain set into the wall.

He secured a firm hold there and held on before moving his other hand over. The drain was damp and clammy so that his grip threatened to slide at any moment. He pulled himself up despite the great strain of the awkward position and grasped the vertical drain with both hands. He moved his right leg and stuck his toe between the drainpipe and the brick wall, jamming it in as tightly as he could.

Once he was braced Manning pulled his boot from the scissor gate and set it on top of the door frame. It was slick along the top and he was forced to knock aside a minor buildup of muck along the narrow lip. Confident with the placement of that foot, Manning pushed down hard against the lip at the top of the door frame and shimmied himself farther up the drainpipe.

Manning's muscles burned and he forced himself to breathe in through his nose. Idly he wondered what his antics must look like to Encizo wherever he had set up his observation post. Manning squeezed the clammy, slick pipe tightly as he inched his way up. He lifted himself until only the toe of the boot on the door frame was in contact with the narrow edge. The muscles of his calf flexed hard under the strain and he released his left hand from the drainpipe and reached out to grasp the ledge of the second-story window closest to him.

He set himself, then knocked a ridge of muck off the window edge. He pushed down against the ledge and inched his right hand farther along the drainpipe. One of his legs found a metal bracket securing the gutter drain to the wall, and Manning wormed his boot toe hard into it. He shoved down with his left arm and lifted his free leg until his knee rested on the second-story window ledge.

His body stretched into a lopsided X, Manning carefully pressed his hands against the windowpane and pushed upward, testing to see if the window was open. He met resistance and realized it was locked. Manning eased his head back and looked up. A light was on in the window on the floor directly above his position. Above that, the fourth floor was as dark as the second. Directly above that was the building roof.

From his careful study of the architect's blueprints given him by Kurtzman, Manning knew that an internal staircase led to a roof access doorway. He debated breaking the glass on the window and working the lock mechanism from inside. He decided the risk was simply too great and made a decision to keep climbing.

"This is a no-go," he muttered. "I'm going all the way up."

"Copy," Encizo answered.

He chose this more difficult route for the same reason he had decided not to use the fire escape. The metal structure was as dated as the building and ran directly next to the softly lit third-floor window; he feared the occupants in the lighted room would be aware of the rattle as he climbed and be alerted to his presence.

Decision made, he shimmied his way up to the third floor despite the toll the physical exertion was taking on him. Manning was in exceptional physical shape but the task of urban climbing was extremely arduous. Hand over hand and toehold to toehold, Manning ascended the outside of the building. He worked himself into position by the third-floor window where the light burned from behind a thin blind, causing butter-yellow light to seep into the wet Dubai City night.

Pausing, he could hear the murmur of voices and sensed shadowed movements beyond the blind, but not enough for him to gather any intelligence. Moving carefully to diminish any sound of his passing, Manning climbed the rest of the way up the building.

Manning rolled over the building edge and dropped over the low rampart onto the tar-patched roof. He rose swiftly, unzipping his jacket and freeing the MP-5 submachine gun. Exhaust conductors for the building's central air formed a low fence of dull aluminum around the free-standing hutch housing the door to the fire stairs.

Manning crossed the roof to the side opposite his ascent, shallow puddles splashing slightly under his boots, and reached the door. He tried the knob, found it locked and quickly worked his lock-pick gun on the simple mechanism.

"All right," Manning said into the throat mic. "I'm going inside."

"Be careful," Encizo's voice said across the distance.

Manning glanced quickly around to see if the occupants of any of the other rundown Dubai buildings surrounding the roof he was on had witnessed his climb. He saw no evidence of either them or Encizo in his overwatch position and ducked into the building, leaving the door open behind him.

The Phoenix Force commando descended into darkness.

CHAPTER NINETEEN

Manning moved down the stairs and deeper into the building. Just inside the doorway he reached up and pulled down the edge of his watch cap, revealing a balaclava mask. He moved past the landing door leading to the fourth-floor apartments and down toward the two levels housing the hole-in-the-wall Dubai City mosque.

NSA programs had intercepted calls originating in the Waziristan province of northwestern Pakistan with their terminus here in Dubai. From that anchor point Akira Tokaido had followed the line to a holding company eventually linked directly to emir al-Thani. A free association algorithm had then placed movements of known terrorists with other calls originating from the building. Secure in his own omnipotence the emir had allowed his tradecraft to grow sloppy.

Now Manning's H&K MP-5 SD-3 was up and at the ready in his grip as he ghosted down the staircase toward the third-floor landing. Intelligence targets were worth more alive than dead. However, it was often more expedient to simply take them out when other means could not be readily facilitated.

Manning stepped softly off the staircase and stopped by the interior door on the narrow landing. From his check of the blueprints Manning knew the third floor served to house offices, a small kitchen and bedroom apartments while the second floor, directly above the grocery, was a wide-open place of worship housing prayer mats, a lectern and screens to separate male and female faithful.

Manning tried the knob to the fire door. It turned easily under his hand and he pulled it open, keeping the MP-5 submachine gun up and at the ready. The door swung open smoothly, revealing a dark stretch of empty hall. Manning stepped into the hallway and let the fire door swing shut behind him. He caught it with the heel of his boot just before it made contact with the jamb and gently eased it back into place.

Down the hallway, in the last room, a bar of light shone from underneath a closed door. Manning heard indistinct voices coming from behind it, too muffled to make out clearly. Occasionally a bark of laughter punctuated the murmurs. Manning stalked down the hall. Prudence dictated clearing each room he passed before he put those doorways at his back, but it was an unrealistic expectation for a lone operator in Manning's situation.

He eased into position beside the closed door and went down to a knee. Keeping his finger on the trigger of the H&K submachine gun, Manning pulled a preassembled fiber-optic-camera tactical display from his inside jacket pocket. He placed the coiled borescope cable on the ground and unwound it from the CDV display.

It was awkward working with only his left hand but the voices on the other side of the door were clearly audible and speaking in what he thought was Arabic, though Manning's own Middle Eastern linguistic skills were low enough that it might have been Farsi. Manning turned on the display with an impatient tap of his thumb and then slid the slender cable slowly through the slight gap under the door.

The display began to reflect the shifting view as Manning pushed the fiber-optic camera into position. A brilliant light filled the screen and the display self-adjusted to compensate for the brightness. A motionless ceiling fan came into focus, and Manning twisted the cable so that the camera no longer pointed directly up at the ceiling.

A modest kitchen set with a dining room table twisted around on the slightly oval-shaped picture and Manning could clearly distinguish four men sitting around a table. All wore neutral-colored clothes and sported beards except for a younger man seated to the left whose facial hair was dark but sparse and whispery.

Manning was able to identify all of the men present by the photographs that had been included in his sitrep workups. One man was Wael al-Zarad, the caliph of the Dubai City mosque, radical Wahhabite cleric with ties to the Egyptian-based Muslim Brotherhood. Sixty-three years old, veteran of the Soviet occupation of Afghanistan, where he had served as spiritual adviser to the muhajeen, al-Zarad was a man intimately plugged into the international jihadist network, and had been for decades. His fiery rhetoric and extreme interpretation of the Koran had earned him followers among the disaffected Muslim youth of the Yemen region.

The next man at the table was the wispy-bearded youth Manning identified as al-Zarad's bodyguard. It was the bodyguard's cell phone calls that had been intercepted with those originating out of the Waziristan province. The youth had a automatic pistol sitting on the kitchen table in front of him. He listened as the cleric spoke, but his eyes kept shifting to the pistol.

Next to the bodyguard sat the man who had so excited the DIA and then Stony Man in turn. Walid al-Sourouri was a known graduate of al-Qaeda training camps in Afghanistan under the Taliban; al-Sourouri had impressed his trainers with his nondescript demeanor and language capabilities. No glorious death by suicide for this warrior. Instead he was employed to help the networks circumvent the technical superiority of Western intelligence agencies by keeping things primitively simple. Sitting at the caliph's kitchen table was the foot messenger of al-Qaeda and their direct link to the emir.

It was the final man who made Manning's heart suddenly pound with anticipation. Raneen Jassim al-Ogedi was a blunt-featured man with a large reputation within the intelligence community. It was a gruesome reputation that had somehow failed to capture the attention of the news media for one reason or another. Despite this, Manning realized he had stumbled upon a killer from the Iraqi A list of wanted men.

Al-Ogedi was a former cell commander of Saddam's fedayeen, and an operator who had exploited his Syrian intelligence contacts to funnel in foreign fighters during the earlier stages of the American occupation and to later on target Iraqi consensus government Shiite officials in hopes of exacerbating a civil war. He had been a virulent Baathist until the fall of Saddam, after which he had suddenly found his Muslim faith again, most specifically the very radical and extreme fringe elements of that religion.

The man was almost never accompanied by less than a squad of Iranian-trained bodyguards, but Manning saw no evidence of them in the kitchen. Like the young bodyguard, al-Ogedi had a weapon positioned in front of him on the kitchen table. The wire stock of the Skorpion machine pistol had been collapsed and the automatic weapon was barely larger than a regular handgun.

The resolution on the borescope was state-of-the-art and Manning was able to make out several books on the table, as well as the weapons.

The cleric was speaking directly to the bodyguard, his words impassioned. The youth nodded in agreement and muttered something in a low voice. The man's blunt finger tapped a worn copy of the Koran for emphasis and next to the bodyguard the terror courier nodded his head in enthusiastic agreement. His bulky parka fell open when he did and Manning got a flash of the nylon strap supporting the man's shoulder holster.

Manning slowly pulled his borescope out from under the lip of the door. He coiled the fiber-optic camera cable into a tight loop and attached it behind the heads-up display with a little Velcro strap designed for the purpose. He slid the device into the inside pocket of his jacket and shifted the H&K MP-5 SD-3 around.

Rafael Encizo's deep voice came across the com connection. His voice remained calm but his urgency was obvious.

"We got trouble," Encizo said. "I got an unmarked sedan seating four guys that just pulled into the alley."

"Copy," Manning whispered.

"You got company!" Encizo suddenly barked. "All four of them just went through the door. Young guys all of them."

At that moment Manning heard the downstairs door break open and the shouts of men as they entered the stairway on the first floor.

"Get Grimaldi into the air and over the rally point," Manning ordered.

"Copy," Encizo acknowledged.

Then everything really began to fall apart.

The voices in the kitchen went silent then burst into frantic curses and Manning heard chairs scrape across the floor from inside the mosque's kitchen and backpedaled from the door as it was thrown open. Light spilled into the gloomy hallway like dawn rising and Manning dropped to one knee and swung up the MP-5.

The first of the kitchen cabal rushed into the hallway. The lead terrorist held his Skorpion submachine gun up as he emerged from the cramped room, his head already turning toward the far end of the hall where the footsteps of numerous men could be clearly heard thundering up the fire stairs.

The terror agent's eyes showed white against the dusky toffee of his skin and the black hair of his short, thick beard. He looked stunned to see the black-clad avatar of the masked Manning crouched in the hallway. The man swept his machine pistol down from a port-arms position to level it at the crouching Manning. Manning's steady finger triggered his submachine gun.

Thwat-thwat. Thwat-thwat.

The sound of the silenced H&K was an eerie mechanical cadence as Manning pulled down on the terrorist. His spent shells were caught in the cloth and wire brass catcher attached to the ejection port of the MP-5. A burst of 9 mm Parabellum slugs ripped into the man's face with brutal effect.

Blood splashed like paint onto the wood of the door and stood out in vivid relief against the pale linoleum of the kitchen floor behind the man. The terrorist turned in a sloppy half circle and bounced off the kitchen door before dropping down to the ancient carpet of the hallway, leaving a smear of his blood on the wood.

The next figure in the frantic line stumbled into the door frame. Manning fired his silenced submachine gun again and put a tight burst into the chest of the pistol-wielding terrorist, racing directly behind the other killer. The man's eyes were locked on the fallen form of his jihadist brother and they lifted in shock as Manning's rounds punched up under his sternum and mangled his lungs and heart.

Blood spilled in a waterfall over the lips of the man's gaping mouth and he tripped up in his jihadist brother's legs and went down face-first. Manning saw the cleric frozen at the edge of the kitchen door, hands held out and filled with a pistol, eyes locked on the visage of death and the grim specter of the Phoenix commando.

Down the hallway the fire door burst open and Manning glimpsed three men in civilian clothes, pistols drawn, as they stumbled into the hall.

Manning rushed forward, hurtling the tangled mass of the two fallen terror agents. He slammed his shoulder into the cleric and knocked his pistol out of the way. His SMG discharged twice into the man's chest and he grunted under the impact and spun off Manning, stumbling backward over a chair and falling heavily to the kitchen floor.

Manning used the momentum of his impact with the man to spin to one side, putting himself at an angle to the fumbling bodyguard, who was attempting to bring his automatic pistol to bear. Manning gripped his MP-5 in both hands and chopped it down like an ax, using the long silencer like a bayonet.

The smoking tube struck the bodyguard in his thick wrist with a crack, and the unprepared terrorist dropped his weapon in surprised shock. Manning swept the submachine gun back and then thrust it forward, burying it in the man's abdomen.

The terrorist folded as he gagged, and Manning lifted the MP-5 up to the end of its sling and cracked him across the back of the neck with the collapsible buttstock. The terror agent went down hard to the floor and the big Canadian coolly dispatched him with a 3-round burst.

Manning heard footsteps pounding in the hall and men shouting. Manning caught a flash of motion out of the corner of his eye and twisted to fire a burst across the room, shattering the window. Beyond the shattered window he saw the spiral reflections of flashing red police emergency lights.

Manning used the distraction to bend and secure the loose cell phone dropped by the bodyguard, a strictly reflexive motion. He rose and sprang toward the window across the kitchen. An armed man rushed the door with his pistol up, a mini-Mag flashlight attached below the barrel of the handgun. As Manning passed the kitchen table he turned at the waist and flipped it up so that it flew back and landed in the doorway.

The man ducked back around the corner of the kitchen door to avoid the flying piece of furniture, and Manning used the distraction to leap toward the window leading out to the fire escape. Manning dropped the MP-5 and let it dangle from its shoulder strap as he scrambled up onto the Formica counter top. The leather sleeve of his jacket protected his arm as he knocked splinters of glass away from the window frame.

Manning stuck a leg through the window and

prepared to duck out onto the fire escape. He looked back toward the kitchen door as he slid out and saw the man he had distracted swing back around the corner, automatic pistol held in both hands.

Manning threw himself to the side as the terrorist fired his weapon. A 10 mm slug cracked into the wall just to Manning's right, creating a pockmark, and the roar of the pistol was deafening in the tiny room. Falling backward, Manning triggered his weapon and killed his attacker even as more surged into the doorway.

Manning felt the hard rungs of the fire escape press into his back and he was immediately aware of a frenzy of activity beneath him. Two separate vehicles had entered the alley in back of the mosque from either direction and men shouted up at the fire escape from below, excited by the pistol shot.

"I have sights on," Encizo said over the com link. "I'm putting their heads down!"

Manning kept rolling as he fell, turning over his shoulder. He reached out with his hands and pulled himself upright by grasping the slick iron bars of the fire escape ladder. Manning hauled himself up and gathered his feet under him. Set, he scrambled upward, running hard up the rungs.

"I'm coming out on the Jaffa side," Manning barked. "I'm still good."

Below him the terrorist gunner thrust his body out of the window and shouted at Manning in Arabic, bringing his 10 mm automatic around. Manning ignored him, his lungs burning as he scrambled upward. He saw sparks fly off the metal rung in his grasp and the fire escape rang as a bullet ricocheted away. An almost indiscernible second later he heard the pistol bark.

There was a supersonic slap below him and the

terrorist screamed. The fire escape rattled as the dead body bounced.

"One down," Encizo said.

At the fourth floor Manning spun around and raced up the last length of fire escape. Bullets peppered the walls around and below him as terrorists on the ground began to fire. The sharp reports of the pistols echoed up between the narrow walls of the alley.

Manning reached the roof and dived over the edge. He hit the tar-papered platform and rolled across on his back, coming up quickly. He crossed the roof and looked down onto the main thoroughfare of Jaffa Street. Two police cars had pulled up in front of the building that housed the mosque, the occupants running to the storefront.

"These response times are insane!" Encizo shouted. "The emir must have paid for extra security!"

"Just keep their heads down!" Manning snapped as he fled.

He turned away from the edge and spun around. He knew the terrorist would be hard on his heels and he crossed the rooftop at a dead sprint heading for the next building, a long, two-story tall, used-furniture store.

By killing the cabal in the kitchen he knew he had separated the wheat from the chaff. All that remained now was to get the hell out of Dubai in one piece.

Manning hit the waist-high wall edging the roof like a rampart. He lowered himself and slid his chest across the cinder-block divider, swinging his feet over until he dangled off the wall, holding on by only his grip. Manning looked down to make sure his landing area was clear and then let go.

He fell straight down, struck the lower roof and rolled over hard onto his back. The maneuver, left over from his paratrooper training, absorbed much of the force of his fall, but he still struck hard enough to nearly drive the air from his lungs.

Manning gasped in the dank air and forced himself to his feet. He rose, set his sights on the tenement building rising up on the other side of the used-furniture store's roof. Windows faced out from the apartments onto the roof and lights were snapping on in response to the gunfire and police sirens.

"I'm heading for the tenement," Manning barked into the throat mic.

"Copy. Our pilot says he's over the rally point. You want me to come get you?"

Manning began to run toward the tenement building, starting to skirt a large skylight set in the middle of the rooftop. From behind him Manning heard the voice of an angry terrorist. A brilliant white pool of light from the guy's mini-Mag cut through the night and lit up the roof around Manning's running figure, and the man began to fire.

"Negative. I'm going to try for my vehicle. Stay in overwatch," Manning answered.

"Copy, but you got a street full of bad guys. I'm thinning 'em out but this has turned into a cluster fuck."

Manning didn't have time to answer.

Bullets struck the roof as Manning ran and he knew he would never make it. Already the bullets were falling closer and if the terrorist settled down, he had a very good chance of striking the fleeing Manning.

He pushed the edge of his jacket back and swept up the MP-5. His heart was pounding as he leveled the submachine gun. He heard the crack of the terrorist's pistol behind him as he squeezed the trigger. The H&K

submachine gun cycled through a burst and the skylight just ahead of him shattered.

Manning felt a tug at the hair on his head as he ran, followed by the pistol report, and knew how close he'd come. He hunched down and dug his legs into the sprint. The lip of the broken skylight rushed toward him and Manning leaped into the air.

Manning hurtled across the open space. The black hole of the broken skylight appeared under him as he jumped and he brought his legs together. At the zenith of his leap Manning plunged down through the broken window.

Glass shattered under his feet as he punched through the skylight hole. He felt sharp glass spikes tear at his leather jacket as he smashed through the smaller opening he'd initiated with his gunfire.

The bottom of his jacket fluttered up behind him as he dropped into the darkness and Manning felt a jolt of apprehension as he fell, completely unaware of where he would land or on what. Splinters of glass fell around him like shards of ice, and the buildup of icy slush on the window cascaded down in an avalanche.

Manning tried to prepare himself for the impact, knew it could be considerable enough to snap his legs or even kill him if he landed wrong, but it was impossible because of the tomblike darkness of the store interior to know for sure.

Manning grunted with the impact as he struck the countertop. He was unable to roll, so his legs simply folded under him and his buttocks hit the hard wood with enough force to snap his teeth closed.

He spilled out on his back and if not for the sling around his shoulder he would have lost the MP-5. His head whipped down and bounced off the counter so sharply he saw stars, and then his momentum swept him off the counter and he fell another five feet to the ground, striking his knee painfully on the concrete floor under the thin, rough weave of the cheap carpet.

His outflung arm made sharp contact with something large and knocked it to the floor. The heavy object landed with a crash beside him and an internal bell rang, telling Manning he had just tipped over the store cash register. The empty door on the register shot open with a pop like a gunshot as he landed and the flesh of his palms split as they made rough contact with the floor. He winced at the sudden sting of his own blood leaking out through the torn skin.

Manning forced himself to his feet, clinging to the counter for support. Adrenaline filled him and he gritted his teeth as he forced himself up. Once he was standing he ripped off his balaclava and stuffed it inside his coat. Through the store's big front windows he saw police lights flashing. They cycled through the dark store, illuminating the interior briefly.

Manning hobbled into a pile of furniture and out from underneath the broken skylight. Outside he saw other cops moving in the street, their attention focused on the building housing the mosque.

Manning forced himself forward, heading directly toward the front of the building, dodging around furniture displays set up to look like living rooms or bedrooms or dining areas. He saw there was no way for him to reach his vehicle. Manning began talking fast despite his blood-smeared lips.

"I'm here," he said. "My ride is a no-go. You ready for extraction?"

"Affirmative," Rafael Encizo answered. His voice was cool.

"Copy," Manning said. "As soon as it's clear I'll blow the distraction."

"I'm coming now."

Manning moved forward until he was clear of the furniture displays and could see out onto the avenue unimpeded. Jaffa Street held five police cars. Most of the occupants had already left their vehicles and stormed out toward the grocery underneath the mosque.

Manning looked toward his own Toyota 4-Runner. No one appeared to be standing near the vehicle. Manning bent his neck and looked down the street. He saw a black Ford Expedition abruptly round a corner three blocks up, lights blazing.

Manning made his decision.

From the skylight behind him a beam of bright illumination shot out from the mini-Mag flashlight attached beneath the barrel of the terrorist's 10 mm weapon. It cut through the shadows inside the furniture store and swept around, hunting Manning.

Manning dived out of the way as the light tracked toward him and the man fired. A 10 mm round burrowed into the floor with relentless force and the shot echoed loudly through the display room. Manning desperately needed something to rattle the gunman's aim. He rolled over his shoulder sideways, away from the illumination of the big front windows.

He came up out of his somersault and shoved a store mannequin toward the searching light of the gunman. The figure toppled and the terrorist pulled down on it, his gun triggering twice. The man's second round struck the mannequin in the head and then cratered into the plastic statue.

Stepping forward, Gary Manning scythed his weapon upward, spitting flame, and drilled the figure with two tight bursts. The corpse dropped through the skylight like a ship anchor.

Manning whirled and shoved a hand into the pocket of his leather jacket. He grasped his key ring and pulled it clear. He looked down and located the electronic fob on the end. His thumb pressed the vehicle remote-start option.

Out in the street the Toyota exploded in a sudden ball of flames with a deafening boom. The vehicle carriage leaped straight up into the air, engulfed by fire and pouring black smoke. It came down hard and sent metal car parts scattering in all directions.

The ruined 4-Runner came to a rest in the middle of the street and burned like a bonfire. Up the street Encizo's Ford Expedition locked up its brakes with an angry squeal. Manning swept his H&K submachine gun up and fired at the plate-glass window. His MP-5 whirred and the spent shells clanged together as they rattled into his brass catcher.

The window shattered outward and heavy shards of glass cascaded down like icicles to burst against the concrete outside the window. Manning dropped the weapon and let it dangle from its strap as he raced forward.

He heard pistol shots from behind him but had no idea if they came close or not as he stepped off his lead foot and sprang into the air.

He hurdled the bottom of the window like a track runner and landed outside. He heard shouts coming from his left and risked a look as he landed in a crouch. He saw a squad of uniformed officers, most of them on the ground and disorientated by the car bomb he had just detonated.

One officer was sufficiently focused to lift an arm

and point, shouting out a warning as Manning pivoted and began to sprint up the slushy sidewalk toward the Ford Expedition gunning straight for him. His breath came in staccato bursts as he charged through them. His breathing was loud and powerful in his own ears and he could feel the hammering of his heart in his chest.

Manning's 4-Runner smoldered, and spilled fuel spread across the street, carrying orange flames along with it. Manning worked his arms hard, increasing his speed and running flat-out. He heard the crack of a pistol but again had no idea how far off the round was.

He saw Encizo clearly through the windshield of the Expedition. The Cuban-American operator locked up the emergency brake and the tires screeched in protest as he swung the back end of the SUV around in a smooth bootlegger maneuver. Manning dived toward the passenger door.

Pistol shots rang out from behind him.

He saw the motion as Encizo leaned across the front seat and opened the passenger door. A bullet struck the rear windshield and spiderwebbed the safety glass. Another creased the bumper. Manning reached the front of the SUV and threw himself inside.

Rafael Encizo didn't wait for Manning to close the door but instead stood on the gas. Tires screamed, turning fast, hunting for traction. They caught and the Expedition lurched forward like a bullet train leaving the station, throwing Manning back into the seat.

"Pilot ready?" Manning panted.

"Affirmative," Encizo confirmed as he sent the SUV into a power slide that took the fugitive vehicle off Jaffa Street and out of sight of the officers firing on them. "He's put the Little Bird down on the top floor of a parking garage six blocks over. We'll be in the air in two minutes." He looked down at a digital clock display. "One minute," he corrected.

Manning nodded. He reached his hand inside his jacket pocket and checked for the cell phone he'd taken off the bodyguard.

"I wonder how everyone else is doing." Manning laughed.

CHAPTER TWENTY

Stony Man Farm, Virginia

Hal Brognola stood at the back of the room, well chewed but unlit cigar clamped between locked teeth as he surveyed the Farm's operations center. Against the wall at the front of the room television screens flickered with images. One screen offered an overview of the island from the Farm's dedicated Keyhole satellite. On another screen was the feed from the nose camera mounted in Jack Grimaldi's Comanche attack helicopter. Two additional screens were linked to similar camera systems in the Predator drones controlled by Carmen Delahunt and Akira Tokaido at their respective workstations. The UAVs were outfitted with Hellfire missiles for the engagement.

The screen featuring a topographical map of the island was controlled by Huntington Wethers and showed the individual operators of both Phoenix Force and Able Team in icon form, allowing the Farm to visually follow their progress as the assault unfolded. The signal enhancers placed on the target site by Rosario Blancanales and Hermann Schwarz sharpened the passive feeds.

Barbara Price stalked back and forth in front of the screens, working her sat-com headset to coordinate last-minute logistical needs. Above her head a digital clock counted down to H-hour.

The Farm's direct-action units had reunited after their separate missions, and with only a few hours of downtime they had been mission capable.

During that time communications chatter originating from the target had confirmed Brognola's greatest hopes. The emir was in place with his al Qaeda counterpart and they were nervous and made reckless by the sudden flurry of attacks on the Saudi's holdings. As Brognola had wagered, the information had not caused the megalomaniacal Saudi royal to stop his plan, but rather to only ramp up his timetable.

The big Fed felt himself grin. The raid was going to unfold like a cruel practical joke, one the emir would find little humor in…before he died.

Barbara Price spoke in a calm, clipped voice. It was the voice of an accountant reading of the quarterly tax audit. She stopped pacing and turned to face the screens, folding her hands behind her back.

"Bear," she said, "go ahead and patch me through to the *Independence.*"

Kurtzman's fingers pounded across his keyboard, then he lifted a hand and gestured toward the Stony Man mission controller. "You're on, Barb."

"Lieutenant-Commander Clancy?" Price paused. "Good. I believe our chronometers have been synced? Good, that is my time, as well. Do you have your code parole with you? Excellent, I'll give you the verification progression now. Bravo, X-Ray, Sierra Seven, Niner Zero Two. Can you confirm that?"

Price paused while she waited for the naval officer to confirm the sequence. She turned, caught Brognola's eye and nodded once, then spun around as the

commander of the USS *Independence*, a corvette-class
littoral combat ship, began speaking to her again.

"Yes, Lieutenant-Commander," Price agreed, "those
are executive paroles. I trust we are on the same page
now? Very good. Your orders are to move immediately
five nautical miles south by southeast to positions being
fed into your navigational stations now." Price pointed
toward Kurtzman, who immediately sent the information. "Once there," Price continued, "you will make
contact with ground elements that will serve as naval
artillery forward control. Is this understood?" Price
paused. "No. You will enter this in your ship's log as
a gunnery training exercise." Price fell silent, cocked
her head to one side. "Yes, Lieutenant-Commander, this
is highly unusual. Keep this channel open for further
instructions. Out."

Price spun and met Brognola's eyes. Over her head
the digital display ran down to 00:00:00. "Has authority
aborted this action?"

The big Fed slowly shook his head no. His cell phone
was on the table beside him but the launch time had
come and the President had not called. "Negative,"
Brognola said. "We are a go."

Price turned on a heel back toward Kurtzman. "Let's
roll."

Caribbean

THE RAMP of the CH-46 Sea Knight began to lower
with a screaming of hydraulic gears. Warm Gulf air
rushed into the back of the helicopter and pitch-black
darkness from an overcast sky stretched beyond the
opening. Below the hovering aircraft whitecaps curled

and split as the Gulf current pushed against the stiff sea breeze.

As CIA pilots worked to keep the helicopter steady just yards above the tossing ocean, the three men of Able Team picked up the F-470 CRRC—combat rubber raiding craft—and began to jog with it down the back of the cargo hold.

They cast it out the back and immediately followed it single file out of the hovering helicopter and into the water. The drop was short and the impact sudden as the men descended into the ocean. As soon as the copilot had cleared the back of the aircraft, the ramp began to rise and the pilot brought the CH-46 away from the surface of the water.

Hermann Schwarz felt the waters of the Caribbean coast, almost blood warm, envelop him. His momentum and the weight of his gear pulled him below the surface immediately. He snapped the cord on his life vest and felt it inflate immediately. He kicked out strongly for the surface, following the buoyancy of the vest toward open air.

He saw a softening of the darkness above him and began to let air escape his lungs as he pushed for the surface. His head broke through the waves and he took a deep breath. He filled his lungs and treaded water for a moment, casting about for his bearings. He located the CRRC bobbing on the surface immediately and kicked out for it.

He reached it in ten hard side strokes, grabbed hold of a gunwale and pulled himself over the side in a movement practiced so many times that it was second nature. Three heartbeats later Rosario Blancanales flipped over the opposite edge and into the fifteen-foot-long Zodiac raft.

"Where's Ironman?" Blancanales demanded.

As he asked the question he was moving toward the stern of the CRRC to where a wooden transom served as a mounting platform for the watercraft's twin fifty-five-horsepower, two-stroke engines.

"Let me see," Schwarz replied.

Schwarz shifted up the center of the raft toward the front where secured bags contained the team's equipment and weapons. He raised his head up and scanned the ocean. He saw Carl Lyons kicking hard for the side of the boat. Leaning over the edge he reached out a hand and grasped hold of Able Team's leader and hauled him over the side. Behind them he heard Blancanales start the CRRC's engines. The sound of the pumpjet propulsor with its shrouded impeller, instead of a traditional exposed propeller, was modest and muted against the white noise of the surf and wind.

Lyons leaned back against the six-gallon fuel bladder set next to the storage bags and began to root around in one of the cargo pouches on his leg. "Let's roll," he ordered. "Get the bearings for our 'Coxswain,'" he said.

"Don't worry, Lyons," Blancanales called. "You'll feel better once you shoot someone."

"Oh, they're going to pay for this," Lyons agreed.

Working alongside Blancanales, Schwarz checked his handheld GPS and then shot a southwesterly azimuth with his compass. While they compared readings Lyons worked the action on his weapons.

"We're good," Schwarz answered, agreeing with Blancanales.

"Hold on," Blancanales said, and grabbed the tiller arm of the twin engines.

The pitch of the engines changed as he goosed it, the

speed skags under the boat began to push down against the waves and the F-470 CRRC took off hard for the over-the-horizon objective.

As Blancanales guided the craft toward the emir's island on an almost due west bearing, Schwarz moved forward and began breaking into the waterproof storage sacks. The CRRC skipped across the surface like a stone hurled from a muscular arm, shooting out like a laser.

Pulling a pair of VisiTech night-vision goggles from the gear bags, Schwarz quickly pulled them into place and cinched them down tight. The rubber straps bit into his head as he secured them and the weight of the NVDs bore down on the bridge of his nose.

The smell of the sea and the humid wind clogged his nostrils. He paused to turn his face into the breeze. He grinned like a boy despite himself. He felt powerful and nocturnal, like some swift, amphibious predator. Adrenaline coursed through his veins like some illegal drug.

Schwarz looked to the north, and as Blancanales skimmed over a roll of waves he saw the blinking infrared signal emitting from the USS *Independence*. He turned back and found Blancanales in the monochromatic wash of the goggles.

"We've established visual with Platform Six," Schwarz said. "Mr. Coxswain," he added, deadpan.

"Good, go ahead," Blancanales instructed, ignoring the good-natured gibe and Schwarz could hear his own laughing exhilaration mirrored in the ex-Green Beret's voice.

Removing an emergency beacon from the bag, Schwarz took it in his hand and found the selector switch on the side. The U.S. A/N-4 light beacon was a smooth cylinder in his grip. He clicked the indicator over two positions and an irregular light began to pulse in the ghostly green illumination of the IR spectrum.

He held the light up for several seconds above his head. After a moment the IR running lights out to his north blinked twice in rapid succession and then switched out. Immediately, Schwarz powered the A/N-4 off and stowed it.

Protocol finished, Schwarz gave Blancanales a thumbs-up. "You stay here, then. I'll start handing the weapons back once I check 'em."

Lyons nodded in reply and Schwarz moved back into position. Out on the horizon he could detect nothing but more water as the CRRC raced across the ocean. He checked his watch, depressing the Indiglo feature and reading the time. If they were on schedule it would be another two and a half minutes before he would be able to see the lights of the emir's island on the horizon.

Schwarz ignored the heavy pull of his wet BDUs. Already he was starting to feel cool despite the muggy temperature. He removed the VisiTech goggles then opened the zippers on the satchels all the way up and began assembling the unit's weapons. For the requirements of the mission they had decided to forgo favorite personal choices in arms and streamline the ammunition and magazines they carried down into identical loads.

Each Stony Man operator would utilize a 5.56 mm M-4 carbine and a Beretta 92-FS Elite 9 mm pistol. While they were signature U.S. military weapons they were also ubiquitous in the Western Hemisphere for exactly that reason. Each man would carry a combat load of 200 carbine rounds in 30-round magazines and five 15-round magazines for the pistols. The pistols themselves sported pachmar grips and shortened but heavier slides than the more traditional models. Each one had been outfitted with a specially threaded muzzle and a four-inch sound suppressor.

Moving with practiced efficiency, Schwarz first locked and loaded a carbine and pistol each for Lyons and Blancanales and then handed them back. After arming some for himself, he loaded his own web gear and began handing back clusters of magazines that were in turn quickly secured by the two other men.

To the weapons Schwarz added an assortment of grenades, satchel charges and det cord.

Out over the bow of the CRRC the modest skyline of the target area blinked into view. Several clusters of lights were stretched in a north-south procession along the black line of the horizon. Blancanales saw them appear and immediately rechecked his azimuth while Schwarz double-checked the GPS display.

Blancanales shifted the arm on his tiller and the craft responded instantly by cutting across the rolling surf like a scalpel through skin. The rubber raft shot off two compass degrees toward the southern edge of the lights. Blancanales ran full-out for ten minutes then brought the CRRC in a degree to the north and ran straight on through to the shoreline.

Carl Lyons slid forward and pulled a bulky pair of Starlite binoculars from a watertight pouch. The night-vision binos worked by gathering ambient light and amplifying it rather than recognizing heat signatures like the IR NVDs. He began systematically sweeping the shore toward their LZ with the binoculars.

Blancanales hit his com link. "Able is prepped for landing."

JACK GRIMALDI WORKED the hypersensitive yoke of the Comanche and banked the fast-attack helicopter into his approach. The helicopter skimmed in tight over the chop, rotor wash skimming troughs out of the warm blue waves of the Caribbean just yards below the belly of his aircraft. Up ahead the outline of the freighter congealed from above the calm sea.

"Stony Hawk on target," he said.

"Copy," Kurtzman said.

On his targeting system a red light went to green as two optic overlays synced. His thumb rotated around and found the ignition. Instantly an AGM-114 Hellfire leaped out from its housing in the Comanche's weapon pylon. The warhead shot through the air toward the freighter just above the chop, its contrail spiraling tightly.

Through the slanted windshield Grimaldi watched the Hellfire skim the ocean and then slam into the starboard side of the freighter. There was a blinding flash as he swung the helicopter, then the deafening explosion pushed an orange-and-black fireball out into the air.

The attack commenced as Grimaldi prepped his second Hellfire.

THE FIREBALL of the first missile strike appeared in vivid relief on the screens of the Stony Man operations center. Instantly, Carmen Delahunt and Akira Tokaido initiated their own phases of the assault. Out over the island the Predator drones responded to their commands and descended from their observation altitudes.

The straight black line of the airstrip pavement appeared out of the green, almost amorphous mass of the jungle swamp. The MQ-9 Predator Bs tightened their circles as they dropped, and the white, sleek silhouette of the emir's Lear turbojet came into focus.

"Acquiring target," Tokaido said.

"Acquiring target," Delahunt echoed.

"Proceed," Price instructed.

Immediately, Hellfire missiles dropped from brackets beneath each UAV and launched toward the luxury-model corporate jet. Deadly payloads hurtled toward the aircraft. On the ground a group of figures had gathered on one edge of the landing strip.

"This is just how I school chumps on Gears of War," Tokaido noted, voice dry.

"Keep 'em coming," Price said. "I want those structures knocked flat before the boys hit."

Delahunt and Tokaido shifted the control throttles smoothly in response and the view from deadly drones shifted on the screen. A row of long, low buildings beside the runway centered themselves on the screen.

A second Hellfire leaped from Carmen Delahunt's platform and streaked toward the structure. An instant later Tokaido's darted out. Immediately there was a one-two explosion as the missiles struck home, thrusting roiling balls of flame into the sky.

As the buildings were consumed by flames Price spun on her heel, turning away from the screens. Her finger found her communications link and she initiated contact with the waiting combined force of Phoenix Force and Able Team.

"Green light," she said.

"Good copy, green light," McCarter answered.

The invasion began.

PHOENIX FORCE READIED themselves as the Expeditionary Fighting Vehicle surged forward and propelled itself into the sea. The twin shrouded Honeywell waterjet propulsors integrated on each side of the hull roared as Encizo gave the vehicle gas.

It surged forward in the surf, pounding against the waves and punching toward the shore half a mile ahead. Calvin James manned the 30 mm gun and sat beside David McCarter in the turret. In the back of the armored fighting vehicle the other members of Phoenix Force chambered rounds into a variety of weapons, each man heavily clothed in body armor.

McCarter looked back into the transport area of the EFV and nodded toward the waiting men. "We're about to hit the beach," he yelled over the engines. "Get ready!"

Beneath them the tone of the tracks changed timbre and the superstructure shuddered as the tracks bit into the sand and the big vehicle lurched onto land. Up front Encizo gunned the engine harder, reviving it as the tracks churned up the sand and spit it out in rooster tails.

Up in the turret James settled himself into his range finder, his hands on the smooth handles of the controls to the 30 mm Bushmaster autocannon. The EFV bounced up over a berm and slammed down hard on the other side.

Encizo powered down the EFV as they pulled into position. Ahead of them UAVs were circling, picking their own targets on the military compound below. Explosions ripped across the topography and fireballs climbed into the sky.

McCarter popped the hatch on the EFV and picked up the handset for his base unit, a PRC-117F. The communication kit interfaced easily with the Single Channel Ground and Airborne Radio System, or SINCGARS, outfitted with a VINSON device for security. The VINSON devices utilized by Stony Man had been modified by Kurtzman to be symbiotic encryption units. Code generated by the sending unit were specific and random to only those VINSON, not generic.

"Stony Falcon, this is Wild Horse, over," McCarter said.

"Wild Horse, this is Stony Falcon," Charlie Mott answered.

"We're at the gate," McCarter said. "We have over-flight confirmation?"

"Affirmative," Mott answered. "Ground vehicles ID match. The money is in the account, Wild Horse."

"Copy, T-time two mikes, over."

"Roger. Two mikes," Mott repeated. "You'll see me. Stony Falcon Out."

"Wild Horse out."

CHAPTER TWENTY-ONE

McCarter secured the handset into its cradle. He looked down the long slope of the desert hill toward the compound of emir al-Thani. An hour ago an MQ-9 Reaper, a larger, more capable improvement on the older RQ-1 Predator, had come on scene. This UAV was fully under the control of Stony Man's resident professor, Huntington Wethers.

After making a reconnaissance overflight its camera had confirmed and triaged the available targets. The money had been deposited in the account.

McCarter looked down at the sprawling, walled compound below him and quickly prepped his laser marker. The handheld laser target designator McCarter operated from the EFV would put the two five-hundred-pound GBU-12 PAVEWAY II bombs carried by the Reaper directly on the al-Thani structure.

Al-Thani's compound was lavish in a stark, industrial way and the contrast it held to the remote desolation of the swampland of the island only emphasized the obvious display of wealth. The main house was a four-story structure with all the hallmarks of traditional Central American architecture. Both the driveway and paved footpaths connected the main structure to secondary houses, maintenance sheds, vehicle garages, tent barracks and a helicopter landing pad. One side of the compound had been dedicated to a short runway capable of hosting small jets.

The main complex, surrounded by a ten-foot-high adobe-brick wall, was not just a residence. In addition to the runway and helipad there was a line of large warehouses set against the east wall beyond the landing strip, which Blancanales's intelligence had shown doubled as a shooting range. One of the secondary houses was believed to serve as a fully functional clinic.

A tent barrack divided the structure from the industrial areas, where semi-trailers used to unload the freighter were parked next to garages with service bays designed to accommodate aircraft and ground vehicles. Their intel indicated that air traffic controllers used to working at remote Colombian drug runways had been imported to man the strip.

Nothing as obvious as gun towers lined the walls, but al-Thani's bodyguards were vigilant. A small gate in the rear, on the northern side of the compound where Blancanales had made his own covert entry, was used for mounted patrols in customized former Soviet republic APCs to conduct security sweeps of the island outside the perimeter walls. McCarter could see two armored vehicles on opposite sides of the flat wetland below his position now, trundling slowly through the swampy geography like giant, six-wheeled cockroaches.

Once again David McCarter had found himself at the tip of the spear.

"You ready?" he asked Calvin James.

"Let's roll," the commando replied.

McCarter activated his laser marker and painted the main house with his laser pointer while beside him Calvin James spoke the activation code into the

PRC-117F radio, alerting Mott in his Little Bird and Wethers back at Stony Man Farm.

While McCarter held the laser marker steady, James climbed out of the front seat, where he'd sat behind the Mk 48 light machine gun. He moved into position behind the driver's seat and he unlimbered the XM-312 .50-caliber heavy machine gun. He racked the charging handle and seated a bullet in the chamber.

Adrenaline began to leak into James's system as he waited for the bombs to fall. The carry racks on the sides of the EFV had been filled with light arms, grenades and rocket launchers. Each commando was outfitted with a lethal personal arsenal in addition to the weapons systems indigenous to the EFV. After the action started in the compound, the weapons would be disposable with reloading being replaced in the initial strike by new weapons.

The target housed foreign jihadists, mercenaries and elite bodyguard troops, as well as the emir and his retinue. With the odds so heavily stacked against them, the ex-SEAL knew the Stony Man kill box could quickly become a deathtrap for the would-be ambushers.

Up in the stratosphere he saw a streak of fire, then a second one, high up in the early morning sky. He forced himself to look away from the rain of death descending and to focus on the two black former Soviet APCs patrolling the ground between their position and the back gate of the al-Thani structure compound. They would be his first target once the hellfire began.

There was a screaming whistle out of the night and a sound like an airplane flying low. The twin GBU-12s landed like the fists of angry gods. The explosions shattered the upper stories of the main structure in twin balls of fiery retribution. The top floor disintegrated under the impact, and flames blew out the windows and doors on the bottom floors. The concussive force of the blast uprooted trees and bushes in the various yards and gardens. The third and fourth stories collapsed inward and the structure raged into a screaming inferno.

"Yes," Calvin James whispered, his satisfaction a bloody, grim emotion in his gut.

The Reaper UAV began to circle down in altitude. Its camera rolled feeds that ran back through an AWACS bounce on the *Independence* to a basement room in the Pentagon, and to Stony Man Farm, where Brognola, Price and Kurtzman watched the unfolding action along with the Stony Man cybernetics team.

In the front of the EFV McCarter hurriedly secured the laser designator and slid into the turret and behind the steering wheel. The geography in the two men's NVDs was brightly illuminated by the leaping flames of the raging fire.

Out on the edge of the flames Charlie Mott's AH-J6 Little Bird swept into view, deadly as a metal wasp. McCarter gunned the EFV and it sprang forward and raced down the hill, tearing into the wet, soft turf and spraying sandy soil wildly. He felt the rear end start to slide and he steered into it so that the EFV straightened itself out and shot forward like a bullet from a gun.

Out ahead of them each of the exterior-mounted patrols in the hard-shell APCs skidded to a stop at the sudden explosion. Top hatches sprang open and gunners took up positions behind the swivel-mounted M-60D machine guns. Neither gunner had seen the approaching EFV, and they both kept their faces pointed toward the burning structures of their compound.

Blacked out and running hard, the EFV swept down on them like a cheetah cutting a pack animal out from the herd. One of the turret gunners suddenly shouted and pointed. From behind the wheel of the EFV McCarter saw the vehicle sentry gesture and followed the line of his pointing arm. The man had seen Charlie Mott's Little Bird.

"Take 'em!" McCarter shouted over the screaming engine of the EFV. "They've spotted Mott!"

The General Dynamic lightweight heavy machine gun had a maximum effective range almost twice that of the M-60D, and Calvin James exploited his superior firepower with ruthless abandon.

Above the compound the Little Bird turned in the air, rotating like the gun turret of a tank. The twin seven-tube launchers for the 2.75-inch rockets lit up like fireworks and began striking the compound in streaks. Mott moved in a methodical sweep from left to right.

As he pivoted his fire, placing rocket after rocket on target, he launched on grounded aircraft, parked vehicles and the guest houses running along the short runway. The effect was catastrophic.

Sitting helplessly on the pad, a fourteen-passenger Sikorsky S-76 Spirit went up as Mott put a 2.75-inch rocket on target in its fuel tank. The helicopter leaped into the air as fire mushroomed out and cast burning debris across the eastern half of the compound.

The nose of a Rockwell International Sabreliner 65 jet stuck out from the open doors of a Quonset-hut-style hangar. Mott put a rocket through the sleek, jet-black windows and into the cockpit. The explosion was contained by the hangar, but the open doors served like a chimney. Black smoke, clearly visible in the light of the raging fires, roiled out. Mott turned the Little Bird on a dime, smoothly swinging the tail around so that he faced the closest rows of tent barracks. Lights had clicked on in the structures as al-Thani's troops and employees scrambled to respond to the raid.

Mott put a rocket through one tent and a second through the front door of another, punching holes and setting a line of the housing units on fire.

Behind him, beyond the wall, the black APC patrolmen twisted their M-60D machine guns around and drew down on the hovering death machine. Orange flames licked from the machine-gun muzzles, and lead began flying in earnest toward the little attack helicopter known as the Deadly Egg by service members.

From behind McCarter, Calvin James opened up with the .50-caliber XM-312. The lightweight heavy machine gun had been pressed into service to replace the military's aging inventory of the M-2 .50-caliber heavy machine gun, which were some eighty years old.

With advanced muzzle brakes and chambering action, the recoil and weight of the XM-312 had greatly improved on the old M-2 while maintaining a respectable rate of fire at just over 400 rounds per minute. The heavy sound of a .50-caliber weapon firing remained a powerful psychological weapon in its own right.

In his driver's seat McCarter felt the recoil even through the heavy vehicle frame of the EFV though it did nothing to slow the vehicle. He saw red tracers burn like laser bolts across his NVD goggle and arc out across the distance before falling on target.

The .50-caliber rounds tore into the first APC. The vehicle soaked up the rounds like a sponge. The weapon cycled close above McCarter's head and he heard the chunk-chunk-chunk of the weapon operating over the dull crack of the rounds firing. Red tracer fire burrowed into the hard-shell APC, some rounds skipping off at wild angles, others disappearing into the vehicle cab.

The top gunner fired his weapon hard, the muzzle blast taking a star-shaped burst pattern in McCarter's goggle. He saw the man suddenly convulse and heave forward, only to bounce off his weapon. A red-hot tracer round burned into the gunner's back and out the front, where it bounced wildly off the roof. One moment the gunner had a right arm and in the next moment it was gone. The man slumped across the hood with wounds large enough to be seen even across the distance and in the uncertain light.

McCarter saw concentrated tracer fire slip through the side of the APC, and after a moment the racing vehicle suddenly veered sharply to the right. It drifted for several dozen yards across the broken ground then its front end hit a narrow depression of a creek and buried its nose in the far bank.

On the other APC the topside gunner's head snapped to the side to follow the sudden erratic path of its fellow patrol vehicle. He saw the wild red tracer fire and the machine gunner swiveled around, searching for the source of the incoming rounds.

Beyond the M-60D gunner McCarter could see Charlie Mott's deadly Little Bird continuing its rampage as more 2.75-inch rockets from its fourteen-missile arsenal fired off. Vehicles exploded as semi-tractors, automobiles and all-terrain vehicles were struck with equal enthusiasm.

By the time the rocket fusillade had finished, multiple bonfires of burning vehicles and structures raged across the compound, all of them miniscule in comparison to the blazing inferno of the main structure. Despite the heavy damage wrought on the majority of buildings, personnel scrambled around the compound, most wielding weapons of one sort or another.

Mott's last rocket went through the front door of a wooden frame structure farthest down the line of the airfield from him. It punched through the door like a breeze tossing paper and detonated inside so that thick smoke billowed out.

Without hesitation Mott switched over to his M-134 7.62 mm miniguns. The electrically powered chain guns whirred to life and a cascade of machine-gun bullets began to douse the compound, tearing into buildings and knots of struggling narcoterrorists.

The machine-gun bursts struck the figures like chainsaw blades, hacking them to pieces and splashing guts and body parts. As he fired, Mott worked the Little Bird, drifting out toward the edge of his effective range to avoid any intensity of return fire likely to bring his lightly armored helicopter down.

McCarter cut the EFV hard, running up onto a track used by the al-Thani APCs. The front tread of the Expeditionary Fighting Vehicle struck a head-size boulder in the dark and the steering yoke lurched hard in McCarter's grip.

The vehicle frame shuddered under the impact, and that side shot into the air, tipping the racing EFV up onto one side. McCarter turned the yoke hard and straightened out the buggy, throwing his weight hard to his right to keep the low-slung vehicle stable.

He saw tracer rounds cut across his front and realized they'd finally sped into the range of the APC's M-60D. Above him Calvin James cut loose with the .50-caliber machine gun again. McCarter worked his brakes and slid into position onto the track, now racing toward the back gate of the al-Thani structure compound, several football fields away.

Once on the dirt road track McCarter took his right hand off the steering yoke and grabbed hold of the M-60D mounted in front of him. He freed it in its mounts and swiveled it around to engage the second APC.

He saw the enemy turret gunner leaning low over his weapon, the star-pattern muzzle-blast obscuring his form in McCarter's NVD goggle. The APC turned in a tight halfcircle, spraying loose gravel like surf as the driver tried to meet the new threat of the EFV head-on.

McCarter saw a bullet spark off the front of his vehicle and his finger found the trigger of the M-60D. The weapon roared to life and rocked in his one-handed grip, straining against the vehicle-secured mounts.

Red tracer rounds from Calvin James's XM-312 tore into the engine hood and then windshield of the APC as the Phoenix Force commando walked his fire up toward the terrorist machine gunner. McCarter followed James's lead, spraying his long, ragged burst in a tight Z-pattern to keep his rounds bouncing inside the APC's cab.

Calvin James found his target. The M-60D exploded into pieces as the .50-caliber slugs buzzed into it, shattering it beyond recognition in the blink of an eye. Half a second later the machine gunner was vaporized above the sternum, shredded into bloody spray and hamburger chunks.

McCarter hit the brakes and cranked his steering wheel hard to slow his momentum as the rudderless APC drifted off before petering out to a stop some hundred yards away. A wave of dust rolled over them as the EFV screeched to a full halt.

Working with efficient speed and ignoring the piping-hot barrel of the XM-312, Calvin James secured the weapon and dropped down into the passenger seat behind the MK 19 automatic grenade launcher.

As soon as the Phoenix Force commando was in place, McCarter punched the throttle again. Both men were pushed hard back into their seats by the force of the acceleration. The engine revved to a full-throated scream as McCarter roared toward the back gate of the Caribbean compound.

Ahead of them they saw flames climbing high into the air, and sitting amid the blank dark of the island's swampy landscape, it seemed as if the chimneys of hell had been opened. Something exploded and a burning, unidentifiable mass shot into the air.

McCarter saw tracer fire pouring out of the dark from over his head toward a section of the compound he knew was the fuel-reserve area where Able Team was making its own coordinated strike.

Above him the minigun burst seemed to go on forever and then there was a whump as the reserve fuel tanks for automobiles, aircraft and semi-tractors began to blow in succession like dominos falling—two-ton exploding dominos that shot flames and jet fuel 150 feet into the sky.

The exploding fuel farm illuminated the area like a noonday sun, and as the Stony Man hit team drew closer their NVDs were overworked by the brilliant ambient light. Almost in tandem James and McCarter stripped off their goggles and tossed them into the seat behind them.

"Stony Falcon to Wild Horse," Mott said, his voice alive with the energy of his adrenaline charge.

"Go ahead, Falcon," McCarter answered.

"Alpha phase completed. I'm going to rise to observation platform as my miniguns are low. All first-strike targets engaged. I can see Able operating through their sector."

"Good copy, Falcon," McCarter said.

Up ahead, the back gate to the compound loomed. It was a solid structure of heavy wood and wrought iron. Calvin James grasped the dual spade grips of the Mk 19 automatic 40 mm grenade launcher and centered them on the gate.

He fired an exploratory shell from the 32-round magazine, sending an M-430 high-explosives grenade toward the gate. The round arced out and exploded in the ground at the front of the gate, firing dirt into the air like lava from a volcano.

James lifted the vented muzzle on the Mk 19 and began to fire in earnest. He put the rounds dead center on his target and blew the gate into flaming splinters. Each explosion showed as a flash of burning light spilling around clouds of dark smoke, then the gate was gone and McCarter could see clearly into the interior of the al-Thani compound.

James fired a second triple-round burst through the fragmented gate to soften up any potential adversaries responding from beyond the wall. The M-430 rounds had kill zones of five meters and possessed anti-personnel capabilities out to fifteen meters.

His high-explosive rounds tore up the ground beyond the back gate, gouging deep ruts in the packed earth and spilling flames in wide arcs. Shrapnel spread out in patterns like an umbrella opening, and concussive hammers rippled out in successive overlapping waves.

"Phoenix, this is Falcon," Mott's voice broke over the earbuds in the two Stony Man operators' helmets.

"Go ahead, Falcon," McCarter answered.

"Inside the gate to your nine o'clock you have a response team orientated toward your position. I see long weapons and a RPG-7."

"Copy," McCarter said.

He wrenched the yoke of the speeding EFV to the side, looped out wide to the right and then brought the nose grille back around toward the gate. Now instead of breaching the threshold straight on through the smoking ruin of the gate, McCarter would guide the EFV through the breach at a diagonal line heading from outside right to inside left. This would have the effect of orientating the weapons of the EFV straight onto the knot of defenders pointed out by Charlie Mott's observation platform above the fray.

McCarter fought the bouncing vehicle back under control, then took up the pistol grip of the M-60D machine gun. Beside him Calvin James adjusted his grip on the handles of the Mk 19 automatic grenade launcher.

The EFV ate up the ground, clawing its way forward and spewing twin rooster tails of dirt behind its tracks. McCarter gunned the vehicle over a slight rocky berm and muscled the EFV into position. The angles lined up and a trajectory window appeared, which Calvin James immediately exploited.

The Mk 19 coughed a staccato pattern of high-explosive death. The weapon cycled with brute economy, throwing 40 mm shells downrange with devastating effect. The relatively slow moving projectiles shot out in front of the speeding EFV and landed hard. The explosions provided deadly, unforgiving cover as Phoenix Force crossed into the al-Thani compound.

CHAPTER TWENTY-TWO

Above Able Team, at the top of a sheer thirty-foot bluff, al-Thani's base commanded the landscape like a haphazard blend of freeway-off-ramp strip mall and fortified gun bunker. On the eastern side of the complex a single dirt road, graded and primed with gravel to facilitate truck traffic, wound from the swamp where Phoenix Force would attack and cut into the compound.

Two gun towers blocked in the compound. One sat above the gate entrance on the west side, while one was set midway down the razor-wire-topped chain-link fence. Each man inside the towers was armed with a drum-magazine-mounted M-249 Squad Automatic Weapon, powerful binoculars for the day and a searchlight similar to door-mounted police models for night sweeps.

Blancanales's and Schwarz's reconnaissance had revealed a less than professional standard of readiness along this stretch where FARC mercenaries patrolled separately from African al Qaeda terrorists.

Schwarz had scouted the wire from all points of the compass and discovered another factor that contributed to the lackadaisical nature of the guards: the northern and southern exposures had been purposefully seeded with a fast-growing, imported strain of bamboo out over the distance of an acre in a wide sweep. The bamboo garden was supplemented by small lawn sprinklers fed through irrigation pipes running out from the compound, making the thickets impenetrable walls. With the sheer bluff to the east, the compound security thought themselves well positioned.

That sense of confidence was about to be exploited.

While the other two members of the assault force provided security, Schwarz first covered their Zodiac CRRC in a patch of camonetting, then removed a Henriksen air-pressured grapnel launcher. The system had been adopted by JSOC forces after cross-training with Norwegian combat divers. The launcher was powered by pressured air for safety reasons, granting relatively low noise and allowing for easy loading with the same filling system used by diving oxygen bottles.

The grapnel was high-strength aluminum alloy capable of projection to a height of at least fifty yards and outward horizontally to a minimum of eighty yards while sustaining a weight of one ton once in place. A climbing-ladder attachment could be elevated to just over twenty yards by the handheld system, and it was in this configuration that Schwarz deployed the launcher.

The Army special operations veteran held up the launcher in both hands like a jackhammer being used on an overhead project and triggered the device. It made a heavy pneumatic cough, followed by the thunk of the release and the whirring sound as the line played out. The grapnel arced up and caught on the chain-link fence set back ten feet from the edge of the bluff face.

Schwarz dropped the sturdy launcher and hauled back on the line, ensuring it was seated. The tactical climbing ladder lay against the rock like stacked *H*s, dull in the low light. Carl Lyons stepped away from the wall and swept up the muzzle of his M-4 carbine.

"Clear," he snapped.

Schwarz scrambled up the ladder with the dexterity of a sailor in a ship's rigging. At the top of the ladder Schwarz moved into place and slid over the lip of the rock wall, pulling his M-4 carbine free. He tucked his broad, muscular frame into a tight curl down on one knee and swept the perimeter along the length of the fence. Carl Lyons quickly shrugged into his rifle sling and pushed it behind him before starting up the ladder, climbing fast.

The rungs of the tactical rope ladder sagged beneath each step the heavy Lyons took, and he was breathing sharply as he powered his way up, the muscles of his thighs and shoulders pumped with blood from the explosive effort of the short climb.

He went over the side and took up a defensive position. Below him Blancanales turned as he rose from his crouch, ducking under the sling of his own weapon. He took three bounding steps and pulled himself up onto the ladder, exactly duplicating the motions and efforts of his teammates.

On top of the bluff Lyons watched the rear line of the compound with a sharp eye. He saw Quonset hut warehouses of corrugated tin. A narrow walkway was formed between the back of the garages and storage buildings and the chain-link fence. Lush, fast-growing saw grass choked the back of the fence, interspersed with brightly colored paper, aluminum cans, plastic wrappers and other bits of assorted litter. The bright red eyes of a swamp rat winked out at him before the little creature turned on its tail and scurried off.

Carl Lyons heard the sound of muted voices coming

from the far side of the structures, and from off to the
south he heard the low hum of a generator. He was
sweating freely in the muggy air under his uniform
and body armor. Above them the cloud cover continued to obscure the sliver of the moon. A harsh male
voice muttered something in oily smooth Spanish, and
several others laughed in response. He looked at his
watch. In minutes Grimaldi would start his run with
the Comanche, attacking the freighter anchored just off
the island's quay. After that Phoenix Force would begin
its frontal assault. Once David McCarter and his boys
had drawn the defenders into a confrontation, Lyons
would lead Able Team into their unprotected rear and
close the jaws of the trap.

Schwarz shuffled forward, bringing his M-4 to bear
just opposite the tightly coordinated position of Lyons.
A second later the grapnel tangled in the top of the
chain-link fence sagged against the wire loops as the
heavy weight of Rosario Blancanales eased onto the
ladder.

After a moment the blocky shoulders of the big
Puerto Rican silhouetted themselves against the open
sky behind them. Blancanales scrambled over the top
and brought his weapon up, settling into position next to
Schwarz. He looked around carefully. From their current
position the flat roof of the northern gun tower could
be seen just over the tops of the compound structures.

The searchlight on the top of the gun tower rotated
in a counterclockwise motion, playing the narrow beam
of illumination first out across the swamp and then
back over the fenced compound. The team remained
motionless as the light skimmed through the air in a
blunt bar four feet above their heads. The searchlight
just caught the top of the chain-link fence and the

interlocked-diamond patterns of the wire loops briefly played across their faces in shadow.

Once it was past, Lyons turned toward Schwarz and nodded.

Schwarz rose in a crouch and jogged forward to the fence just off to the side from where the grapnel had landed. He went to a knee and let his carbine dangle from his shoulder strap as he pulled a pair of wire cutters with rubber grips from a pouch on his web belt. Lyons tapped Blancanales on the shoulder once.

The ex-Green Beret immediately rose up out of his crouch and shuffled forward, holding the M-4 carbine vertical by the pistol grip. He slid into place beside the hunched-over Schwarz and reached down to curl his fingers around the edge of the chain-link fence at the bottom near the ground. He waited for the first snick of the wire being cut and then began to peel the loose edge upward.

Working with the smooth economy of a Saville Row tailor, Schwarz cut a line up through the chain-link fence four feet high while Blancanales continued peeling back the lower edge. Holding one end of the fence up, he reached down and slapped Schwarz on the back.

Schwarz immediately replaced his wire cutters, took up his carbine and slid through the rent in the fence. Pushing himself through the loose thorns and paper trash, Schwarz shifted down the inside of the fence line about two yards to where the edge of one building ended and took up a defensive overwatch position flat on his stomach.

Blancanales turned and nodded, and Carl Lyons was through the fence in a flash, like a middle linebacker running a Hail Mary. He put his back to the wall next to Schwarz and kept his muzzle pointed in the opposite direction from his partner.

Blancanales looked toward the partially blocked gun tower, then got up and unhooked the aluminum alloy grapnel from the top of the fence and repositioned it through the wire at the bottom. He followed Lyons through the hole and then carefully pulled the bent section of chain-link fence back into place. He turned back toward Lyons and gave the dark-clad commando a thumbs-up.

Lyons nodded and carefully surveyed the scene.

His M-4 was nestled in his hands, up and close to his body, his finger on the trigger. Adrenaline smoothly leaked into his system, feeding his reflexes, senses and capabilities like high-octane fuel into a racing engine. He looked up and down the line of buildings. Each one had a single wooden door set in the center of the rear wall under a single, naked light bulb. Night bugs fluttered around the exposed illumination in twisting, darting clusters.

He heard the sound of footsteps coming down the narrow alley to the south of the building they were backed up against. He snapped his head to the side.

From the ground Schwarz held his arm up and closed his fist: the military hand-and-arm signal for "freeze in place." Able Team went still as statues. Lyons kept his own gaze locked on the prone Schwarz, the only unit member who could see the approaching threat.

The footfalls were obvious and unconcerned as they strolled between the buildings. Schwarz's reconnaissance hadn't revealed regular patrols inside this section of the compound wire; the approaching individual was a twist in their plans.

The footfalls approached the back of the building. A

bit of cloud above them parted for a breath and a pale
bone-colored light fell from a sliver of moon. Suddenly
the shadow of the approaching figure exploded out of
the gloom with distorted features and exaggerated size.
Lyons saw Schwarz's hand reach down and rest on the
handle of the double-bladed Gerber fighting knife he
kept sheathed on his waist. Reflexively, Lyons brought
his left hand to the butt of his silenced 9 mm pistol.

Gravel crunched loudly under a thick boot sole. The
clouds congealed above them again and the stretched-
out shadow of the figure disappeared. The FARC thug
stepped forward into view, a Remington 870 pump
shotgun hanging casually off one shoulder. He wore a
yellow straw cowboy hat and a checkered shirt tucked
into denim jeans. Besides the Remington, he wore a
heavy-caliber revolver on his hip.

The man stepped to the edge of the building opposite the Able Team infiltrators. He reached into a shirt
pocket and produced a pack of cigarettes. He slapped
one free, replaced the pack, then hunched his shoulders
around a silver lighter. Able Team remained motionless
as display-window mannequins. Schwarz held his knife
half drawn. Lyons remained statue-still with his hand
held carefully around the grip of his silenced pistol.

They heard the striker click and an orange reflec-
tion flared off the corrugated tin wall of the storage
building. The lighter snapped out and the man released
a cloud of cigarette smoke the color of milk. In a lazy
fashion the man opened the fly on his jeans and began
urinating on the wall in front of him.

When the man finished, he tucked himself away and
re-buttoned his pants. He took his cigarette out of his
mouth and scratched his forehead under the cowboy
hat with a blunt thumb. With a casual gesture he tucked

the butt of his cigarette into the corner of his mouth underneath a bristling mustache.

He shrugged the Remington 870 off his shoulder and tucked it under his arm like a man setting out for a stroll during duck-hunting season. He plucked the cigarette out of his mouth, dragged it across the wall of the building to extinguish it and dropped it to the ground. He ground the toe of a cowboy boot into the smoldering butt and then spit. Satisfied, he began to amble back down the narrow run toward the center of the compound.

Schwarz let his knife ease back into its sheath. Lyons exhaled and released the butt of his silenced pistol. He turned and caught Schwarz's eye and grinned. The other Able Team member returned the smile. Schwarz shook his head slowly in bemused wonder at the close call with the oblivious sentry.

Blancanales looked at Schwarz and held up an open hand. Is it clear?

Schwarz gave him a thumbs-up in answer and slowly rose off his belly. His clothes were covered in dust and grit in the smeary shape of a watercolor letter *T*. He maneuvered himself into a crouching overwatch position and aimed the barrel of the M-4 down the alley.

"Go," he urged.

Behind him the commando unit unfolded into motion. Like dark shadows they darted past Schwarz and across the opening. Lyons moved all the way down the back of the next building, where he dropped once again into a defensive crouch followed immediately by Rosario Blancanales. Once they were into position Schwarz hurriedly joined them, taking up the rear security position.

Twelve hours ago a shipment of crates large enough

to fill the rear of two five-ton military trucks had been unloaded by the emir's freighter under the watchful eye of the FARC soldiers and al-Thani's top three al Qaeda lieutenants. The size of plain wooden, rectangular crates had reminded the Farm's analysts suspiciously of long-range armament on the order of Scud or some compatible missiles.

This had raised the specter of chemical weapons. A hard probe had to be conducted before the components were destroyed to ensure it was done properly and deadly poison wasn't spread into innocent population centers.

On his initial probe Schwarz had hidden out on the flying deck of the emir's yacht and used a sniper scope to watch the FARC cohort unloading the boxes into the warehouse from the far southern corner of the compound.

The Able Team commandos were going to get some questions answered before they knocked over the first house of cards in al-Thani's personal neighborhood of make-believe.

Rosario Blancanales reached up with one long arm and unscrewed the light bulb directly above the back door to the last structure. From the other side of the buildings the team could hear the rumbling exhaust of a diesel engine as someone in the compound started up a truck.

Blancanales turned and threw the bulb into the choke of weeds against the chain-link fence and Hermann Schwarz knelt in front of the paint-chipped door while Lyons pulled security on the flanks. From inside his black khaki uniform shirt Schwarz pulled a lock-pick gun and carefully inserted the metal prongs into the door's lock housing after checking to make sure it was in fact secured.

He made a fist and squeezed the trigger lever against the handle. There was a muted metallic snap as the lock mechanism was manipulated, then the bolt clicked over and he turned the doorknob sharply to the right as far as it would rotate. He removed the lock-pick gun and secured it before looking up at Lyons and nodding.

The big ex-cop let his M-4 dangle muzzle down, cross body from the rifle's shoulder strap. He drew his silenced 9 mm pistol and stepped away from the building's back wall. Schwarz lifted his knee off the ground, resting in a crouch on the soles of both feet. Blancanales gathered himself and armed his own silenced pistol.

"Do it," the ex-Green Beret said.

Schwarz rose like a dancer and stepped to the side, pulling the building door open and pushing himself against the wall and out of the way. Blancanales shuffled forward, moving in a quick heel-toe shuffle. He darted into the room and immediately stepped to his left.

He was inside a warehouse with an exposed skeleton of metal alloy girders. Long, skinny fluorescent lights in banks of three burned overhead and spilled harsh illumination in oblong pools. Wooden crates and fifty-five-gallon industrial drums on shipping pallets were lined against the north and south walls and down the middle run of the building. A small electric forklift sat in a corner at the front, plugged into a wall outlet by a long orange extension cord. The front door of the storage building was a single framework wide enough for a truck to back in between and set into a track of overhead rollers. It was closed.

Blancanales put his back against the inside wall

and scanned his vectors with the silenced handgun. Right behind him Schwarz entered the building, his own weapon up. The Able Team commando mirrored Blancanales's choreography, stepping inside and to the right. He had barely set himself into position when Carl Lyons entered.

The Able Team leader rushed forward, snapping his weapon back and forth across a precise ellipse as he pushed deeper inside. He cleared out to the middle of the room and then went to one knee. Schwarz turned and pulled the door closed behind him, then took a knee beside the egress point and monitored the outside through a crack, his M-4 ready.

"In," he said.

"Clear," Lyons said from the middle of the building.

"Clear here," Rosario Blancanales said. "Let's do this, Gadgets," he said to Schwarz.

Immediately, Schwarz holstered his silenced pistol and pulled his knife from its belt sheath. The blade of the Gerber gleamed dully in the overhead lights. The claustrophobic structure smelled of sawdust, oil and body odor.

He eyeballed the crates and boxes of various sizes, looking for the ones he'd seen off-loaded at the docks. He moved to a five-foot-high stack set directly in front of Lyons's position toward the front of the warehouse.

He slid the tip of his blade into the jam of a crate and pried off the lid. The metal spikes released from the soft pine with a dull screech. Schwarz quickly circumnavigated the box, popping it open with efficient thrusts of his blade. Finished, he put the Gerber fighting knife away and pulled the lid free of the crate. He looked down and whistled softly.

"What about you, bro?" he asked Lyons. "You ever see a storage setup like this?"

Curious, Carl Lyons rose, pistol still held ready, and walked over to look into the box. His brow furrowed in consternation. He slowly shook his head. "No," he replied. "Mortar round. Obviously, but only five to a crate? And what's up with the warhead? And that plastic casing?"

Blancanales moved forward to look. He saw an 80 mm mortar round in a plastic sheath set in gray, cut-sponge packing material next to four identical munitions. The round was dark gray with a single black stripe just below the warhead.

"Chemical or biological?" he muttered. Then he shrugged and swung around toward Lyons. "What's your call on this? Can we blow them in place without spreading the shit in a cloud all up and down the coast?"

"High explosives will do just that. What we need is a thermobaric charge. We get a quick hot ignition, preferably shaped for an implosion, then the stuff will instantly cook to an inert format."

Blancanales nodded. "We pack our Semtex in an earmuff configuration and call on the Sea Witch?"

"It would work on this bunker," Schwarz said. "But without the earmuff configuration, the crap could spread on rocket impact."

"What if there were no real explosion?" Blancanales countered. "Just heat."

"It'd cook up into tar and we'd be good," Schwarz answered.

"Time we need for that, I wouldn't try it surreptitiously," Lyons said. "We get our cover blown with even one warehouse bunker left unchecked and we'd be screwed."

Schwarz nodded. "Ironman's right," he said. "Let's blow the known quantity, then call in light missile from the *Independence*."

"Adapt, improvise, overcome," Blancanales replied.

"Take down the compound and burn the lot?" Schwarz asked.

Blancanales nodded. "Seems the only way."

"Oh, *now* we're talking." Lyons grinned.

CHAPTER TWENTY-THREE

Schwarz worked quickly to place the Semtex shaped charges while Lyons covered the front of the bunker and Blancanales secured the rear. Outside a westerly breeze breathed in, stirring the weeds and trash, and bringing the smell of the ocean to Blancanales through the crack in the door.

Lyons's earbud gently purred. He lifted a thick finger and settled the device. His other hand kept his trigger finger in place. "This is Able. Go ahead," he murmured.

"Heads up. Stony Hawk is about to start run on maritime assets. Phoenix in place," Barbara Price said.

"Copy. We're good here," Lyons replied.

"Stony out." Price clicked off.

Lyons turned and looked back into the warehouse, making sure each man had understood the transmission. Schwarz slid a pencil-shaped timing rod into his carefully crafted shaped charge. He looked over and gave Blancanales a thumbs-up and nodded. Schwarz shifted down the line of biohazard motors and nodded once, as well.

Lyons flashed him an okay sign from the front of the warehouse. Everything was rolling forward on a smooth track. No problem yet, he decided.

Then he heard the approaching helicopter through the opening in the door. At the door Rosario Blancanales watched a hostile helicopter suddenly lift off a pad and swing out, coming back in from the west, a searchlight slung under its belly like a cyclopean eye. The searchlight spun and rotated as the helicopter approached, the light playing across the swamp floor like the gaze of a hungry predator. His mind went instantly to their vehicle parked at the bottom of the cliff by the beach. The camouflage netting was only a superficial precaution and he didn't think it would hold up to sustained scrutiny.

"Heads up, boys," he said. The heads of the teammates turned in his direction. "We got a chopper running down our alley from the west right now. Let's get this show started."

He turned and noted the progress the unit was making, then returned his focus to the approaching helicopter. He saw it start to fan out away from its linear approach and begin to track back and forth across the swamp in a zigzag pattern. He didn't like what he was seeing at all.

OUT ON THE OCEAN the captain of the *Independence* put his gunner mate crewmembers into motion. The four men sprang into action. Three of them moved forward and removed the front cargo hatch cover while the fourth directed the hydraulics control from the flying deck of the littoral combat ship.

An M-270 multilaunch rocket system lifted smoothly from the hold and rose up to lock into position. The system was capable of launching twelve guided munition rockets in less than sixty seconds. Each XM31 solid-fuel rocket was 3.94 meters in length and 227 mm in caliber. GPS guided, the warhead could deliver two-hundred-pound unitary HE rounds over twenty-eight miles.

The fire team finished prepping the system for launch and then gave the high sign to the OIC on the bridge, who in turn notified the captain that they were ready for action on his command.

Outside from the north they heard Jack Grimaldi open up on the freighter from the weapons platform of the Comanche helicopter. The final assault had begun.

"I'VE GOT MOVEMENT on the outside to the front!" Carl Lyons reported.

In the next moment the rest of the team could hear the rumble of a big diesel engine coming from outside the front of the bunker unit. Rosario Blancanales let the back door close and slid behind the concealment of a row of pallets. Carl Lyons backed up to the cover of a long line of fifty-five-gallon drums, his silenced pistol never wavering from the door.

Hermann Schwarz coolly continued to prepare the last shaped charge. They heard the sound of vehicle doors slamming and the excited calls of men in Spanish. There was the loud hiss of an airbrake and then of an idling engine from the other side of the bunker's front door.

Schwarz carefully placed the earmuff-configured Semtex charge. The lock on the sliding door was popped open and the metallic snap of the release echoed through the inside of the bunker. Schwarz primed the timing pencil. The door began to rumble as it slid along its track runner and the sound of the idling truck engine grew louder as the entrance slid open.

The shadowed form of a stocky man in a cowboy

hat with the familiar Remington 870 shotgun over one shoulder was silhouetted in the opening. The guard began pushing the heavy metal door to one side. The brake lights on the passenger side of the vehicle appeared, glowing red.

Schwarz somersaulted backward over his shoulder behind a stack of crates and froze in the shadow. His eyes darted around, seeking out the other members of his team. He couldn't find Blancanales from his location, but he could see Carl Lyons behind an oil drum. Lyon's silenced 9 mm pistol was up and ready as the FARC narco-soldier finished pushing the door open.

"Más rápido," the man snapped.

Schwarz heard the truck driver respond and then the grinding of gears. The old U.S. Army deuce-and-a-half truck began to back into the storage building, its rear gate already down and its cargo area covered by an OD-green canvas tarp. The vaquero with the pump shotgun walked backward, guiding the driver, who watched his hand-and-arm signals in the big sideview mirror on his door.

A yard from the boxes of mortar rounds Able Team unit had just finished priming for detonation, the vaquero halted the truck by closing his fist. The air brakes on the truck again hissed. The driver swung open his door and dropped down inside the Quonset hut bunker. He wore a checkered flannel shirt like the first man and dirty blue jeans tucked into brown Cochran leather work boots. He wore a battered baseball hat and his square face was framed by a close-trimmed beard. A S&W Model 696 .44-caliber 5-shot revolver rode in a black nylon holster on his hip.

From the passenger seat of the truck cab a third man opened the door and hopped out. A cigarette was tucked haphazardly into the corner of his mouth, the cherry gleaming red, the brown smoke almost invisible in the dim light.

He wore a blue chambray work shirt and had pulled his long black hair back in a tight ponytail. In the low light Hermann Schwarz could see the gleam of his gold teeth. The outline of a pack of cigarettes was readily evident in the chest pocket of his shirt, and an automatic pistol was tucked into the front of his jeans. A large clasp knife rode in a leather sheath on his belt.

Schwarz blinked and when he opened his eyes again Carl Lyons had appeared like a ghost over the man's shoulder. Schwarz narrowed his eyes, tense as Lyons's hand suddenly appeared from behind the truck passenger's back and covered his gold-toothed mouth, smothering any cry and knocking the cigarette loose. Schwarz saw the man's eyes suddenly grow wide in surprise then his facial features twisted into pain as Lyons drove the point of his Gerber fighting knife into the man's kidney. Suddenly the bloody blade appeared and carved a second smile in the taut muscles of the man's neck.

Blood turned the color of obsidian in the low light gushed from the long, clean laceration and spilled down the front of the FARC drug runner's shirt. It stained the shirt dark as the man's knees buckled and he fell forward. The spilling blood splashed down and extinguished the smoldering cigarette with an almost audible hiss. Lyons carefully eased the man to the concrete floor and the body hung as limp as a rag doll in the big American commando's grip.

The truck driver began walking down the length of his vehicle. Behind him the muzzle of Lyons's pistol tracked his every step as the Able Team leader retreated into shadows at an obtuse angle. At the rear of the truck Schwarz caught a flash of motion out of the corner of his eye. He saw Rosario Blancanales silently stalking forward toward the vaquero next to the demo-packed crates. A Gerber fighting knife of his own was naked in his fist.

The vaquero walked up to the first crate and looked down. Schwarz kept his finger on the trigger of his M-4. The Colombian terrorist frowned and Schwarz knew he'd seen the earmuff charges. Suddenly the man's eyes went wide with understanding and he turned to call out to the driver coming down the side of the truck.

From outside across the compound the laser-guided bombs began to fall and the shock waves traveled across the compound, shaking the earth in heavy tremors.

Stunned and shocked, the man found Rosario Blancanales standing in front of him. The vaquero opened his mouth and his hands clawed for his shouldered weapon. Blancanales pounced forward. His right hand sprang out, recoiled and sprang out again. He struck throat, heart and diaphragm in three quick heartbeats. He first slashed the man's upraised wrist, then stabbed his biceps on the opposite arm, smoothly crippling his ability to defend himself. Blood geysered out under the fury of his rapid, multiple attacks. The man tried to call out but found his larynx savagely ruined. He gagged and sagged to his knees, and with two quick thrusts Rosario laid the terrorist's neck open on either side.

The man's eyes rolled up in his head and he fell over.

The truck driver saw the vaquero's outflung arm as he approached the rear of the truck.

"¿Lo que es hasta?" the man called out. His hand went reflexively to the butt of the S&W Model 696 on

his hip. He saw blood spilling in a dark rush across the dusty concrete floor.

Carl Lyons quickly executed his own personal version of the hearts and minds philosophy: two to the heart and one to the mind.

The 9 mm pistol made a triple cough. Two red gouges appeared in the truck driver's back just below his shoulder blades. The man gasped in shock and went to his knees, and the third Parabellum round caught him in the top of the head and lifted a broken chunk clear of the scalp. The man fell forward and hit the concrete with a wet, muffled slap.

Rosario Blancanales rushed forward, his M-4 up on his shoulder to cover the opening at the front of the bunker. Outside the searchlight-equipped helicopter was directly overhead. A beam of sharp white light caught the hood of the truck and illuminated it before sliding off and skipping across the compound.

"We've got to take the towers out," Blancanales said. "Once those are down we can shoot and scoot around, mopping up."

"We could blow these charges," Lyons offered, "then call in the rockets. As far as we know that batch of mortars was the only shipment of NBC weapons this crew has. Risky, but I think the odds bear me out."

"Let's save the call for fire as an ace in the hole," Blancanales countered. "We got a shit storm of ordnance coming down already!"

"Nothing to it but to do it," Lyons agreed.

Blancanales looked out the open door to the storage unit from behind the cover of the truck. He tried to ascertain the positions of the rest of the compound personnel but his angle restricted his view.

Overhead the helicopter had begun moving out

from the center of the compound in growing circles, its searchlight sweeping across the ground. Through the open door the team could hear rough male voices talking back and forth to each other and they knew they could not hope to delay for very long.

"There's no way around it," Lyons said. "We're too close to complete compromise. But we can't roll out of here without securing the NBC threat. Not with Phoenix going inside the main house to try for a snatch. We've got to check each one of these warehouses for duplicates of those mortars before we can risk calling in the rockets."

"Plan?" Blancanales asked.

"You and Hermann enter the warehouses. He knows the most about the packaging. I'll provide overwatch on the compound for your entries. We'll try to take out the towers and hold off the guards." He frowned and looked up, clearly troubled. "And the helicopter, Mott's going to be on scene in 2.2 seconds. Once we've secured the storage units we can detonate the thermobaric charges and call in a rocket barrage from the *Independence*."

"What if there's a whole bunch more of them?" Schwarz asked.

Blancanales pointed with a thick finger out the open door. "Fuel depot. We cover 'em with gas and diesel so that when the HE rounds hit we get a burn factor."

Schwarz nodded his head vigorously, face a deadpan flat affect. "Good. I like it. Completely ad hoc and seat of the pants. This is most definitely how we roll."

Blancanales smiled and held up one massive fist. Schwarz returned the grin and reached out to tap knuckles with his old friend.

"If you two are through flirting," Lyons interrupted, "I think we've got some people to kill."

"I heard that," Schwarz said. His teeth were a sharp gleam in the gloom as he smiled.

McCARTER COULD JUST make out the knot of armed figures in the light of the burning fires. Smoke hung thick as London fog between the walls of the structure compound and obscured the area from the sky. Both Charlie Mott and the camera eye of the Reaper UAV could only make out the unfolding action in random, patchy glimpses.

McCarter shouted his alert to Calvin James and triggered the M-60 machine gun mounted in front of him. The heavy 7.62 mm slugs lanced out before the EFV and sliced into the knot of confused figures on flat, smooth rails of flight.

The first bullet struck the lead gunman low in the stomach where the thirty-two-foot length of the human intestine rested like a water hose packed accordion fashion on the back of a fire truck. The round struck with the force of a baseball bat and penetrated the soft flesh and viscera without slowing.

The bullet gored through the man's guts, tearing a channel large enough to stick a fist through as it cut its way out of the body, slicing through the spleen in the process. The man folded like a lawn chair, gasping at the sudden agony, and a wave of bullets tore his screaming face from his body.

Calvin James saw a black Hummer pull out from around the back of a row of Quonset huts. James shifted the blunt muzzle of the 40 mm grenade launcher to face the vehicle, its occupants hidden behind a deeply tinted windshield.

James pulled the trigger as the truck gunned toward him. The first 40 mm HE round arched over the vehicle roof and struck the ground well behind the Hummer, exploding in a fiery ball and rain of steel shrapnel. James lowered his sights by half an inch and put two shots straight into the big truck.

The first round punched through the windshield and filled the cab with a sudden flash of fire that blew out the side windows and rear windshield. The second round struck the grille of the workhorse and detonated up against the big-block engine. Instantly the engine fluids caught fire as the vehicle was driven off to one side by the force of the explosion.

The hungry flames sped along melting lines toward the gas tank, and the whump of the fifty-gallon container going up tripped hard on the heels of the first explosion. The Hummer lifted into the air, propelled on an orange tower of flame like a rocket leaving the launch pad. It spun like a burning pinwheel and then fell.

The mangled frame tumbled back to the ground and bounced with crushing force, causing tendrils of flame to spread out across the ground in burning spines of fire. James turned the Mk 19 on its axis and lobbed two rounds at the group of fighters McCarter was engaging with his M-60 machine gun.

McCarter's fire scythed into the formation, cutting them off at the legs on one sweep of a Z-pattern burst, then finishing them off with the second pass. Two grenades slammed into their midst and exploded, tossing bodies into the air like parade confetti. McCarter gunned the patrol vehicle forward, skirting a low ornate iron fence running around a series of aluminum containers used to store potable water.

He saw a line of burning tent houses running between the structure and airstrip. He looked overhead but couldn't see Charlie Mott's Little Bird. He made to initiate radio contact but was suddenly taken under fire.

A stream of bullets cut toward him from a concrete utility house just behind him. The rounds struck the back of the EFV and hacked apart equipment boxes. The bullets ricocheted wildly and cut the air immediately between the two men.

"Christ!" James shouted.

Instinctively, McCarter started to cut to his right and face the attack but realized just as quickly that such a maneuver would leave Calvin James open to fire from that side and unable to use the grenade launcher as it was currently mounted.

McCarter slammed on the brakes, leaving the rear of the EFV orientated toward the utility shed as more rounds burned around him. James tripped his trigger and lobbed two 40 mm spheres into the attacker, vaporizing him in a quick, hot flash.

"Phoenix, we are here!" the ex-SAS member yelled. "Deploy, deploy, deploy!"

CHAPTER TWENTY-FOUR

The back ramp of the EFV began to lower and Gary Manning and T. J. Hawkins scrambled out in one direction, toward the main compound structure while Rafael Encizo, armed with a .50-caliber sniper rifle, peeled off in the opposite direction.

As he bailed out of the vehicle, snatching up his M-4/M-203, Hawkins threw himself sideways across the seats to avoid the angle of fire, and green tracer rounds tore apart the steering wheel inches from his head.

Manning flopped out of the EFV and hit the ground on his belly. He raised his head to look for a target over the knobby rear track of the APC. Instantly bullets blew by him on all sides. He felt a slap and a sting on his right shoulder and something punched him in the head above his ear.

He felt hot blood pour down the side of his face and soak the sleeve of his uniform blouse. He ducked, his cheek resting on the dirty tread of the rubber traction plate on the linked track of the EFV. He felt the rough impact as more bullets slammed home into the solid rubber and thick steel links. He brought his M-4/M-203 around the corner of the thick tire and angled its fire by estimation.

His finger found the metal trigger behind the shotgun breech of the attached grenade launcher and pulled it.

The weapon recoiled in his hands with the solid kick of a .12-gauge shotgun. He heard the round land and explode, and he risked a peek around the tire. He saw earth falling in an avalanche along with pieces of a deck chair, about four feet in front of the gunman's position behind the concrete-block utility house.

Manning threw his carbine's collapsible stock to his shoulder and began pouring fire around the building, keeping the rifleman pinned down. His bullets knocked chunks off the square building and skipped across the concrete deck encircling the water tubs. The open grass lawn began to burn.

"Get the three-twelve up!" Manning shouted.

Hawkins scrambled over the bullet-ripped EFV seats and brought the XM-312 back on line. The black bungee tie-down shot out of the EFV like a rubber band and landed on the ground yards away. Hawkins turned the heavy machine gun in a tight traverse and unloaded on the pool house.

At the front of the vehicle both James and McCarter were heavily engaged suppressing fire from that front. The Phoenix Force element was under fire from three sides of the compass now.

The .50-caliber machine gun manned by Hawkins blew the concrete-block-and-rebar structure to dust. The rounds smacked hard into the building, punching through the walls without slowing. Baseball-size chunks of mortar disintegrated, leaving gaping holes shot throughout the structure. Manning saw a figure, shirtless and barefoot, wearing only pants, spin wildly out from the maintenance shed.

The man was tossed bleeding into the potable water tub, where he hung suspended in the water, floating face-down and turning the blue reclaimed liquid darkly scarlet. Manning rose swiftly and spoke into his throat mic.

"Falcon, this is Phoenix Bravo," he said. "You have our twenty?"

"Copy. I have you by the water tanks but observation is spotty," Mott replied. "You want extraction? It's a hornet's nest."

"Negative. Bravo Two and I will do target site assessment prior to extraction."

"Copy. I'll try to cover your back when you go in, but the smoke is bad."

"Copy. Understood. Out," Manning finished.

Hawkins dropped out of the EFV. In addition to his M-4 he armed himself with a folding-stock Remington 870 pump-action shotgun, a Glock 18 pistol capable of 3-round bursts and a 10 mm Glock 17, as well as the grenades, knives and equipment already secured to his web gear.

"Let's go make sure no one misses the party," Manning said.

Hawkins nodded once. "Let's go," he said.

"Roll, McCarter," Manning yelled, and the EFV jumped forward, rolling toward where two more enemy APCs had raced out of a burning garage to join the battle.

The two commandos cut across a strip of neglected lawn separating the rear pool complex from the concrete apron and steps at the back of the now collapsed and burning main structure. It was becoming immediately clear as they navigated the compound grounds that intelligence gathered on site by Blancanales and Schwarz had been too rushed, leaving their estimates dramatically incorrect about the number of enemy combatants contained in the compound.

After the overwhelming force and violence of the initial strike, resistance should have been sporadic and ill coordinated. Command and communications centers, staging areas and arsenals had all been struck and reduced to rubble. Despite this, there were so many uninjured gunmen sweeping the structure complex that it was very apparent that there had been a vastly greater number of paramilitary agents than reported.

Manning and Hawkins found themselves in an anthill of running, screaming men calling out to each other in an attempt to reorganize and repel the threat. Machinegun teams were set up rapidly and engaged Charlie Mott in standoff duels, forcing the helicopter pilot to zip in and out of range as he took gun runs at multiple knots of fighters. McCarter and James in the EFV had not stopped firing their weapons since the raid had begun, and now there were more targets than ever.

Moving in a precise drill, the duo moved under fire toward the structure. They approached a long series of veranda doors issuing smoke through the blown-out glass. They moved in a bounding overwatch, modified to exploit speed, but basically consisting of one commando holding security while the next leapfrogged forward to the next point of offered cover.

Twice their path was cut by armed men rushing to help engage the swooping Little Bird. The first time Hawkins took a shirtless man down with a short burst, followed up immediately by Manning's finishing shot to the head. The second time a shoeless, bearded fighter with the build of a professional bodybuilder sprinted around a tight cluster of native Brazilian hazelnut trees with a drum-fed AKM in his massive fists.

Both Phoenix commandos turned and fired simultaneously from the hip without breaking stride. The two-angled fire cut the giant of a man into ribbons and knocked him back among the tangled stand of trees.

As Manning and Hawkins ran they could hear people screaming from around the compound, and once they heard a long ragged machine-gun burst answered immediately by Charlie Mott's M-134 minigun. At one point an RPK-armed African terrorist popped around the corner only to have his head vaporized by a single well-placed shot by Encizo in his sniper hide.

Manning cleared the deck over a column of concrete pillars supporting a low, wide stone rail encircling the patio. The explosive force of the GBU-12s had cracked and pitted its surface but failed to break the stone railing.

Manning landed on plain terra-cotta tile, waves of heat from the burning building washing over him and casting weird shadows close around him. He saw a flat stone bench and took up a position behind it, going down to one knee. He scanned the long line of patio doors with his main weapon while Hawkins bounded forward.

Hawkins passed Manning's hasty fighting position in a rush and put his back to a narrow strip of wall set between two ruined patio doors. He kept his weapon at port arms and turned his head toward the opening beside him. From inside the dark structure flames danced in a wild riot.

The ex-Ranger nodded sharply, and Manning rose in one swift motion, bringing the buttstock of his M-4 up to his shoulder as he breached the opening. He shuffled past Hawkins, sweeping his weapon in tight, predetermined patterns as he entered the building.

Hawkins folded in behind him, deploying his weapon to cover the areas opposite Manning's pattern. It felt as if they had rushed headlong into a burning oven. Heavy tapestries, Persian rugs and silk curtains all burned bright and hot. Smoke clung to the ceiling and filled the room to a height of five feet, forcing the men to crouch below the noxious cover.

In a far corner the two men saw a sprawling T-shaped stair of sturdy, unidentifiable wood now smoldering in the heat. A wide-open floor plan accentuated groupings of office furniture clustered together.

Slowly the two men turned so that their backs were to each other, their weapon muzzles tracking through the smoke and uncertain light. Smoke choked their lungs and stung their eyes. They saw the inert shape of several bodies cast about the room among the splinters of shattered furniture. One body lay sprawled on the smoldering staircase, hands outflung and blood pouring down the steps like stream water cascading over rocks.

Manning moved slowly through the burning wreckage, approaching twisted bodies and searching the bruised and bloody faces for traces of recognition. Manning searched the dead for the faces of his enemy's leadership cadre, for the emir or the leader of al Qaeda in Africa. Around him the heat grew more intense and the smoke billowed thicker. Hawkins moved with the same quick, methodical efficiency, checking the bodies as they vectored in toward the stairs.

Manning sensed more than saw the motion from the top of the smoldering staircase. He barked a warning even as he pivoted at the hips and fired from the waist. His M-4 lit up in his hands and his bullets streamed across the room in curtain of lead.

Manning's 5.56 mm rounds chewed into the staircase and snapped railings into splinters as he sprayed the second landing. One of his rounds struck the gunman high in the abdomen, just under the xiphoid process in the solar plexus. The Teflon-coated high-velocity round speared up through the smooth muscles of the diaphragm, sliced open the bottom of the lungs and cored out the left atrium of the gunman's pounding heart. Bright scarlet blood squirted like water from a faucet as the target staggered backward.

The figure, indistinct in the smoke, triggered a burst that hammered into the steps before pitching forward and striking the staircase. The faceless gunman tumbled, limbs loose, and his head made a distinct thumping sound as it bounced off each individual step on the way down, leaving black smears of blood on the woodgrain as it passed.

Manning sprang forward, heading fast for the stairs. Hawkins spun a tight 180-degrees to cover their six o'clock as he edged out to follow Manning. He saw silhouettes outside through the blown-out frames of the patio doors and let loose with a wall of lead in a sloppy figure-8 pattern.

One shadow fell sprawling across the concrete divider and the rest of the silhouettes scattered in response to Hawkins's fusillade. Hawkins danced sideways, found the bottom of the stairs and started to back up. Above him he heard Manning curse and then the Canadian's weapon blazed.

To Hawkins's left a figure reeled back from a window. Another came to take its place, the star-pattern burst illuminating a manically hate-twisted face of strong Middle Eastern features. The Phoenix Force commando put a 3-round burst into his head from across the burning room and the man fell away.

"Let's go!" Manning shouted.

He let loose with a long burst of harassing fire aimed at the line of French doors facing out to the rear patios and lawns as Hawkins spun on his heel and pounded up the steps past Manning. Outside, behind the cover of the concrete pillared railing, an enemy combatant popped up from his crouch, the distinctive outline of an RPG-7 perched on his shoulder.

Down on one knee, Manning fired an instinctive burst, but the shoulder-mounted tube spit flame in a plume from the rear of the weapon and the rocket shot out and into the already devastated house. Manning turned and dived up the stairs as the rocket crossed the big room below him and struck the staircase.

The warhead detonated on impact and Manning shuddered under the force and heat, but the angle of the RPG had been off and the construction of the staircase itself channeled most of the blast force downward and away from where Manning lay sprawled. Enough force surged upward to send Manning reeling even as he huddled against the blast. He tucked into a protective ball and absorbed the blunt waves.

He lifted his head and saw Hawkins standing above him, feet spread wide for support as he fired in short bursts of savage, accurate fire. Manning lifted his M-4 and the assault carbine came apart in his hands. He flung the broken pieces away in disgust and felt his wrist burn and his hand go slick with spilling blood.

He ignored the hot, sticky feeling of the blood and cleared his Beretta 92F from its underarm sling. He pushed himself up and turned over as Hawkins began to engage more targets. As he twisted he saw something move from the hallway just past the open landing behind his fellow Stony Man operator.

Manning extended his arm with sharp reflexes and

stroked the trigger on the Beretta autopistol. A 3-round 9 mm Parabellum burst struck the creeping enemy in a tight triangle grouping high in the chest, just below the throat.

The narco-terrorist's breastbone cracked under the pressure and either insertion point of the sternocleido-mastoid neck muscles were sheared loose from the collarbone. The back of the target's neck burst outward in a spray of crimson and pink as the 9 mm rounds burrowed their way clear.

"Go! Go!" Hawkins shouted.

The tall Phoenix Force commando swept his M-4 back and forth in covering fire as Manning scrambled past him to claim the high ground. Manning pushed himself off the stairs and onto the second floor. Stepping over the bloody corpse of his target, he turned and began to aim and fire the Beretta in tight bursts.

Under his covering fire Hawkins wheeled on his heel and bounded up the stairs past Manning. At the top of the landing he threw himself down and took aim through the staircase railing to engage targets below him in the open great room.

From their superior position the two Stony Man warriors rained death down on their enemies.

ABLE TEAM ENTERED the maelstrom, quickly cutting back through the storage bunker toward the door where they had made their entrance. Blancanales checked out through the crack in the door, saw no one and pushed past. He flipped around the door and took up a knee, weapon up and pointed down the narrow, weed-choked run formed by the back of the storage units and chain-link fence.

Behind him the other two members of Able Team

surged out of the doorway in linear procession and squatted next to the building while the back door swung closed. Blancanales frowned. The helicopter was growing louder, but the building blocked it from his view. If the pilot lifted the chopper straight up for elevation the entire compound would be spread out below him like a chessboard and the infiltrators would have no place to hide.

Blancanales risked a look around the corner of the building and down the alley toward the center of the compound. He saw several men armed with the 870 Remington shotguns go rushing past the opening on the far end. Light stabbed at his eye and he looked up to see the helicopter sweeping in from the west.

Blancanales spun and caught Schwarz's eye.

"We're done for. Blow it!" he snarled.

Rosario Blancanales threw himself back around the corner of the building as the helicopter raced toward the fire team's position. Behind him Carl Lyons stepped away from the shelter of the building wall and threw the butt of his M-4 carbine to his shoulder. The sound of the helicopter rushing down on them was deafening, and the craft was barely thirty feet off the deck as it approached. A detached part of Blancanales's mind identified the hovering platform as an OH-58D Kiowa Warrior light reconnaissance and attack helicopter.

Blancanales saw the bright, hard beam of the searchlight flicker upward from the belly and move directly toward him. He triggered a 3-round burst from his carbine and blew out the light. A hail of bullets rushed out in answer from the copilot seat to buzz around the Puerto Rican commando like angry hornets.

Behind him Schwarz pulled out the digital signal detonator and bypassed the timing pencils on his shaped charges. The explosion was immediate and overwhelming. The building's back door was blown off its frame and thrown into the fence, followed instantly by a jet of flame like dragon's breath. There was a near instantaneous whump as the fuel cells on the old truck inside caught and went up. The building shuddered and the roof ripped free of its seams.

Shock waves rolled into the men of the Stony Man fire team and staggered them. For a second the concussive force made it seem as if cotton balls had been stuffed into their ears. Screaming shrapnel from the curved roof burst forth as ammunition stores began exploding inside.

CHAPTER TWENTY-FIVE

The Kiowa shuddered under the impact, then canted hard to the side as the pilot fought the sudden, stunning shock. The 650 hsp Allison C30R engine screamed in protest, but it was futile. The spinning rotors of the low-flying aircraft tipped and caught the top of a building. The ripple of the impact shivered back up through the blades and vibrated into the body of the Kiowa. The chopper lurched again, and then listed nose first into the storage unit.

A ball of fire lit up the Caribbean night like a Roman candle, and burning fuel fell in a jellied, flaming rain. Rosario Blancanales was thrown to the ground. He tucked his carbine in close and prepared to move.

"We have to get the towers!" he shouted over his shoulder.

"I'll do it!" Lyons shouted back before folding around the corner of the burning building and sprinting down the narrow run between the two buildings.

A FARC soldier came around the corner, weapon up, and Lyons shot him in the head from twenty-five yards. The man stumbled backward from the impact of the high-velocity rounds and went down, his Remington 870 shotgun tumbling out of his hands and onto the ground. Lyons continued forward.

Behind him Schwarz reached down and put a hand under Blancanales's shoulder and helped the other man rise to his feet. They stumbled, found their footing and began racing forward. The pair moved past the blazing wreckage of the helicopter and Schwarz saw one of the pilots writhing in his seat restraints as he was burned alive.

The sickly sweet smell of burning flesh mixed with the toxic stench of aviation fuel and the man's screams became as piercing as a siren. Schwarz granted him mercy with a double tap of 5.56 mm bullets from his M-4 carbine.

At the far end of the back run, near the north fence line, two vaqueros appeared. One wielded what seemed to be the standard-issue Remington 870 shotgun and the other, perhaps a supervisor or sergeant of some sort, carried a mini-Uzi submachine pistol.

"¡Hijo de mil putas!" the Uzi-gunner shouted, and pointed.

"¡Cantamañanas!" Schwarz snarled across the distance.

Both groups fired their weapons.

Schwarz and Blancanales went down to one knee, sweeping their rifle muzzles up and triggering bursts with simultaneous timing. The 870 jumped and boomed in the shotgunner's hands and the mini-Uzi chattered its own response. Schwarz felt buckshot pellets rip at his clothes and heard Blancanales cry out in surprised pain as some of the shotgun spread caught him, as well.

Schwarz's M-4 burst struck the shotgun-toting-vaquero center mass, one of his rounds burning into the breech of the Remington and snatching it from the man's hands as four more 5.56 mm rounds burrowed into his chest and shredded his lungs.

The supervisor with the mini-Uzi shifted his fire, but his excitement had caused him to let the recoil lift the muzzle of his weapon. Schwarz hissed against the wound in his side and gunned the man down. The mini-Uzi dropped as the dead man spun and landed face-first on the still leaking body of his partner.

Schwarz turned toward Blancanales. Behind them they could hear Carl Lyons firing his weapon toward the center of the compound. Schwarz looked down at the growing stain of red spilling across the side of the other man's fatigue shirt.

"How bad?" Schwarz demanded.

Blancanales shook his head fiercely. "I'm fine. Let's roll," he said, and pushed himself up.

With weapons up they proceeded toward the fire storage unit beyond the burning wreckage of the helicopter. The flames cast behind them threw distorted shadows on the wall. Schwarz went to one knee again as Blancanales ducked back around the corner of the building as the west and north towers pinned him under a brutal cross fire. Red tracer rounds knifed through the air in brilliant tracks of rigid illumination. FARC drug soldiers began advancing on Blancanales's position under the cover fire, adding the staccato booming of their Remington 870 shotguns to the raucous din.

From across the narrow breezeway Lyons fired into the compound. "Cover me while I move!" he ordered.

Blancanales shifted automatically and began raking the muzzle of his M-4 back and forth in a sloppy Z pattern, triggering repeated 3-round bursts. Lyons fired two shots at the north tower and saw sparks arc off the metal safety railing in front of the SAW gunner. Surprised, the man stopped firing and jumped back.

Lyons charged forward, firing from the hip as he ran. Blancanales could see he was running for the cover of a GP medium forklift. As he sprinted a vaquero appeared from behind the rear of the utility vehicle, a mini-Uzi machine pistol chattering and bucking in his hands. A crumpled straw cowboy hat was kicked back far on his head, and a ZZ Top-style beard reached down to his chest.

Lyons caught the man first with his fire and drove the Colombian back into the knobby rubber tires of the industrial forklift. The man staggered, patches of pink and red blossoming like flowers on his chest under a series of thick gold chains.

As the man stumbled Lyons finished his sprint and reached the dying man, driving the butt of his weapon into the side of his head and knocking him down. Rosario Blancanales put his hard sights on the north tower gunner, who had recovered from his close call and was now spraying the forklift with a vengeance. Blancanales pulled his first shot left but his next burst caught the man center mass and drove him back against the sliding door of the tower housing.

The SAW gunner tumbled backward and dropped his weapon to the grating before sliding down slowly, leaving blood smeared behind him on the metal door. Blancanales turned and fired at a FARC vaquero who had gotten too close, driving the man back behind the cover of a random line of fifty-five-gallon drums.

Blancanales did a snap check on Lyons just as the Able Team warrior popped up out of a crouch and stepped from behind the cover of the forklift. He saw the egg-shape sphere leave the ex-LAPD detective's hand like a shotput. He visually traced its arc as it covered thirty yards and bounced off a concrete apron around a set of three fuel pumps and rolled under a black Lexus SUV parked there.

"Jesus—" Blancanales swore.

The ex-Green Beret twisted away and threw himself backward from the hellfire he knew was coming. There was the hard, sharp boom of the grenade going off followed by the whump of the luxury SUV's fuel tanks igniting up. The night was illuminated by a glare every bit as bright as when the helicopter had exploded.

Blancanales felt a wave of heat wash into him like a Santa Ana and in a sudden, second-long vacuum of sound he heard a man screaming in agony. Stony Man's warriors had brought flaming justice to the Caribbean swamp.

All of this paled with what came hard on the heels of the first explosion a heartbeat later. The high-explosive grenade shredded the hose lines to the free-standing fuel pumps and mangled the pump housings themselves. Fuel spilled out like a river rushing over a waterfall and the torrent was instantly ignited. The flames spread at the speed of breath and the massive reservoirs under the fueling station were ignited. The explosion ripped the ground like a JDAM bunker buster bomb falling from the belly of a B-52.

ON THE OVERSIZE plasma screen at Stony Man Farm, the Caribbean night lit up like an erupting volcano as the fuel cells under the gas pumps exploded. The images from the circling drones were digital clear and digital sharp. The rolling column of bright orange flame and thick black smoke filled the screen's parameters completely.

"That Ironman," Kurtzman said dryly. "He makes a big splash."

On the screen they saw Rosario Blancanales and Carl Lyons cross streams of autofire to scythe a gun tower sentry out of his post. Price nodded once then spoke into her mic.

"*Independence,*" she said, switching channels.

"Go for *Independence*," the tech answered.

"Is your payload prepped?"

"Affirmative."

"Copy. Stand by for signal."

Barbara Price switched over to the open operational channel. "Ground Element," she said. "Confirm you are aware of incoming."

"Copy. Folding back now," Blancanales answered immediately. The sound of weapons fire was clearly audible in the background.

Blancanales switched over to his tactical channel and his voice filled the earbuds of the Stony Man fire team. "Fall back to exfiltration point," he said. "We've got too many vaqueros rolling on our site to complete this as planned."

"Copy," Carl Lyons answered.

"Copy," Schwarz echoed.

Blancanales began falling back. He triggered four 3-round bursts at some of the men advancing on his position, forcing them to scatter for cover. Bullets whizzed through the air around his head and dimpled the siding of the buildings next to him or kicked up gouts of dirt around where he crouched.

He cut loose with more covering fire as Carl Lyons fell back from his own forward position. Across the compound and outside the fence on the road a Hummer rolled up to the interior gate, floodlights blazing. A terrorist outfitted in old Soviet style camouflage sat in the open gun turret of the vehicle behind an M-60E 7.62 mm machine gun.

The man swiveled the general-purpose machine gun

around to provide cover as a narco-soldier hopped out of the back and sprinted toward the gate to open it. Behind them several more Hummers rolled up ahead of two troop transport trucks. Men began jumping out of the vehicles, all of them armed with M-16 assault rifles. From behind them, on the Phoenix side of the compound it looked as if the gates of hell had been opened up.

The cavalry had arrived, Blancanales thought wryly.

He put the iron sights of his M-4 on the head of the M-60 gunner and shot him from 150 yards out. The man was knocked backward against the turret lip and then bounced forward to sag against the butt of his weapon. Blood gushed from the head wound.

The soldier struggling to unlock the gate snapped his head back to look at his teammate, and when he turned back toward the lock, Blancanales shot him, too. The man dropped to the dirt road and flopped like a fish in the bottom of a boat.

Blancanales burned two 3-round bursts into the windshield of the lead Hummer. The first 5.56 mm rounds spiderwebbed the safety glass, and the second grouping punched through to hammer the driver in his exposed face and throat. Off to Blancanales's left he heard an explosion, then, just as quickly, a domino pattern of secondary explosions. A ball of fire rose into the sky from his right-hand side.

"I'm at the grapnel site," Lyons said over the tactical channel.

"We have eyes on you," Schwarz said, voice loud over the com link as he ran. "If we're going to go, let's go."

"Copy," Blancanales answered. "I'm falling back

now." He used his thumb to dial up the fire selector on his weapon one notch. "You copy that chatter, *Independence?*" he asked.

"I did. You ready for danger close?" the naval tech asked.

"Bring it," Blancanales said.

Then he turned and ran.

"HOLD THE STAIRS!" Hawkins growled, rising to his feet. "I'll check the site, then we'll un-ass the AO."

"Copy," Manning acknowledged as he coolly worked the trigger on his M-4.

"Pescado coming in!" Encizo shouted from the ground floor. Manning looked down and saw the Cuban-American combat swimmer run through the busted door frame. "I just shot, like, twenty people, out there and I can't make my defilade position," he shouted.

"Right," Hawkins answered. "Cover this area with Manning. I'll be right back."

Hawkins moved quickly down the hallway. Smoke burned his throat and irritated his eyes, obscuring his vision as he hunted. He worked quickly, checking behind doors as he moved down the hall. Flames kept the corridor oven-hot and the hair and clothes on still, broken bodies smoldered as Hawkins hunted to verify the dead.

In several places he found that the collapse of the two floors above had penetrated down onto the second story, cracking open the bedroom ceilings and dumping broken furniture and flaming debris like rockslides. Hawkins scrambled over mounds of rubble and skirted charred holes dropping away beneath his feet.

Behind him Hawkins heard Manning's smooth trigger work keeping the animals at bay. The heavier cracks of Encizo's .50-caliber weapon punctuated the fight like thunderclaps.

He came upon a body and picked up the head by the hair. The face looked as if it had been taken apart by a tire iron and was puffy, bruised and covered in blood, but Hawkins was still able to identify the head of al Qaeda in Africa. He mentally crossed the man off his list.

He turned the corner in the *L*-shaped hallway and saw the corridor blocked. An avalanche of ceiling beams, flooring, ruined furniture and body parts had dropped through the third floor and completely obstructed the hall. Flames ran in fingers off the cave-in, spreading heat and destruction with rapid ferocity.

A bit of debris fell through the roof and Hawkins looked up. His eyes widened and he stepped forward to get a better look. Dangling from the hole was a mahogany-colored Gucci executive briefcase made from dyed alligator hide. The Gucci case hung from a pair of blue steel handcuffs attached to a blood-smeared arm.

"Well, look at that," he murmured.

Hawkins raised his arm up and touched the bottom of the alligator-hide case. He stood on his toes and grasped it with a firmer hold. Realizing he was going to have to yank the whole body down to get the case, Hawkins pulled hard.

There was a brief moment of resistance, then the case came loose in his hand so suddenly he was overbalanced and went stumbling back. His heel caught on a length of wood and he almost fell. He backpedaled like a pass receiver then cut to the side and came up against the wall.

He looked down at the case in his hand. The case was still attached to the blood-smeared wrist by the dark metal handcuffs. A man's arm hung from the dangling chain. It ended in a ragged tear at the elbow. Bloody muscle and tendon hung in scraps from the open wound.

Sweating, Hawkins looked up through the hole and saw only more flames. He saw the bloody, smashed face of the emir, one side of the prince's head crushed like an egg. He dropped his gory artifact onto the hot ground and knelt to one knee, pinning the disembodied forearm to the ground with his leg.

He drew his boot knife and freed the arm from the handcuff, then clutched the Gucci briefcase under one arm and rose.

He backed up to the edge of the corner and pulled a grenade from his web gear suspenders. The AN-M14 TH3 incendiary hand grenade weighed as much as two cans of beer and had a lethal radius of over twenty yards that spread its burning damage out in the hallway; its destruction would be concentrated, spreading fire and contributing greatly to the overall structural instability of the building.

Hawkins yanked the pin on the hand grenade and let the arming spoon fly. He lobbed the compact canister underhand and let it bounce down the short stretch of hall before ducking around the corner to hide. The delay fuse was four seconds, which gave him plenty of time to achieve safety.

Both he and Gary Manning carried the incendiary grenades. They were heavier than some other, more modern hand grenade versions, but their power was undisputed and they made a nice compromise to larger but more powerful satchel charges.

Hawkins moved in a fast crouch toward the once ornate landing where Gary Manning and Rafael Encizo fired down from their defensive vantage point to cover Hawkins's search-and-destroy mission.

Hawkins spoke into his throat mic. "Phoenix to Stony Hawk. I have two primary target kills confirmed. Our operation is finished. Site destruction verified to acceptable factor of certainty. Over."

"Hawk to Phoenix, copy," Jack Grimaldi answered. Hawkins could hear the beating of the Stony Man pilot's rotors and the muffled sound of his minigun bursts. "I am disengaging covering operations and proceeding to extraction overwatch. Over."

"Phoenix Bravo, copy," Hawkins answered. "Phoenix Actual, how copy, over?"

McCarter's voice came through instantly. "We're rolling hot to the back door."

Behind Hawkins the incendiary hand grenade exploded and jellied flames spewed out past the turn in the hall. Hawkins felt the rushing waves of heat strike his back, increasing the intensity of the fires already burning by several factors.

"Coming toward you!" Hawkins shouted as he moved.

Hawkins jogged down the hallway toward where Encizo and Manning lay in prone marksmen positions. He moved at a quick pace, but the thickening smoke forced him to keep his head down and run bent over almost double.

As he approached them, Hawkins pulled his second incendiary grenade from his web belt and yanked the pin. He kept the handle down as he called out to the Phoenix Force commando, counting down the fuse.

"I found this briefcase. Let's scoot," he yelled, expanding on the message he had uttered over the com link to Grimaldi.

Manning nodded without looking back as Encizo scrambled up and Hawkins let the spoon on his grenade fly free. Below him through the smoke he saw figures maneuver and the muzzle-bursts of weapons firing. The heavy grenade arched out over the stairs and dropped like a stone into the smoke and milling confusion.

CHAPTER TWENTY-SIX

It hit the stairs with a clearly audible thump and rolled across the now scarred and pitted tile of the open space. Manning rolled back away from the edge as beneath them the grenade detonated with sudden, stunning sound and liquid fire splashed across the room.

Men screamed in pain and horror at the eruption as hungry jelly flames began to feed. The bottom of the stairs was instantly ignited by the intense heat and a sheet of flame sprang up, cutting the combatants off from the three members of Phoenix Force.

The men turned and raced back down the hall, stopping at the first door, which they hurriedly entered. Hawkins had already cleared the room on his initial sweep and they moved into the vacant room quickly. A glass veranda door of the same design as those on the patio below opened up off the bedroom onto a small terrace. The veranda overlooked the pools of potable water and off to one side more men were running up from the hell fields of the airstrip and burning tent barracks to assault the house.

Hawkins and Manning each removed an M-18 smoke grenade and primed the canisters while Encizo covered them. Hawkins threw his out the window and off to one side while Manning repeated the process to the other side. They held back from engaging targets to avoid drawing attention to themselves until they were ready.

The grenade canisters bounced out and immediately began spewing thick green smoke, obscuring the area around the window from any enemy eyes. Patiently the two men waited for the billowing smoke to grow thicker. Gary Manning primed an incendiary grenade as they waited.

From the cacophony of the battle they heard the screaming diesel engines of the EFV gunning toward them.

"Let's go," Hawkins barked once he had judged their covering smoke was thick enough.

"Go!" Manning agreed, and rolled his grenade across the floor back toward the room door.

Encizo went over the side and disappeared into the smoke. Following him, Hawkins rose, holding his pistol and the briefcase in the same hand. He moved forward and grasped the wrought-iron railing around the second-story veranda in his free hand and leaped over the side. Gary Manning's AN-M14 TH3 incendiary canister trundled across the distance between the window and the door.

Manning turned and rose as the grenade reached the doorway. He stepped forward and grasped the same railing Hawkins had vaulted over just a heartbeat before. The flesh of his palm found the warm metal bar just as the bullets hit him.

The burst of machine-gun fire struck him hard at a sharp angle so that the 5.45 mm rounds penetrated his torso armor just to the left of the ceramic plate insertion and entered the big muscle near the spine before traveling along the curve of ribs to exit underneath the armpit. A fourth round hit the left cheek of his buttocks.

Manning felt the shock of impact, then heard his attacker screaming as the sound of the AKS-74 chattered hard across the room. The shock of impact sent the wounded American over the railing and he lost his weapon as he fell.

The ground rushed up to meet him and he hit with the force of a car wreck. Pain lanced like lightning strikes through his body from the bullet wounds, and then the blunt trauma of his impact drove his breath from his lungs. Manning's eyes welled with a thousand points of brilliant light, and then a black void rushed in and darkness took the soldier.

HAWKINS HIT THE GROUND and rolled, coming to his feet in the smoke. He popped up, bringing his weapon to bear, and heard weapons fire from the balcony above him. He heard Gary Manning grunt with pain and then had an impression of something falling.

Encizo spun in a half circle in front of him, firing from the hip and putting out a wave of covering fire.

Hawkins felt Manning sprawl out across the ground at his feet and heard the man's weapon clatter as it fell away. He went to one knee beside his brother-in-arms and the smoke eddied just enough for him to see Manning lying still, his eyes closed.

The incendiary grenade detonated with a signature whump, and blazing banners of flame shot out the open window above Hawkins. With grim satisfaction he heard someone screaming in agony from above him and he knew the man who had shot Gary Manning was burning to death.

Hawkins moved quickly. He didn't stop to see if Manning was alive or dead. It did not matter. If the ex-Special Forces soldier was still alive, then Hawkins had no time to treat or dress his wounds yet. If he was dead, then Hawkins had no intention of leaving his body to the wolves to be displayed in mutilated splendor on terrorist Web sites.

The sound of the charging EFV was loud in the swirling smoke, and the chatter of the armored unit's weapons was continuous.

Hawkins grabbed Manning's arm and muscled the man over his shoulder in a tight fireman's carry position. Using the flaming beacon of the burning room above his head as a compass point, Hawkins turned and began to jog through the smoke out toward the back gate and the waiting EFV.

Encizo scooped up the briefcase and followed Hawkins. "We're coming toward you out of the smoke," he warned over the com link.

"Copy. Ramp coming down," McCarter responded instantly.

A figure rushed past Hawkins in the smoke, nearly colliding with him. Hawkins put a single 9 mm round through the confused man's head at the temple, then stutter-stepped over the body as it fell.

Gary Manning was a big man and Hawkins gasped for breath in the choking smoke as he labored to carry the fallen soldier clear of the assault site. The Phoenix Force veteran's blood soaked into Hawkins and ran down his back, gluing Hawkins's black fatigues to his sweating skin with syrupy stickiness.

Hawkins ran clear of the area obscured by his and Manning's smoke grenades. The air still stank of ash and blood, and burning fires continued polluting the air, but Hawkins was now better able to see. His eyes were red-rimmed and his throat raw from his coughing.

He used a grimy sleeve to wipe the trail of snot coming from his nose.

He hacked and spit as he turned, searching through the haze for the back gate. He heard the motor cadence of Jack Grimaldi's Comanche as it passed overhead. There was a burst of minigun fire and a hailstorm of spent shell casing rained down on Hawkins from above.

He ran forward, the Beretta machine pistol up and tracking as he moved. Each step sent thumping shock waves up from his heels through his body and into his tightly clenched teeth. The added weight of Manning's body slowed Hawkins down, compromised his reactions, but not once did he think of dumping it and running on his own.

He passed the burning remains of the Hummer and the flames had died down enough that he could easily see the charred, skeletal remains of the enemy gunmen trapped inside the vehicle cab when Manning's 40 mm rounds had found them.

Hawkins saw a man with a scope-mounted SKS carbine stumble out of the fog, coughing harshly and streaming tears from the vicious airborne irritants. Encizo extended his rifle and triggered a round from the hip.

The big gun cycled smoothly, Encizo's grip fighting to absorb the recoil action. The slide pistoned back and forth in a single action, spitting a smoking shell casing as large as a cigar out in a loose curve.

The man dropped over to the side in the smoke, leaving blood behind him in the air like fog as he fell. The body sagged to the ground and the dying man's leg spasmed harshly as Encizo stepped over it on his way toward the compound's back gate.

He cut across the stretch of irrigated lawn and saw the EFV on the dirt road leading toward the rear gate.

Just beyond the ruins of the structure the smoke was being beaten back by the spinning rotors of Grimaldi's fast-attack helicopter. Hawkins ran toward the chopper and he realized with a jolt of random thought that everyone back in the War Room at Stony Man would be able to see that Manning was down.

Running up the lowered ramp of the chopper Hawkins laid the wounded Manning out on the floor and began applying first aid. Behind him Encizo clambered inside.

His hands found the butt pouch attached to the back of Manning's web gear and he ripped it open. He saw the OD-green packets of coagulation powder packed between bandages and a cravat. He snatched three of them up, ripped them open with his teeth and began dumping them into Manning's wounds, trying to get the leaking blood to clot as they extracted from the assault.

The ramp snapped up and Hawkins heard the engines whine a heartbeat before the chopper ascended.

He felt the blood of Gary Manning clotting his already gummy clothes against his sweaty flesh and then Encizo was beside him, working feverishly, and Manning began to cough. The ex-Airborne Ranger knew they'd cheated death one more time.

CARL LYONS SENSED movement and twisted around, bringing up the muzzle of his M-4. He saw Rosario Blancanales come out of an alley between two storage units, and his finger went lax on the trigger. Red tracers burned through the air and split the space where the ex-Green Beret had been just as Blancanales hooked through the fence and sprinted toward Lyons.

A clean-shaven Colombian in olive-green fatigues appeared on the rear run, an M-16 up and ready in his hands. Lyons triggered a burst that burned inches to the left of the running Blancanales and hammered into the confused soldier. The man was knocked over backward and his assault rifle fell away.

A second soldier appeared in the opening between the buildings, saw his brother go down and threw himself behind cover as Lyons triggered a burst at him, as well. Blancanales hit the ground next to Lyons and fired toward the north, in the opposite direction covered by the Able Team leader.

Black men armed with assault rifles and dressed in old Soviet-style uniforms began to swarm out from between the burning storage vehicles and both Stony Man operators found themselves forced down on their bellies by the withering automatic fire.

LYONS LOOKED DOWN the run and saw Rosario Blancanales lying prone on the ground. The ex-Green Beret fired his weapon in cool bursts, using the dead bodies of the FARC sentries as a hasty fighting position. The Able Team commando was positioned so that his fire was directed down the alley, in the direction from which the team had first penetrated the buildings.

Lyons threw himself against the right side of a building next to an opening and angled his weapon outward to add his fire to that of Blancanales. Schwarz crouched on the left and swung the barrel of confiscated AKM around the corner. He began triggering long blasts of full automatic fire as Able Team fought hard to shift the momentum of the battle away from the attackers.

"I can't see them!" Lyons shouted above the roar of the weapons. "How many of them are there?"

"Four!" Blancanales shouted back. "They came in off the compound!"

"Gadgets," Lyons said, "cover our six while we fight to the grapnel point."

Schwarz stopped firing and repositioned his weapon so that it was articulated in the opposite direction. The Able Team veteran threw himself belly down on the ground and peeked his head around the edge of a burning storage unit to try to cover the unit's rear.

Lyons leaned out of the door and sprayed bullets down the narrow run. He saw two of the enemy narcoterrorists firing down the alley from positions behind the open doors leading out of a miraculously undamaged Quonset hut and they answered the Americans burst for burst.

Blancanales abruptly lifted his M-4/M-203 up at an angle, turning the weapon sideways. Lyons heard the distinctive bloop as the commando triggered the 40 mm grenade launcher. The rifle recoiled smoothly into Blancanales's shoulder, and there was a flash of smoke as the round arced down the run.

Instinctively, Lyons turned away as the HE round rammed into the wall at the end of the run and detonated with a thunderous explosion and flash of light. The crack was sharp and followed by screams. The Quonset hut doors acted like a chimney, filling with dark smoke from the detonation and funneling it in the team's direction.

Lyons seized the initiative hard on the heels of the grenade explosion. He leaped over the rifle barrels of both Schwarz and Blancanales and slid across the dirt path, bounced a shoulder off the fence and centered his weapon down toward the hut. He shuffled forward, firing his weapon in tight bursts toward the enemy positions he had witnessed before the explosion.

Behind him Blancanales rose to his feet and began to move down the hallway, as well, firing in tandem. Behind them Schwarz rolled into position and covered their rear security with his drum-magazine-mounted AKM assault rifle.

Lyons caught a silhouette in the smoke and raked it with a Z-pattern burst of 5.56 mm rounds from his M-4 carbine. Beside him Blancanales matched him step-for-step, his weapon firing. Lyons's target spilled out onto floor, his chest and throat looking like an animal had clawed it out.

"Magazine!" Lyons warned.

Lyons hit the magazine release with his finger and dropped his almost empty magazine. His other hand came up with a fresh magazine and slapped it into place. Lyons's thumb tapped the release and the bolt slid forward with a snap as a round was chambered.

Lyons brought his weapon up, scanning quickly for a target. The smoke from the grenade blast hung in the air, reducing vision. Blancanales put a man down, then finished him off with a 3-round burst to the back of the head. Lyons risked a look over his shoulder to quickly check on Schwarz's status.

Just as Lyons turned he saw Schwarz come up out of a crouch. The commando lunged toward the open door to a burning storage unit where he and Lyons had found the NBC ordnance.

"Grenade!" Schwarz screamed.

Lyons saw Schwarz stretched out vertical as he dived, five feet up in the air, his weapon trailing behind him as he sprang and his other hand out ahead of him as if he was doing the crawl stroke while swimming.

Directly under the leaping man's boots Lyons saw the black metal egg bounce once, then get caught on the sprawled leg of a dead narco-terrorist. There was a flash of light and suddenly Lyons was slapped down.

His world spun and he hit the floor hard enough to see stars. His vision went black for a heartbeat, then returned. Once again he had been struck deaf. He lay still for a moment, stunned by the concussive force of the blast. He blinked and the ceiling came into focus.

He saw a dark shape move beside him and turned his head in that direction. The hallway lit up as the muzzle-flash from Rosario Blancanales's weapon flared like a Roman candle. Lyons saw ex-Green Beret's face twisting as he screamed his outrage but he heard no sound.

Lyons blinked. When he opened his eyes again he saw Rosario Blancanales roll onto his back and fire his weapon back down the alleyway from between his sprawled open legs. With a rush, sensibility rammed into Lyons and snapped him back into the present.

He sat up and his hearing returned instantaneously. He looked down and saw he still held his weapon. He looked down the run and saw starbursts of yellow light through the fog of smoke as more enemy combatants charged the American position.

He sat up and leaned against the wall before lifting his weapon and returning fire. He squinted and saw Schwarz lying motionless, his legs trailing out from the doorway of the room.

The torn and headless torso of one of the terrorists lay on top of the American's body. Another one of the bodies that had been caught up in the blast had had its clothes lit on fire.

Lyons sprayed gunfire down the run. He saw his red tracers arc into the debris and dust and smoke, and saw green tracers arc back out at him. Suddenly he saw a muzzle-flash to the right of a wrecked storage hut and even closer than before. He twisted at the hip and fired in response.

A man folded at the waist out of the smoke and pitched forward. As he tumbled to the ground Lyons put another burst of 5.56 mm slugs into his body. Beside him Blancanales rose up off the ground, keeping the barrel of his weapon trained down the alley.

Lyons held his fire for a moment and forced himself to stand. No enemy fire assaulted him and he took a look behind him, counted the three dead men he and Blancanales had shot.

Lyons took a step down the run in that direction, weapon ready. He saw the crater where Blancanales's 40 mm round had impacted and the black scorch patterns spreading out from the blast center. He saw a severed arm lying next to a chunk of skull in the torn-up dirt amid a puddle of blood and he turned back down the hallway.

Blancanales jogged forward, weapon up. Lyons followed him, his weapon on his shoulder. He reached the motionless Schwarz and leaned down to pull the dead man's torso off his friend's body. Lyons drew even with him as Blancanales knelt beside the wounded Able Team commando.

"Gadgets!" Blancanales shouted. "Gadgets, can you hear me, brother?"

Lyons passed the two without looking, his eyes searching for targets. As he passed a downed narco-terrorist he heard a moan and saw the man move. Lyons whirled like a whip snapping and triggered a burst into the terrorist, who shuddered and then lay still.

CHAPTER TWENTY-SEVEN

Lyons snapped his weapon back around. At the end of the run, through the smoke and haze of dust, he saw a bearded face peek around a corner of a burning storage unit and instinctively fired a burst. The head ducked back to safety behind the corner, and Lyons pulled himself out of the run into a tight breezeway between the walls of two Quonset huts.

"How is he?" he shouted to Blancanales.

"Bad," Blancanales replied.

His voice was flat, lacking inflection. Lyons felt a chill pass through him. Not a brother down, he thought. He pulled his tactical radio from off the web gear H-harness fitted over his now filthy and blood-soaked black fatigues. He keyed the mic.

"You in our AO?" he asked without preamble.

"Affirmative," Charlie Mott answered. "Doesn't look good for a touchdown except on the beach. Those empty lots around you are too filled with debris."

"I got a man down. Is that the best you can do?" Lyons said, his voice almost cracking. "The front is filled with bad guys."

"I can do some passes over your AO to try to clear it up while you get back to the CRRC."

"Copy that. Make it happen."

Lyons tucked his radio away and fired a blind burst down the run as harassing fire. He turned back and saw

Rosario Blancanales frantically working on the inert Schwarz. What Lyons saw made his throat close tight so quickly he almost gagged out loud.

"We have to go," he said. "Charlie's got the Little Bird outside."

Before Blancanales could answer, Lyons heard a loud thump strike the door behind him. He didn't think; he simply reacted. Lyons rolled up onto one hand, his leg curled beneath him, and leaped forward. He landed on top of the startled Blancanales and forced the Stony Man operator down over the mangled and bleeding Hermann Schwarz.

Behind Lyons the hand grenade went off like a peal of thunder and blew a section of building off and sent it flying into the runway, followed by a billow of smoke. Lyons lifted himself off Blancanales and Schwarz as debris and dust rained down on the men. Lyons swooned and shoved hard against the mangled fence, forcing himself upright.

He felt as if he'd just downed a bottle of tequila and taken a ride on a Tilt-A-Whirl. He gritted his teeth, snarling against the pain and disorientation. He scooped up his weapon and moved back to the edge of the building, where he thrust the barrel around the edge of the door and pulled the trigger.

The weapon bucked in his hand as empty shell casings arced out and spilled across the bloody ground. He fired a long burst, burning off half a magazine. Immediately machine-gun fire answered his burst and a maelstrom of heavy-caliber bullets sizzled through the narrow passage and hammered around him.

"Take him and go!" Lyons shouted. "Get to the beach—Charlie's there. I'll hold them off!"

"No good, Ironman!" Blancanales shouted back. "I

have to get a pressure dressing in place or his guts are just going to leak out when I run. He'll die!"

Lyons gritted his teeth, fury rising in him with tornado force. He levered the M-4 carbine around the corner of the building and triggered a burst of harassing fire. He heard the whine of bullets cascading off some hard surface and the dull thuds as the ricocheting rounds burrowed into the hallway walls.

As he fired for cover he took a quick glance around the corner. What he saw made his heart stop cold. At the end of the run formed by two ruined structures a narco-terrorist was inching forward behind the cover of a Level III ballistic shield. Behind the shield bearer, working in coordinated tandem, shuffled a gunman firing an American M-4 carbine in neat 3-round bursts.

The 5.56 mm bullets chewed into the edges of the building wall above Lyons's head, spraying his face with sparks. Lyons fired a return burst and saw sparks of his own shower off the gray metal material of the ballistic shield. He saw more gunmen down the run starting to edge out from behind the corner, emboldened by the shield bearer's success.

The M-4 gunner ducked as Lyons fired, crouching behind the shield bearer. His arm arched up and the black metal sphere of another hand grenade flew into the hazy air. Lyons saw the spoon fly off as the fragmentation bomb lobbed through the space between them.

He sprayed wildly down the hall, forcing the M-4 gunner to remain crouched behind the ballistic shield. The M-67 antipersonnel grenade landed and bounced, Lyons caught the segmented body in one hand and cocked his arm back. The M-4 gunner held his carbine above his head and fired a wild burst. Lyons dived forward onto the ground and released the grenade.

The M-67 fragmentation grenade hit the passage behind the assault team, bounced once, rolling away from them, and then detonated. The tight corridor instantly filled with black smoke and a deafening explosion. Shrapnel erupted outward, whizzing through the air, peppering the aluminum-and-corrugated-tin walls of the already mangled structures across the grenade's blast radius. Most of the blast and shrapnel was soaked up by the two-man terrorist assault team.

The M-4 gunner was picked up and hurled over the top of the shield man, spinning like a rag doll, his back torn open into a blanket of red, raw meat and splashing blood. He landed hard and loose on the floor of the hall, limbs splayed and head cocked unnaturally.

The shield carrier was propelled forward by the blast, falling forward across his shield, which rang with the impacts of metal shrapnel. Lyons lifted his head and saw the man reaching weakly for an autopistol lying on the ground next to him.

Lyons shot him in his upturned face, then ducked back around the corner of the doorway. He dropped the magazine out of his carbine and inserted another. He turned to see how Blancanales was advancing on the wounded and unconscious Hermann Schwarz.

He saw Blancanales's blood-soaked hands tying off a knot over Schwarz's injured abdomen. Blood was puddled on the ground around the wounded man and Rosario Blancanales's legs were soaked in it.

Moving fast, Blancanales used surgical tape to secure a final twelve-by-twelve-inch gauze pad into place. It was instantly stained red.

Machine-gun fire rattled through the open alley,

punctuated by the slash of green tracers. Lyons turned
and fired a burst around the corner. He looked back at
Rosario Blancanales.

"You ready?" he yelled.

Blancanales, face ashen, looked over at Lyons and
simply nodded before moving into action.

Letting his weapon dangle from its strap, Blancanales bent and pulled Schwarz into a sitting position. The American's head rolled loose on his neck and
underneath a shroud of his own blood, the man's skin
was deathly white and starting to tinge with blue.

Blancanales squatted, tucking his butt underneath his
shoulders and securing his grip on Schwarz's shredded
and smoking clothes. He grunted and lifted straight up,
driving with the powerful muscles of his buttocks and
thighs. Schwarz rose as Blancanales did and at the top
of the arch he ducked under the limp soldier, shoulder-
ing his bodyweight easily.

Lyons sprayed the hallway through the door without
looking. Again his burst was answered with a longer
and heavier caliber in return fire. Blancanales turned,
Schwarz's blood flowing out over him, and looked
toward Lyons.

"Go!" Lyons shouted. "Go. I'm coming."

Blancanales nodded once and turned, running toward
the hole in the fence through which Able Team had first
accessed the compound. He slid in the bloody mud of
the torn-up ground but did not go down, and Lyons
turned his attention back to the ground he held as last
defense.

Whatever else happened, he had to give his teammates time to get aboard the Little Bird helicopter. He
would hold off the narco-terrorists located in the front

of the fuel depot as long as he could, then make his own break for freedom.

Everything had gone to hell in a handbasket in the blink of an eye and all Lyons could try to do now was pick up the pieces. It didn't matter why he had come to this place to begin with; all that matter was what was happening *now*.

A burst of machine-gun fire tore down the long passage then trailed off, and Lyons heard the familiar thumping bounce of yet another hand grenade coming his way. He looked down at the threshold of the path and saw the black metal sphere roll into the path beside him.

He swung his left arm down like a handball player and slapped the grenade back down the corridor. He didn't look to see how far it traveled but instead tucked his head between his arms and rolled away from the opening. There was a boom and he felt the explosion shock waves traveling out of the passage and through the buildings to slop over and push hard into his back.

He lifted himself up off his belly and twisted back toward the contested alley. Standing, he thrust the muzzle of his weapon around the corner and fired until he burned off the last bit of his magazine.

He turned and began to sprint down the back alley toward the infiltration point. He dropped the spent magazine as he ran and fumbled for another one in his web gear. His combat boot came down awkwardly and he went down hard, landing on one knee. Pain lanced out from the hinge joint and he gasped in surprise at the intensity of it after all he'd already suffered.

He forced himself up and kept running.

"Get down the rope!" Blancanales yelled from just ahead. He spun and shot two men.

"Go ahead!" Lyons said. "I got it!" He put a 3-round burst into the belly of a vaquero wielding an Ingram M-11 machine pistol.

Blancanales made as if to argue, saw an opening, shot a soldier, then closed his mouth. Arguing with Carl Lyons was like pissing up a rope. "The rockets are inbound!" he yelled.

"I'm coming!" Lyons yelled over the sound of his firing weapon. "Just go!"

Blancanales spun on his belly and began high crawling on his elbows to the spot where the rope went over the edge of the bluff. Secured to his back by interlocked web gear suspenders and belt, Schwarz's head lolled.

He ducked his head under the sling of his rifle and grabbed the rope with both hands. Lyons triggered burst after burst to cover him while edging backward in an awkward shuffle under the intensity of the returning fire.

A deadly sphere the size of a baseball suddenly arced out of the night, backlit by the burning fires. It landed and bounced wide, out of Lyon's reach, and there was nothing for him to do but duck his head.

The explosion was so loud Lyons felt a scream ripped from his lips in the instant before his right ear went deaf. He felt shrapnel rip into the length of his body along the right side and he felt the concussion try to pull his carbine from his hands, but he stubbornly held on.

He felt slow and stupid, almost drunk from the shock. He forced himself to turn, to bring his weapon up and around, but it felt as if he was swimming through mud. He couldn't hear very well, then suddenly his ear popped and the sound of the battle came rushing back into his consciousness. He realized with a sort of sick certainty that virtual walls of lead were burning past his body in deadly fusillades.

He saw the crater formed by the exploding hand grenade and frowned. Something was wrong. He shot someone with a blazing M-16, then twisted and fired at someone else. He saw the aluminum-alloy grapnel hook lying loose on the ground, its prongs twisted like Italian noodles.

He rolled over onto his stomach and fired wildly. The climbing rope attached to the grappling hook was nowhere to be seen; it had been blown apart by the grenade blast. His first thought was to wonder if Blancanales had gotten Schwarz off the line in time.

His second thought was the realization that he was trapped on the bluff.

Another black sphere arced toward him out of the night.

The grenade landed and rolled to a stop in front of him.

Ignoring the machine-gun fire hammering his position he surged up and forward. He grabbed the hand grenade and whipped it out from in front of him. It sailed back toward the fence and landed hard, bouncing once before exploding. Geysers of dirt jumped into the air. Shrapnel ripped out in an umbrella pattern.

Then the missile barrage from the USS *Independence* landed danger close.

The warheads struck in a wave of overwhelming explosive destruction. Fireballs streaked out of the sky and rammed into the compound. The earth shuddered under the impact and Lyons felt the vibration come up through the ground and shake his body hard enough to rattle his teeth.

Clots of dirt fell around him like rain and washes of

heat rolled into him in waves. The sound was deafening and brutal. He tried to lift his head and another shock wave slammed into him. In between the hammer falls of the explosions he could hear secondary detonations as the fuel tanks on vehicles were ignited.

Burning fireballs turned the night as bright as day and Lyons felt naked and exposed in the brilliant illumination. He lifted his head and dirt hammered into him. He spit and blinked, and saw figures spinning and rolling as building after building inside the compound was hammered into collapse. Armageddon was at hand.

Lyons jumped up and looked around quickly. He saw nothing moving on the rubble-strewn and burning landscape. He spun and jogged over to the edge of the bluff and looked down, afraid of what he would find. He saw Blancanales crouched by the front of the CRRC with his weapon trained on the cliff top, kneeling beside the prostrate form of Schwarz.

"Throw the grapnel down!" Blancanales shouted up at him. From out to sea Mott was driving his Little Bird toward their position.

Lyons turned and scanned the fence line, searching for the grappling hook. After a tense moment he found it stuck in the ground where it had been blown clear by one of the explosions. He ran over and picked it up before returning to the edge of the bluff. He saw Blancanales moving forward with an end of the rope in his hand, and Lyons tossed the grappling hook down. Blancanales sprang forward and retied the end of the knotted rope through the eye-loop, then lifted the injured Schwarz and started for the black SUV.

"Here it comes!" the ex-Green Beret yelled.

He spun the rope around on a tight axis and then released it. The grappling hook arced up and shot forward to land at the top of the cliff. Working quickly Lyons snatched it up and then secured it to a sturdy swamp scrub that had somehow survived the bombing attack. He took one quick look around, shouldered his weapon and went over the side of the bluff cliff.

He felt the hard wind of the Little Bird's rotor wash as Mott guided the helicopter into the beach and brought it down.

Dropping hand over hand he quickly made his way to the bottom of the rope and dropped the last few feet to the ground. He turned around and ran for the CRRC to help Blancanales help secure the injured Schwarz behind Mott in the Little Bird.

Engine screaming in protest Mott gave the two men a thumbs-up then powered the helicopter up and out toward waiting triage aboard the *Independence*. Working quickly, Blancanales and Lyons pushed the CRRC into the surf and gunned it toward their own rendezvous. Behind them the very earth was burning.

CHAPTER TWENTY-EIGHT

Stony Man Farm, Virginia

Barbara Price turned away from the wall of the War Room, phone to her ear. "Uh-huh," she said, and held out a thumbs-up to both the waiting Lyons and McCarter. "Very good, then. Thank you," she finished, and hung up.

She flashed a big smile. "That was Bethesda," she said. "Both Manning and Schwarz have been stabilized and are expected to make a full recovery."

"Either one of them is too mean to die," Lyons observed.

"Gary'll probably be pinching butts in no time," McCarter allowed.

"Great." Price rolled her eyes. "A harassment suit against a man who doesn't officially exist—it should be lovely."

Lyons simply shrugged. "That was one hell of a close call back there."

"Right bloody war," McCarter allowed.

Barbara Price's eyes twinkled. "Not half as brutal as the one Hal's going to have to fight to explain what happened on that island to the Covert-Action Oversight subcommittee."

Washington, D.C.
Capitol Building

BROGNOLA HURRIED down the hall, the upcoming meeting was going to be uncomfortable enough; he didn't need to ruffle any feathers by arriving late. He put his head down and walked faster.

"Hey, Hal," a familiar, raspy voice called out.

Brognola turned and faced the now familiar figure of Kubrick.

"Hey yourself, Brigadier," he replied. "I hate to rush but—"

"Here." Kubrick shoved a sealed envelope into the big Fed's hands.

"What's this?" Brognola demanded.

"Let's just say I'm returning our favor."

Brognola looked at the thick package with a dubious eye. "Oh, yeah…"

"When you get inside those chambers you're going to get the most heat from the representative from New York. Right before he starts to go off, have an aide carry this over to him."

Brognola looked at the envelope as if it was a ticking bomb. "What's in it?"

"Proof his nanny is in the country illegally. Photos of him engaged in an affair with same said nanny, and the activation codes to overseas accounts where he got campaign donations from foreign entities. Most namely the Saudi royal family."

"You're shitting me?"

"I most certainly am not."

"How—"

"Don't ask, don't tell," Kubrick deadpanned.

The brigadier general turned and strolled down the hallway.

"Pleasure doing business with you," Brognola finally said.

The big Fed straightened his shoulders and turned toward the doors to the hearing chamber. The meeting was secret so he wouldn't have to worry about reporters. He fixed his tie. In his mind he was already working on the next mission for his Stony Man teams.

The war was never ending.

* * * * *

The Don Pendleton's Executioner®
CARTEL CLASH

A Mexican drug dealer sends a deadly message to the U.S....

Tensions are high after a powerful Mexican drug cartel kills an undercover DEA agent in a declaration of war against the United States. A shipment of missiles is bound for the region, and Washington's hands are tied with red tape. With the border beyond American control, only Mack Bolan can stop the destruction before innocent blood is shed.

GOLD EAGLE®

Available November wherever books are sold.

TAKE 'EM FREE

2 action-packed novels plus a mystery bonus

NO RISK

NO OBLIGATION TO BUY

AleX Archer
PHANTOM PROSPECT

A sunken treasure yields unfathomable terror....

Intrepid treasure hunters believe they have discovered the final resting place of *Fantome*, a legendary warship that wrecked off Nova Scotia almost two hundred years ago. When Annja is asked to help with the research, she must brave the cold, deep waters—as well as the menacing shark known as the megaladon—in order to uncover the truth.

Available November wherever books are sold.

GOLD EAGLE ®

www.readgoldeagle.blogspot.com

GRA27